THE
DAUGHTERS

BOOKS BY JULIA CROUCH

THE
DAUGHTERS

JULIA CROUCH

bookouture

Published by Bookouture in 2022

An imprint of Storyfire Ltd.
Carmelite House
50 Victoria Embankment
London EC4Y 0DZ

www.bookouture.com

ISBN: 978-1-80314-125-1
eBook ISBN: 978-1-80314-124-4

For Clark

ONE

For ten years now, Sara has spent half an hour on 30 May on her iPad, watching her family lay flowers at her mother Alice's memorial tree. For ten years now she has wished that, like that first, awful grief-scarred time, she could be there in person.

The discovery she made last night about her mother's death means that the urge to be there this year, on what would have been Alice's fifty-sixth birthday, is so strong that it physically hurts her.

Sara's stepmother Carys stands by the tree, her lean brown fingers wound around poor Lucy's blue-white hands, her close-cropped hair resting against Lucy's orange frizz. Carys is a good six inches shorter, but the way Lucy – Sara's eighteen-year-old baby sister – leans against her makes it clear who is doing the supporting.

Carys has made herself indispensable to the family since she moved in less than a year after Alice's suicide.

Supposed suicide, Sara corrects herself.

And that's the uncertainty now burning a hole in her mind.

It's early morning over there, and the camera lens is misted by a late-spring drizzle. Binnie, the five-year-old half-sister Sara has never met, stands next to Carys in a practical lime-green cagoule. Her head is somewhere else, in the land of My Little Pony or Pokémon, or whatever girls her age are into. She's very sweet. She's also proof, if any were needed, that Carys has truly embedded herself in the family.

And unlike Sara, Binnie – short for Robina – is actually there.

Also absent is Bill: Sara, Lucy and Binnie's father, Alice's widower, Carys's much older husband. As with most years, his back is too bad for him to stand for the ceremony. He attends instead in one of the boxes on Sara's iPad, looking on from the Muswell Hill house. The tears in his eyes as he watches the ceremony show everyone how much he loved Alice.

Everyone loved Alice.

Carys knows this, yet still, every year, she arranges this ritual, and in doing so keeps her predecessor's spirit alive.

With her new knowledge adding fresh layers to the situation, Sara thinks this is trying too hard. Like Carys has got something to hide.

Carys peers into the screen and steps forward to adjust the phone, which must be on a tripod this year. Fancy.

'Is that OK?' she asks.

The video, which looked like everyone was leaning sideways, is now straight.

'Perfect.' Sara slugs her beer and looks out over the network of highways beneath her balcony. The evening rush hour is just beginning to calm down. Behind her, the personality vacuum of her serviced city-centre apartment yawns.

Nearly thirty. To think her life would come to this.

She shakes her head and refocuses her attention on what is happening in the Alice Herman Health Centre garden in Hackney, London. Lucy is singing 'Amazing Grace'. A central part of the ritual, it was cute the first time, but she was seven then. She has lost the remarkable confidence she had as a child, and now peeps the song in a half voice, approximating the notes.

Sara, who sang along with her sister for the first two years, now just hums quietly so the Airbnb couple enjoying a sundowner on the neighbouring balcony don't think she's some kind of religious nutcase.

Then, as always, it grabs her. The cold grip of grief, the clamping-up of the throat that when it first happened had her going to the doctor to check if she had some sort of cancer. 'Globus hystericus,' the doc said, looking kindly at her. 'Literally a metaphorical lump in your throat. Meditation could help?'

Usually it's like a tennis ball, but this year, thanks to what she now knows, it's football-sized, swollen with questions and suspicion.

Another metaphor made literal is that Carys has stepped into Sara's mother's shoes. She's got on the ankle wellies Alice wore to walk Nonna, the now-elderly Italian water dog – or, more fancily, Lagotto Romagnolo – who is lying patiently over her toes. Those boots were still warm, that dog still pining, when Carys moved in and took them over.

Two months, two weeks and four days after Carys moved in on her family, Sara left on her pre-uni year out in Australia. It was all planned, but even if it hadn't been, she would have run as far away as possible. Her year out turned into another, and another. She fell in love, married Pete the Cheat, got her citizenship, started in the police force and has somehow never managed to go home.

But now she's divorced and homesick and fed up with her job, which is all about cleaning up the messes made by morons.

Also, from Zooms over the last six months or so and from what Sara can see in front of her right now, Lucy is clearly in a bad way again, heading back to some of the problems that blighted her early teenage years. Sara was too tied up trying to get pregnant with her cheating-rat husband to even think about it back then. But now, freed from all that, she has an increasing urge to return to help the troubled little sister she feels she abandoned.

Her new discovery about Alice's death makes it seem all the more urgent.

None of them have ever visited. The flight would be too hard for Bill, apparently, with his back and his leg. When Binnie was born, Carys went on about wanting to bring her over with Lucy to 'meet her big sister'. But Sara spoke with Bill and they both agreed it would be weird and uncomfortable, so thankfully it never happened.

Lucy finishes the song and lays down the customary armful of irises at the base of the blackthorn. Carys has always called it 'Alice's tree', but whenever she does, Sara hears her mother's voice protesting that a blackthorn is a bush, not a tree.

Since this 'tree' started producing berries a couple of years in, Carys has gathered them to make sloe gin, and every New Year Sara pays the duty to receive a small bottle, which she and Pete used to down with ice and tonic water.

Pete never really got sloe gin.

Pete never really got Sara, truth be told, but it took him seven years to find that out.

Carys strokes Lucy's hair, then looks into the camera. 'Do you guys want to say anything?'

'I love you, Alice, my darling,' Bill says, and Carys smiles, pure warmth, pure understanding. She's either a saint devoid of jealousy, or she's two-faced.

Sara's pretty sure she knows which it is.

'Love you, Mum,' Sara says. 'I wish you were still with us.'

She could say a whole bunch more, but this is not the time. Not yet.

'Beautiful,' Carys says. 'We'll do our one-minute silence now, yeah?'

Sara rests her iPad against the plastic cactus on her balcony table and stands.

The sign on the health-centre building behind the blackthorn is beginning to show its age. Carys has been talking about the family funding a new one. Sara is all for it. Despite everything, she is inordinately proud of her mother.

Because even looked at objectively, Dr Alice Herman was a formidable woman. She built this visionary GP practice, which alongside the traditional NHS surgery stuff offers a range of holistic treatments such as acupuncture, osteopathy and hypnotherapy. The fees paid by the owners of the top-dollar private houses around the centre subsidise access for the low-income families in the council estates that jostle up alongside them. Alice's vision has since provided the model for countless other centres in the UK. A year after her death, they put her name on that sign.

Lucy is sobbing now in her stepmother's arms. Binnie, a chip off Carys's caring block, also hugs her half-sister.

Sara glances over at the Airbnb couple on the neighbouring balcony, who are smirking at her standing with her hand on her heart and tears rolling down her cheeks.

She mutes her mic.

'You two can piss right off,' she says out loud to them. They look away, shocked.

If only she had discovered this aptitude for face-on confrontation before she left the UK, she could have told Carys exactly what she thought of her. But England doesn't really nurture that sort of honesty.

Even so, she misses the place, with its seasons and its drizzle and its two-faced passive aggression.

Lucy takes Carys's hand. 'I need to go now,' she says.

Carys nods, every bit the stand-in mother, and, after saying goodbye to Sara and Bill, steps forward to switch off the phone.

Sara wishes she had someone to look after her like that.

When she found herself unmoored after Pete left her, she filled her empty evenings trying to answer the questions she had about her mother's suicide. Using her police access and her detective skills, she trawled through old newspapers and legal and police documents. And last night she discovered that her mother's coffin, which she, along with everyone else, cried over at the small family funeral, had been empty.

So however much everyone believes that Alice jumped from the cliffs at Beachy Head, her body was never found. A certainty – even if it is that your mother killed herself – can give great solace.

Not knowing what happened is the worst.

Alice could even still be alive.

That thought really freaks Sara out. Her mother choosing a new life over her husband and daughters seems way more upsetting than opting for death.

So would it be a comfort if Sara were to discover that, instead of deserting her family, Alice was murdered?

She doesn't know if she wants to know more, or if she just wants to tuck it away.

For a brief moment, she and Bill are alone together on the Zoom. Over the years, her anger at what she saw as his grief-fuelled desertion of her and Lucy settled, and she came to view him more as a weak, sentimental old sucker. But now she also knows he has lied horribly to her and Lucy, and the fury is leaching back in.

It's tempting to ask him right now why he has done that. But, a good detective, she bides her time.

Instead, she exchanges the usual few stilted words with him, then they say goodbye.

As is her custom, once alone, she starts the slideshow she has made of photographs of her mother. It ends on her favourite image: Alice looking tiny next to Sara, her strapping, sporty sixteen-year-old daughter. She has her arm around her, and on her wrist is the crappy little friendship bracelet Sara made for her when she was ten. Alice had said she would wear it forever, and this photograph proves that, six years later, she was as good as her word.

'What happened to you, Mum?' Sara says, touching her mother's image.

Perhaps she was washed away, out to sea. It happens.

But the truth is, anything could have happened to Alice Herman.

Sara shivers and lets herself back into her soulless rented apartment.

Stuff to sort out, leave to arrange. It's time to go home.

TWO

'You've done it again.'

Bill puts his arm around Carys's waist and draws her close, placing a kiss on the top of her head. She will never tire of pleasing him. This, plus the excited laughter of Binnie's friends as they rush for the eight remaining chairs lined up in the open-plan living space, brings on a full-body shiver of pleasure.

He starts the music again as Carys dashes in and removes one of the chairs. The room smells of sugar, veggie sausage rolls, crisps, the sweaty heads of children and the raspberry Spider-Man cake Bill spent most of yesterday constructing.

They make a great kids' party team. The first one they threw together was Lucy's eighth, just a few months after Carys's arrival in the family. The poor girl's seventh had passed almost unnoticed due to being just four days before Alice's big public memorial, so Carys started a tradition of pulling out all the stops, trying to recreate the big, happy, messy parties of her own childhood.

Then as now, she threw her all into the food, decorations and games, and Bill made the first of his famous showstopper cakes. But only half the invited children turned up. Being the grieving child of a suicide mother doesn't bring popularity in the cruel world of the playground. After everyone had gone home and Carys was tucking her in, Lucy whispered that in future she would rather take one or two friends on a trip, say to the zoo, than have another big party.

Carys agreed, of course, but one of the many things she looked forward to when –after five years of trying – she found herself pregnant with Binnie was throwing proper birthday bashes. And Lucy loves coming to her little half-sister's parties.

Which makes it odd, Carys thinks, as Bill turns off the music and there's another wild scramble for the insufficient number of chairs, that she isn't here yet. Lucy is never late for Binnie's birthday party.

'She'll be here soon,' Bill says, as if he can read her mind. 'She just hasn't got her head round the buses is all.'

Carys leads the child left standing to the side and gives her one of the consolation badges she and Binnie have spent the past month making. 'It's only two buses and she's got Citymapper,' she says to Bill as she resumes her umpire's station beneath one of Alice's beautiful botanical paintings.

She has always been in two minds about Lucy moving away from home after her A levels to do her art foundation year. Fair enough, she's totally safe in the Stoke Newington flat Carys still owns from before she met Bill. But it took a lot of turning the subject over with him before she could bring herself to agree that allowing Lucy to live on her own terms might be the thing she needs.

Bill's argument that Lucy had become too dependent on Carys made a lot of sense. Carys didn't miss the other, implied part of his reasoning – that she had become too used to being in charge of Lucy. Because in many ways, she had. While Sara was clearly ready to forge her own way in life when Carys married Bill, Lucy appeared then, as now, to have just a very thin, translucent skin protecting her from the world.

Bill's was only a little thicker at that time. He was self-medicating his grief with alcohol, and was further broken by his resulting drunk motorbike crash – not least by guilt at the harm he could potentially have done to other road users. But Carys has had far more success building him up than she has his younger daughter. Optimist though she is, she can't see an entirely trouble-free future for Lucy.

But where is Lucy right now?

She tells herself to chill, to stop her catastrophising. But it's hardly surprising that her thoughts are going in that direction. Lucy has been a Child and Adolescent Mental Health Services stalwart since she was eleven. And Carys and Bill have paid for all sorts of additional therapies to try to address her identity crises, psychotic episodes, anorexia and bulimia, periods of mania and extreme anxiety. Putting it like that, Carys thinks as she once more extracts a chair – leaving just Binnie, little Amira and the boisterous, competitive Jaden to compete for the two that remain – letting her live on her own was a crazy decision. How did she let it happen?

'We should have insisted she stayed here,' she says to Bill.

'She's fine,' he says. 'She said she's been having the time of her life since she moved out.'

Carys knows this, but it hurts. Was it being with her that was Lucy's problem?

The music stops, and Binnie cleverly slides between Jaden's bum and one of the two remaining seats. Jaden is not best pleased, but Carys avoids a repeat of last year's scene by immediately leading him to a pile of Bill's doughnuts.

The final chair is played and the Lucy-shaped knot of worry in Carys's chest is briefly replaced by a swell of pride as Binnie subtly lets Amira take it. She knows that Amira has a hard time of it.

'Pizza time!' Carys cries after a glowing Amira has been awarded her trophy. She and Bill herd the twelve children to the kitchen table, where he has set out pizza bases and bowls with different toppings.

'It's build your own!' Binnie tells her friends, and little hands reach into the bowls, pulling out contents of varying nutritional value. There's the usual peppers, tomatoes, cheese and mushrooms. But Bill has added surprise toppings of some of his favourite junk food: chocolate, marshmallows, cheese puffs and crisps. Carys, a vegan, mostly indulges his crap eating. She particularly enjoys it when, as he tucks into a McDonald's, he tells her that Alice wouldn't allow him within ten yards of a burger.

'Whatever you want,' she says, steering her fellow vegans to the non-dairy cheese and making sure that the eight who choose to add sweet toppings to otherwise savoury pizzas cordon them off. 'Like a pudding slice,' she tells them.

'Do you have anchovies?' one little girl asks.

'I'm afraid it's all vegetarian,' Carys says.

Another child, in a dress Carys knows comes from a seriously expensive ethical organic children's clothing shop on the Broadway, approaches her with a slice from the mozzarella bowl. 'Is this buffalo-milk cheese?' she asks.

That's Muswell Hill for you, Carys supposes. A far cry from Southcoates, Hull, where she grew up. Not for the first time, she thanks her lucky stars for her father, who encouraged her artistic and academic ambition to study architecture at uni, and for Bill, the world-renowned architect she met and married and through whom she won a free pass into this world.

'I'm afraid it's just cow-milk cheese,' she tells the child, whose name is India.

India looks disappointed, but brings herself to put the slice in the middle of her pizza, a paragon of minimalism, decorated otherwise only with black olives and basil leaves.

While Bill gets the pizzas into the oven, Carys tops up the glasses of the three parents who either couldn't bring themselves to leave their child, or who just wanted to hang out and semi-legitimately drink wine on a Saturday afternoon. Just three, though. Carys has given up trying to be accepted in this mostly white, middle-class enclave. She briefly makes friends, and then they always turn away, seeming to ghost her. Bill tells her not to worry, that they're all over-privileged tossers who don't know quality when it stares them in the face. That helps.

'Top party as ever,' Elsa says. Elsa is her current one true mum friend, mother of Binnie's BFF Hetty and recipient of the Bill stamp of approval for the PR work she has been doing for their architect firm.

'We try,' Carys says.

Two hours later, Carys, Bill and Binnie see everyone off with party bags origamied from newspaper. There's no plastic inside, just little craft projects, coloured pencils and a slice of Spider-Man cake.

Bill has successfully steered entirely clear of the wine. Nearly six months dry now, and she couldn't be prouder of him. Brilliant people like him tend towards excess, so she's glad that this time he's called it quits for good.

'Can we look at the stars?' Binnie asks him. Her birthday present is a telescope that cost more than Bill knows. They're supposed to be tightening belts while they invest almost all they have in Five Oaks, the housing development that is going to make them. But you're only six once. And Bill is a big fan of astronomy – he had a very similar telescope when he was growing up.

'Why not?' He smiles. 'Jupiter might be up already.'

'You guys go have fun with the planets and stars,' Carys says. 'Leave the clearing-up.'

'You're not going to do it on your own.' This is an order from Bill, not a question.

'Of course not,' Carys says, although ultimately she knows that she probably will. 'I'm just going to see if I can find out where Lucy is.' She has tried calling countless times, but has had no reply. It's possible she has completely forgotten, and is at the cinema, or perhaps shopping, or out for one of her long walks up Hackney Marshes and beyond, and has left her phone behind. But still, it's not like her to miss Binnie's party.

Lucy and Binnie are best sisters, always have been. Indeed, after Carys taught her how to deal with Binnie's hair, Lucy is the only one now allowed to touch it.

Bill looks at her and nods. His lack of objection is notable.

'I'll drive over,' she says. 'If that's OK.'

'You're OK to drive?' he says, Binnie tugging his hand, trying to drag him upstairs to the little observatory they built into this, their prototype eco-house.

'What do you think?' Carys says.

She is the queen of moderation. She will leave food on her plate if she feels full, and rarely drinks more than one small glass of wine. She can't remember when she was last drunk.

'Keep me updated, yeah?' Bill says as he and Binnie disappear into the hallway.

His anxiety – he's usually the one to play down concerns – only adds to Carys's worry.

THREE

Carys pulls the Volvo Recharge up outside her old flat. She'd normally bike it, but this evening there's a thin summer drizzle. Plus she might be able to persuade Lucy to come back with her.

It hits her every time she steps onto the pavement on this tree-lined road: how lucky she and Edina were to buy it before prices in this particular pocket of London went ballistic. Carys was just a twenty-one-year-old student back then, so it was Edina's salary – with her being ten years older and in a proper job – that got them the mortgage. Carys paid her way, though, however broke she was. She's no freeloader.

That proper job of Edina's was the one difficulty Carys had in what was otherwise, until Bill came along, a pretty perfect relationship. Although Edina is principally a psychology academic – they met as the only two black women at the university women's group during Carys's freshers' week – her side hustle is as an expert witness in historic child sex abuse cases, specialising in false memory. In other words, defending the monsters by unpicking the witness statements of the alleged victims.

'Everyone deserves a fair trial,' she told Carys during one of their regular arguments about the subject. 'Otherwise what are we?'

When she left Edina for Bill, Carys found herself in a position to buy her out, which helped smooth over a terrible, emotionally exhausting break-up. Edina lives just across the high street now, over Clissold Park way, but they both decided that because of the bitterness all round, it was better to break off contact completely.

Carys regrets the whole episode, but the way she fell completely for Bill – her first-ever male partner – took her completely by surprise. She suddenly felt like every one of the ropes connecting her to the earth had been cut.

So that's what love is, she remembers thinking. The depth to which she had fallen for him completely drowned out her internal arguments about betraying her sexuality, the complication of Alice, the age difference.

That he was, as Edina cruelly said, extremely solvent and owner of the internationally acclaimed practice where Carys was doing her Part One architecture student placement was neither here nor there. Carys fell for his looks, his bravery, his vision and drive. All of that was whisked away, however, less than a year after she first met him, by Alice's death and the subsequent near-catastrophic grief-fuelled motorbike crash that left him with periodically intolerable back pain and a walking stick. But that just made him more attractive to her. Someone to care for, to build up, to restore to his former glory.

Bill was, and continues to be, the real deal. He is Carys's soulmate. And so what if, as Edina helpfully pointed out, she might have daddy issues? To her, the twenty-five-year age gap and the fact that she is just five years older than his elder daughter are meaningless. He is her one, her all. She will go to the ends of the earth for him and Binnie.

And Lucy and Sara, of course.

Which is why she is here, sheltering from the rain under her canvas jacket, on the street outside the flat that holds so many mixed memories and that now houses her troubled young stepdaughter.

Lucy's bike is there in the little front garden, locked to the rusty railing that tops the boundary wall.

The bike means very little, though. Scared of the traffic, Lucy rarely uses it. Given her dyspraxia, this pleases Carys.

Feeling in her waters that Lucy is in, she presses her finger on the doorbell and squares her face for the camera so that her stepdaughter, who would never answer the door to a stranger, can see it is her.

No reply.

She tries again and again – perhaps Lucy's in the bath.

No one comes.

The drizzle turns to full-on rain, and the jacket Carys is holding above her head with her free hand is now soaked. She remembers standing on this very doorstep twelve years ago, also dripping with rain, begging Edina via the entryphone to let her in when, after hearing about Bill, she had changed the locks.

She turns round and sees Constance across the road – who must be well into her nineties now – peering as usual through a lifted corner of her sparkling white net curtains. Carys waves her hand in greeting, and Constance's face lights up. Carys tells herself she will pop by next time, take her some bun, like she used to.

The smell from the fried chicken shop at the end of the street throws everything into focus, stirring old bones long buried. Carys can't bear it any more, standing on this doorstep. Part of her wants to believe that Lucy is simply out and she needs to stop worrying, but something is making her uneasy. She hates doing it, because this is Lucy's place, but it is time to use her keys.

She lets herself in and stoops to pick up the litter of post and flyers on the doormat of the communal hallway. Why do people not bother to do this? There are even a couple of NHS letters for Lucy. That she hasn't collected them makes Carys hurry along the little corridor to the flat door.

When she unlocks it, she is greeted by silence underscored by Lucy's familiar scent of patchouli and oranges. The stair light is on.

'Luce?' she calls up.

No reply.

She hangs her soaked jacket on the pegs in the tiny hall at the bottom of the stairs and slips off her soggy Birkenstocks, then, barefoot and silent, makes her way up to the flat, which occupies the first floor and loft of this terraced Victorian house. When she was Lucy's age, Carys had a tiny bedroom in the house she shared with her mum and dad and nan.

Lucky Lucy, she thinks, before correcting herself. In fact, material comforts aside, Lucy got into the wrong line when they were handing out good fortune. Since the death of her mother, the poor girl has found every single aspect of living a challenge.

Which is why, as Carys puts her feet on the restored wooden floorboards of the landing and smells the hot iron whiff that women know only too well, she lurches towards the little bathroom at the back of the flat.

It's locked.

'Lucy!' she calls, rattling the door. But there is an ominous silence from inside. Luckily, Carys knows this bathroom lock; she knows that the key you can stick in the middle of the handle and wiggle to open it lives on a hook in the meter cupboard back down at the bottom of the stairs.

A lot less quietly, she races down to get it, then back up to the bathroom. Her hands shaking, she clicks the lock.

As she flings open the door and sees what's inside, she thinks for a moment she is too late. Her brain going into emergency coping mode, she clocks the details like she is counting off a list. There are the dozens of candles, lit and flickering. There, laid out neatly like a surgeon's tools on a tray resting on the dirty laundry bin, is Lucy's kit of clean white handkerchiefs, cotton wool balls, surgical spirit, plasters and wound glue.

And two razor blades.

There is the red of Lucy's hair, and there is her face, even whiter than usual, her eyelids pale and blue and closed. And there is the red of the blood as it crusts round the new wounds in the thin skin of her inner left arm, cross-hatching the scars from her earlier cuttings. But the razor blade in her right hand has gone in too deep near the wrist, and there is too much blood. It pools around Lucy's body, which is lying on the pale green lino.

This all takes a fraction of a second, after which Carys springs into action. She pulls her phone from her pocket and dials 999. The phone wedged between her ear and her shoulder, she falls to her knees and checks Lucy's neck – she doesn't want to go near the arms, not yet – for a pulse. It's there, just. A faint thrum confirming that despite Lucy's best efforts, she is still alive.

'What have you done? What have you done?' Carys takes one of Lucy's handkerchiefs and, as she asks for an ambulance to come immediately, does her best to fashion a sort of tourniquet around her cut wrist.

It seems pointless, though. It's hard to believe that there can be any blood left in Lucy's poor, pale, drained body.

It all takes so much of Carys's attention that it is only when she is in the car following the ambulance to Homerton Hospital that she thinks about calling Bill.

FOUR

It's early morning and Carys is out walking Nonna in Coldfall Wood. Nonna has been brought here her whole life, first by Alice, then by a bereaved Sara, then willingly and with a lot less emotional baggage by Carys.

But today Carys feels like she is dragging a whole juggernaut of feelings behind her. Her eyes feel tight and small with it.

It has taken three days of blood transfusions, wrist surgery and many, many conversations with specialists from several different branches of medicine to get Lucy out of the woods, but she is now stable – physically at least – and Carys is trying to stop her being sectioned.

Lucy swears she didn't mean to nearly kill herself.

'I was just cutting,' she told Carys and Bill from her hospital bed, all sorts of wires and tubes doing their business in and out of her self-mutilated body.

Just cutting.

They had thought they were past all that. As far as they knew, it had been two years since the last time. But then secrecy and a complicated relationship with truth are part of the package when it comes to someone with Lucy's sort of issues.

'I just got carried away. I wanted to see how deep I could go.'

'But why?' Carys said.

Despite all her reading, Carys has no way of truly understanding why you would want to slice yourself open, create pain to release pain.

'I just had to dig deep,' was all Lucy could say. Then she closed her eyes, her marble face outdoing the hospital pillow for whiteness.

Carys lets Nonna off the lead and wearily uses the thrower to lob a ball.

'We're going to bring her home with us,' she said to Bill when they finally got back to the house after two nights sleeping on hospital chairs. Even he, with his ideas about Lucy needing her own space, couldn't argue with that. 'She needs us and home.'

Carys's accent gets broader when she's talking about family. It's like part of her is returning to the council house she grew up in, which was a place of unconditional love where a home-cooked British/Jamaican hybrid dinner everyone called tea was served up every night at five on the dot before an evening of homework, TV, story, cuddles and bed.

'Of course,' Bill said, as he placed a cup of tea in front of her. 'Let's keep her close.'

The timing is so rotten, though. Right now, Five Oaks has taken over their lives. With Lucy stable, the juggling – even with Binnie around – seemed possible. But now, even thinking about the weeks ahead exhausts Carys.

Nonna runs on over the earth bank to get the ball. She's sprightly for her great age, which is, according to Lucy, eighty-eight in dog years. Her retrieving days long behind her, she reaches the ball and lies on her front with it between her paws, waiting for Carys.

Like Alice before her, Carys loves it here. But for the distant rumble of traffic, this ancient woodland in the heart of Muswell Hill could be in the middle of the countryside. These trees have been here longer than any of the buildings for miles either side.

Alice knew all about trees, and Lucy has told Carys what little she remembers from her walks with her. Before, Carys only really thought about them as big plants that either enhanced the architectural space or created logistical or planning problems. Through Lucy, Alice has reached out from her grave, and now Carys really *sees* them.

They even make her feel safe. When Lucy first brought her here, she was forever looking over her shoulder. Urban wildernesses spook her. But twelve years on, she happily enters the wood with only a dog who would absolutely greet an attacker by rolling on her back for a tummy rub.

So when she sees a tall, dark, slender man up ahead of her, a crash helmet slung on his arm, she is taken aback by an animal rush of adrenaline.

'He's just out for a walk,' she whispers. Just out for an early-morning walk on his own in these deserted woods.

There's something in the way he moves – all legs, quickly, silently – that makes her think of a spider.

She squats to pick up the ball. Nonna is sitting upright, nose quivering, looking in the man's direction. Does she feel it too?

Carys sticks one hand into her jacket pocket. Her fingers burrow through dog treats to find her keys, which she threads through her fingers. With her other hand she slips the ball into her bag, then clasps the thrower, ready to wield it like a blunt plastic machete.

But then a dog who could be Nonna lollops up behind the stranger. Carys and Nonna are so taken aback that they both let out a short, sharp exhale.

He's just a dog walker. 'And he's got to be a good person, if he's got a dog like you,' Carys whispers to Nonna.

But why, if he has a dog, does he carry a crash helmet? She imagines the animal riding pillion, and smiles.

'Fig!' the man calls as the dog trots towards them and greets Nonna with a low-status roll onto his back. She graciously accepts his offer, puts a paw on his chest and lowers her face towards his to lick his nose.

'My God,' the man says, his voice surprisingly high for one so tall. 'Another Lagotto.'

'Definitely not a Labradoodle,' Carys says.

They laugh. The breed is often mistaken for the more fashionable Labrador/poodle cross.

'First I've seen in London for years,' the man says, striding up with his dog's lead in his hand. 'Are you OK with him saying hello?'

Bit late for that, Carys thinks. But she is fine, and the two dogs look like they are getting on well. Except for the fact that Fig is very definitely a boy, it would be hard to tell them apart.

'Ajay,' the man says, holding out his hand. 'And this is Fig.'

Carys surprises herself by shaking his hand. 'Carys,' she says. 'And Nonna.'

'Ah, a good Italian name for a venerable Italian lady,' Ajay says.

They stand like doting parents at a playgroup, watching the dogs tumble over each other, swapping information on their pets' ages and how they have come to own Lagottos.

'A friend's dog had puppies, and I just saw them and fell in love really,' Ajay says.

'This one belonged to my husband's first wife.'

'She went and left that lovely dog behind?'

Close up, Ajay looks kind. He has soft brown eyes, and his grey-streaked black hair flops over his face in a way that makes him look like a shy schoolboy, even though he must be at least Bill's age. Carys decides to go in with the truth.

'She, um, died.'

'I'm so sorry.'

Carys only realises she has heaved a giant sigh after it's out.

'If it weren't for Fig,' Ajay says, 'I don't know how I would have got through the past decade. They kind of help you over life's challenges, don't they?'

He looks at her so kindly, she can't help herself. 'I don't think my stepdaughter Lucy would be here if it wasn't for Nonna,' she says.

Ajay nods in a way that Carys thinks of as therapist style. Fig jumps up and heads off along the earth bank, back the way Carys and Nonna have just come. Nonna follows. Carys tries calling her, but she's not having any of it. She's found a friend, and she's sticking with him.

'Ah well,' she says. 'It's time we were heading back anyway.'

'Work?' Ajay says.

Carys nods. 'But first hospital, to see Lucy.'

'Oh no,' Ajay says. 'You mean...?' He nods his head towards Nonna.

'She swears she wasn't trying to do herself in,' Carys says. 'But yeah, whatever her intentions, that's what she nearly did.'

'My God.'

'I'm sorry. You didn't need to hear that.'

'No. It's fine. How is she now?'

They stroll into an area where the early-morning sunlight – the beginnings of a beautiful summer's day – dapples through the trees like nature's disco ball. For a moment Carys is dazzled. Her eyes prick and the bloody tears start.

'I'm sorry,' she says, scrabbling in her bag for a tissue she knows she doesn't have.

'Here.' Ajay fishes in his pocket and finds a perfectly clean, neatly ironed handkerchief.

'I couldn't.'

He presses it on her. 'I'll be offended if you don't.'

She dabs at her eyes, stupidly trying not to get the handker-chief too wet.

'You can tell me, if you like,' Ajay says. 'Sometimes an unconnected stranger can be a useful sounding board.'

Carys smiles through her tears. 'Good job you turned up, then.'

On the other side of the clearing is a park bench. The dogs have gone ahead and are competitively sniffing the ground around it.

'Shall we?' Ajay indicates the bench. 'I've got a flask of coffee.'

Carys nods and follows him towards the bench, where the dogs loll on the ground like a conquering army awaiting their rulers. She settles on the wooden slats a safe distance from him.

'Here.' Ajay rummages in his rucksack, pulls out a mug and a metal flask and sets them out on the bench. 'I'll have mine in the flask lid,' he says as he pours the coffee. 'It's black. I hope that's OK.'

'It's how I like it.' Carys takes the mug from him.

'So tell me about Lucy.'

His eyes are so kind that she finds herself obeying him. She has to be so positive and supportive around Bill and Lucy that she takes the opportunity to properly open up about how she is actually feeling. She tells him all about Alice and Bill, and how scared she is about Lucy, how she feels so useless, how she wishes she could wave a magic wand...

Nonna is now asleep, snoring as she does these days. Fig lies on his side next to her, unable to tear his eyes from this rare doppelgänger. A middle-aged woman passes on the other side of the glade and raises her hand in greeting without turning to face them. There's something in the way she moves that reminds Carys of someone, but she can't put her finger on it.

'So how long is your stepdaughter going to be in hospital?' Ajay asks her.

'We hope she'll be out within the week, so long as she can commit to taking her meds. It's when she stops that the problems start.'

'It can be a difficult process.'

'You sound like you're involved in the area?'

Ajay smiles. 'Yeah, in fact. I should have said. I'm actually a clinical hypnotherapist, and although I treat a range of mental health conditions, I specialise in young people with suicidal ideation.'

Carys almost chokes on her coffee. She doesn't really believe in fate – her life experience has taught her that if you want something to happen, you usually have to work bloody hard for it. But could that be what this is?

'Wow,' she says. 'And can hypnotherapy work with girls like Lucy?'

Ajay nods. 'As part of a solution, it can be very helpful indeed.'

Carys nods. Nonna stirs, putting one paw on Fig's back, like she is claiming possession. 'Where do you work?'

'I started out in the NHS, but sadly the hoops we had to go through to get my work funded turned out to be too much, so I've got a private practice now. Most insurance schemes cover me, though. I kind of even it out by doing pro bono work with a halfway house for kids coming out of care.'

Carys's little sister Emily never reached the top of the NHS waiting list for the surgery to stop the seizures that killed her. Because of this, knowing that however much Ajay costs Carys will be able to afford it without a second thought makes her feel decidedly uncomfortable.

They wander back to the park entrance, where Ajay has left his motorbike.

'My husband used to have a set-up like that,' she says. 'Before we got together.'

'The only way to travel.' Ajay straps Fig into the sidecar. 'Hey,' he says, reaching into his pocket. 'Here's my card. In case. You know. Lucy.'

She takes the card and hope sweeps through her heart.

FIVE

'They make me fat, stupid and sleepy.'

Lucy sits at the table in Carys and Bill's dark-wood-lined dining area and eyes the weekly pill dispenser Carys has placed in front of her. Each of its twenty-one compartments – three for each day of the week – contains, variously, one, two or three of the pills that keep her head screwed on, her outlook calm, her serotonin levels in the right ballpark.

Her face is arranged in such a way that Carys knows she is determined not to take a single one.

Bill pushes the container a couple of millimetres towards her. 'They'll stop you going la-la, though, Luce.'

Over at the hob, where she is making Lucy's favourite pancakes, Carys rolls her eyes. She doesn't like Bill and Lucy using this language about mental health, but it's not her place to step in.

After ten days in hospital, Lucy has discharged herself. The one suggestion she has agreed to is staying with Bill and Carys rather than going back to the flat. She is approaching the rest of her recovery the Lucy way – which is to say not listening to anyone else.

Carys kind of admires her for this, but it can also be infuriating for those who love her and don't want to watch any more repeats of near-fatal self-destruction.

She looks down at the frying pan, where the pancake she is trying to cook is still runny on top but threatening to burn underneath. She checks the recipe she is using – a butter-stained old one from Alice's box file, written out in her distinctive handwriting – and wonders if, in the adaptation from omnivore to vegan, she shouldn't have added more aquafaba to replace the egg.

These Muswell Hill musings almost always pass her by unnoticed, but sometimes, like now, the Hull girl in her stands back and has a proper laugh. Hearing her snort, Bill shoots her a look.

This is serious.

Carys switches the heat right down to give the pancake time, and picks up the cafetière. 'I hear what you're saying, Lucy,' she says, going over to the table and pouring three coffees. 'But can you give them a try, just for say a week?'

'And then what?' Lucy says. 'I'll be suckered in by then, Stockholm syndrome.' She makes a zombie face.

Bill reaches across the table and takes her hand. 'Dr Chen will keep an eye on things, and if you don't get on with the meds, there are others she can try.'

'Fucking shrink. Fucking drug pusher.' Lucy takes her hand away, grabs her coffee and leans back in her chair. 'I've tried all her little pills. Every single one messes with my head.'

'That's kind of what they're supposed to do,' Bill says.

'In a good way,' Carys adds. She heads back to the damn pancake and sees that it is starting to behave and is making little bubbles on its surface. She flips it, and, amazingly, it stays together. 'We could add other approaches too, perhaps, see if they help.'

Lucy folds her bandaged arms across her chest. 'Not acupuncture again.'

Bill faces Carys with a look that in everything but the teenage stroppiness exactly mirrors his daughter's attitude.

Carys laughs as she turns the now-perfect pancake out onto a waiting warmed plate. The acupuncture was an expensive disaster, the irony of sticking pins into a habitual self-harmer eventually revealing itself to everyone concerned – even the poor acupuncturist, who Lucy played mercilessly.

She spoons blueberries cooked down in maple syrup over the pancake. Lucy can be a total pain in the arse, but Carys swears to herself that she loves her just as much as Binnie, her easy-going, mini-me blood daughter, who is currently round at Hetty's for a sleepover while her more challenging half-sister is welcomed back into the fold.

'Ta-da!' She puts the plate in front of Lucy.

'Wow!' The stroppy, hurting teenager temporarily leaves the building, to be replaced by a totally delighted child. 'Thanks, Carys.' She tucks in.

'I was thinking of hypnotherapy,' Carys says, slipping in beside her to subtly watch her eat – something she knows is wrong, but which gives her so much enjoyment after the food refusal Lucy went through between the ages of fourteen and sixteen.

Bill looks at her open-mouthed. 'What?'

Carys sighs. Almost ritually opposed to any mention of alternative therapies, he always reacts like this, which is ironic, given how Alice's whole approach was built on incorporating them into traditional medicine. But a mix of approaches is the only way they are going to get Lucy out of this whatever-it-is.

'It really worked for me when I wanted to give up smoking,' she says.

'You smoked?' Lucy says, her mouth full of blueberry and pancake.

'My point exactly.' Carys sips her coffee a little smugly.

Bill looks at her, his eyes wide.

'When I met Edina,' she tells him. 'She can't bear the smell of smoke.'

'Well, it wasn't a long-standing habit then,' he says. 'Seeing how you were only twenty-one.'

'From the age of fifteen,' Carys says. 'A quarter of my life smoking roll-ups.'

Bill smiles. 'You northerners.'

'Yeah, booze, ciggies, lard...'

'Whippets,' Lucy says. They all laugh. Genuinely, not just to humour her.

'But no way I'm allowing Lucy to see a hypnotist,' Bill says.

'Hypnotherapist,' Carys says.

'I mean, OK for stuff like stopping smoking and, I don't know, weird compulsive habits, but Lucy needs more serious help than some old look-into-my-eyes quack.'

'Does she, now?' Lucy says.

'Actually, yes.' Bill puts his cup down. 'Yes, she does, because I love her and I want her to get better, and—' He suddenly stops talking like someone slamming the brakes on a speeding car. 'I'm sorry, dear girls. I just...' He puts his hands on the table and hauls himself to standing, reaches for his cane and heads across the living space. 'I just need a few moments. You know...'

Carys and Lucy watch as he makes his way across the polished concrete floor and through the door that leads to the hallway and then on to his studio. 'I'll bring you in some toast,' Carys says, aware that in all the cooking pancakes for Lucy, she has completely overlooked feeding herself and Bill.

'I'm not hungry, thanks, love,' he says. 'Just give me ten minutes, yeah? Sorry, Luce.' He closes the door behind him.

Carys sighs. 'He loves you so much.'

'And there's me, such a nutjob.' Lucy looks down at her lap.

'Shh.' Carys puts her hand on Lucy's knee. 'We're going to get through this.'

'Hmm.'

She leans in to her stepdaughter, puts an arm around her shoulders. 'This hypnotherapist,' she tells her. 'He specialises in young people like you.'

'Oh, you have one in mind?'

Carys fetches her phone from the kitchen counter and pulls up Ajay's website, which was listed on his business card, and which she has thoroughly gone over. 'He's got all sorts of qualifications, great testimonials, has worked in the NHS and now has a highly successful private practice up near Parliament Hill.'

'Posh.'

Carys takes Lucy's hands. 'Lucy. Please take this seriously. Don't you want to get well? It's tearing your dad apart, and if we don't do anything, God knows what you might end up doing to yourself. Won't it help to get to the bottom of what's making you so unhappy?'

'Is that what he does? Deep psycho digging? If that's the case, then big no. I've had enough of that these past five years. I've been filleted by shrinks and I'm missing my skeleton.'

'It's more practical than that,' Carys says, lowering her voice so that Bill can't hear. 'He reprogrammes how you perceive your past experiences.'

'You mean he can make me all glad that my mother topped herself when I was a nipper?'

Carys closes her eyes for a brief second. 'Not quite. But he can probably help you. At the very least, he can teach you how to relax and throw back a bit, and that won't do you any harm.'

They both look in the direction of Bill's studio. Even though there are two doors in the way, and both are firmly shut, his grief and desperation seep into the living space so surely that Carys can almost touch them.

'What about Dad?' Lucy says. 'That was a pretty firm no.'

Carys leans against her. Lucy's patchouli and orange scent is underscored with sweat and a note of something chemical that she puts down to medication. 'He gets these bees in his bonnet about things,' she says. 'And he's a bit of an old traditionalist when it comes to medicine.'

'Tell me about it.'

'So we could just...' She raises an eyebrow and looks at Lucy.

'Lie to him?' Lucy says, all mock shock.

'Just not tell him. It's not actually lying, as such. More an omission.'

'Poor Bill.'

'Yes, poor Bill.' Carys smiles. She picks up the pill dispenser and gives it a rattle. 'And if I set this up and pay for it and all that, will you promise me you'll give these a go? For two months at least, see how it goes?'

Lucy looks at her. 'It's not as if I've got anything to lose, I suppose.'

'The worst possible outcome is no change. Anything else is a bonus.'

She picks a last stray maple blueberry from her plate and pops it in her mouth. 'All right then. Let's give it a go.'

SIX

'Here we are.' Carys drives past the pub and approaches the glorified lay-by that passes for a car park.

Lucy looks up from Alice's book, which she is balancing on her lap. A labour of love, built up over eighteen years of motherhood, it's a beautiful hardbound volume of inked and watercoloured maps and illustrations outlining the features, histories and locations of her favourite trees. Written on the first page – presumably when she started the book, shortly after Sara's birth – are the words *My legacy for my children*. Today is the first day of the project to visit each tree. It is also the twelfth anniversary of Alice's death – her death day.

'I wish Sara could have got here for today,' Lucy says.

'She couldn't just drop everything. She'll be here on Wednesday.'

'And she can come to the rest of Mum's trees with us.'

'Of course.'

'I can't wait to see her again.'

'Me neither.'

Although actually Carys has mixed feelings about her other stepdaughter – just five years younger than her – re-entering their lives after a decade away. She's managed to swing a six-month sabbatical from the New South Wales Police Force, so it's not exactly a flying visit, either.

Lucy strokes the book, which she has kept in a box under her bed since she was a little girl. Carys has coaxed her out with it and hopes that, along with the hypnotherapy and the promise she has wrung from her to keep going with her regular shrink and meds, visiting Alice's trees will help get her properly better this time.

Carys has tried so hard, but it is to her eternal regret that she has never managed to make amends to her stepdaughter for the suicide of her mother. There's a ghost rattling around Lucy's head and it needs exorcising.

So here they are, using the marks Alice made in the book to really try to meet her. She cared deeply about many things beyond her family. Medicine, equality and social justice, of course. But she was also passionate about painting, the environment and, as her book demonstrates, trees. *Our guardians*, she wrote on one of the pages, *our gentle giants who remind us of our place in the world.*

She was also, Carys knows, passionate about regret. The queen of regret, in fact, but she tries not to think about that too much.

She unclips her seat belt and looks at Lucy. 'Ready?'

Lucy closes her eyes and nods. She grabs the irises from the footwell and, book and flowers in hand, levers herself out of the car.

They let the dog out of the back, and while she runs over the grassy downland looking for a perfect place to pee, Carys and Lucy stretch themselves out after two hours cooped up in the car.

Carys tries to sense the desperation of those who find their way here, but all she gets is a benign sense of peace. To the south, the grassy hills lope away towards the hazy sea in the distance, the only hint of peril the white pip of a lighthouse. Out on the horizon, where the deeper blue of the sea blends into the sky, a boat moves silently across the water. Above them, a pair of skylarks trill, wary of the dog, who has got too close to their nest.

Lucy turns and looks across the road. 'That's the path she took. And those are her hawthorns.' Handing the book, open at the appropriate page, to Carys, she points at a bank of spindly trees leaning northwards away from the cliff edge like a quiff.

'"The survivors in an unforgiving world."' Cary's reads Alice's words, written in her distinctive hand beside her immaculate if quirky watercolour of the hawthorns.

For the past four years, they have come here on this anniversary. Bill has no idea. He wouldn't understand.

'She parked the car where we did and that's the path she must have taken,' Lucy says, hugging the flowers as they look eastwards towards where the green meets the sky. This talking through the steps Alice took is part of the ritual.

'Although another time, she must have sat and painted the hawthorns.' Carys looks at the book and works out the spot from Alice's illustration. It's a park bench a few steps away. 'Come on,' she says to Lucy and the dog.

They sit on the bench, look at the book, look at the hawthorns and agree that yes, this is where Alice sat.

'"Fairies live under the hawthorn to guard it",' Lucy reads. '"In Celtic mythology, it is one of the most sacred trees and symbolises love and protection."' Despite the dizzying blue of the vast morning sky, a shadow falls over her face.

Carys stands, stretches, ramps up the energy. 'Come on, Luce!'

They make their way along the path to the edge of the cliff. A section scarred by a nasty-looking crack in the chalky turf has been fenced off. One of the fence posts has bunches of flowers and soft toys lashed to it.

'This is where she stood.' Lucy positions herself on the cliff, to the right of the fence, and looks down. It's low tide right now. Carys shudders at the thought of how the rocky chalk beach might feel as your body meets it.

Lucy unties the string that binds Alice's favourite irises – twelve of them, one for each year – and throws them off the edge, one by one. They take their time to almost float down, until they are blue blots hundreds of feet beneath them. Holding her phone, she leans over to photograph them.

'Careful.' Carys holds fast onto the strap of Lucy's bag. Standing here, she can almost understand the pull that death exerts over some people. Almost.

'Hashtag for Alice,' Lucy says, as she takes the photographs. She puts the book on the turf and snaps Alice's paintings at her feet.

Carys doesn't approve of Lucy documenting her grief and various 'episodes' – as they refer to them in the family – for everyone to see on social media, but what can you do? When she tries to broach the subject, Lucy wastes no time in pointing out that though Carys is just sixteen years older than her, so much has changed that millennials like her have no hope of understanding what Gen Z are getting up to. 'Boomer Bill', as she calls her father, has even less chance.

Even so, the photograph she posted two weeks ago of her stitched-up arm, the drip held in place at her wrist by transparent tape, made Carys want to storm into the hospital and rip the phone away from her.

And now it looks like she is making Alice's tree book public too, putting it all out there for anyone to see. Carys wants to tell her it's private, that it's family stuff, but she knows she can't. Because as she and Bill have discussed, however much it hurts, Alice has first place in Lucy's heart. As with everything to do with her predecessor, Carys just has to suck it up.

'Plus,' Bill said just the other night, 'this is the meat that will make an artist of her.'

For Lucy, who has inherited both her parents' gifts with line, form and colour, is set on studying fine art at Central St Martins after her foundation year. Bill says the fact that she is going with the purity of art, rather than the more vocational route he and Carys took through architecture, is something to celebrate. Carys, however, is worried about whether she will ever make a living.

But again, it is not her place to ask those questions. And anyway, if they pull off the Five Oaks development, it may well mean that making a living will be optional for Lucy.

Once again, she has to stop herself from thinking how lucky her stepdaughter is.

Lucy steps back and turns around, taking photographs of the green, the blue, the white. A couple of seagulls streak across the hill towards them, screaming and squawking like angry old women.

She turns her camera on the decorated fence post, which, Carys now sees, also bears a garland of crocheted flowers.

'Mum used to crochet,' Lucy says. Unnecessarily, because several of Alice's blankets still cover sofas and beds both in Bill and Carys's house and at the Stoke Newington flat. She frames and snaps several images, then stops and bends to take a closer look.

'Come here,' she tells Carys, who joins her and squats to look at the note she is pointing out, where someone has written *Not waving but drowning*.

'It's a poem by Stevie Smith about how someone who everyone thought was larking around was actually in serious trouble,' Carys says.

'Thanks for the Eng. lit. lesson,' Lucy says. 'But the thing is the handwriting.'

'What?'

She takes her bag from her shoulder and pulls out Alice's book. 'Look. It's the same.'

Carys squints at the note, then at the book. 'There's a similarity.'

'Similarity? They're exactly the same.'

But having been through an art foundation course herself, and then architect training, Carys just sees a certain kind of arty handwriting done by someone who is used to holding a pen or pencil to express themselves. Art teachers, architects, painters. Alice's handwriting had not the tiniest hint of doctor in it, which is possibly why she was such an outstanding GP.

To please Lucy, though, Carys nods and tells her she's right.

Lucy breathes deeply, in and out, like something inside her has settled. Like she is looking for confirmation that her mother, dead all these years, is somehow still around.

As they head back to the car, a slight woman passes them on the other side of the hawthorns, her face hidden under a straw sunhat. They turn to watch her as she heads towards the cliff edge.

She pauses and looks out to sea, her arms flung wide.

'Should we go and see if she's OK?' Lucy says.

But the woman shakes her hands in the air, then turns to the left and carries on away from them, along the path that leads to Eastbourne.

Carys calls Nonna and they all pile into the car, looking forward to the final part of the ritual: coffee and cake at Birling Gap.

SEVEN

'When I grow up, I want to be like Lucy.'

Still in her tunic from her after-school ballet class, Binnie swings on the back of the mid-century sofa in Ajay's bright waiting room, stretches out her piece-of-string legs and shows Carys a couple of positions involving what her teacher calls 'pretty hands'.

'That's a nice thing to say,' Carys tells her.

'I'm not just saying it. I really do want to be like Lucy.'

'Of course you do. Do you want your hummus and rice cakes now?'

Carys can't bear to even think it to herself, but the last person in the world she wants her daughter to turn out like is Lucy.

Lucy is in with Ajay. Of course, he says he needs to be alone with her, but even though she is eighteen – so technically an adult – and even though Ajay's qualifications hang framed on the wall opposite her, Carys can't help feeling like she has abandoned her.

She is also experiencing mild buyer's regret. Ironically, when she booked Ajay, she had forgotten that when Lucy was six, she might have seen the beginning of an encounter between Carys and Alice. It was not a pretty sight, and *if* she saw it and *if* she remembers it, there may be trouble ahead.

Lots of ifs, so Carys tucks it away for now.

In any case, Edina used to say that the accusers she provided expert witness against would create fictional memories to make sense of their unhappy present. Carys can use this against any story Lucy might unearth about her stepmother shouting at her soon-to-be-dead mother.

It can be dealt with.

She peers through the open waiting room door, across the blonde parquet hallway towards the closed treatment room door. It must be soundproofed, because however much she strains her ears, she can't hear even a murmur, let alone the screams the worst-case-scenario imaginings she is trying to suppress would produce. She has a horrible image of Lucy pinned out on Ajay's treatment couch like a Victorian biology specimen, her insides exposed.

'Of course it's not like that,' she whispers to herself.

'What?' Binnie says.

'Eat.' Carys points at Binnie's snack.

Hypnotherapy clearly pays, because Ajay's treatment room is on the ground floor of a large Edwardian house on one of the leafy streets leading on to Hampstead Heath. The waiting room contains a forest of house plants and three sofas arranged around a rectangular bay window. The view is over the jungly front garden. Ajay's motorbike – a classic Enfield with matching sidecar – sits in the driveway under the foliage.

Carys looks at her watch. Lucy has been in now for one hour and five minutes. The appointment is running over.

Beside Binnie's rice cakes on the coffee table, a neat pile of leaflets printed by Ajay's professional association claim that hypnotherapy can help you become happier and healthier and unlock your potential.

Carys hopes so, because it's costing her enough.

'Where is she?' Binnie climbs to her feet and dances round the table to sit next to Carys on the sofa, licking the last of the hummus from her fingers.

Carys checks her watch again. From her extensive experience with Lucy, she knows that private therapists tend not to go over time. There's no one else in the waiting room, though. As it's gone six, Lucy's appointment is probably the last of the day. 'Looks like they're overrunning. Want to look at your homework?'

Binnie makes a face. So instead Carys gets her notebook out and sets out a grid of dots to play a game of boxes.

They're just getting to the interesting bit where you start claiming whole lines of boxes for yourself when the door to the treatment room slowly opens, over half an hour later than scheduled.

Ajay is alone.

The tension that Carys has not wanted even to acknowledge erupts, making her heart skip a couple of beats.

'Is it OK if you stay here alone for a few minutes while I talk to Mummy?' Ajay asks Binnie.

His face and tone give nothing away. It's the kind of attitude Carys uses before telling a client that because of unforeseen circumstances – say a high water table only discovered after digging foundations – their build is going to cost a whole load more than expected and come in way past its due date.

Binnie looks at her. Carys squeezes her knee, lines up a vintage YouTube *Sesame Street* video on her iPad and hands it to her. 'Won't be a minute,' she says, then stands and follows Ajay through into his treatment room.

Lucy smiles at her from an expensively Danish-looking plywood and sheepskin reclining chair on the other side of the room. Set on a plinth to her side, a cylinder of quartz crystal the size of a man's forearm points its diamond-cut tip to the ceiling.

'She did really well,' Ajay says.

Lucy beams like something long extinguished has lit up inside her. 'I was with Mum. We were so happy. She was pushing me in a swing, and then before that she took one of my paintings – of Nonna and her puppies – and put it up on the fridge with magnets and said it was the best painting she had ever seen. Then we were running in the park, and I fell over and cut my knee and she looked after me so well, cuddling me and kissing me and then cleaning the blood and putting on a *Monsters, Inc.* plaster so that in the end I felt like I had actually been lucky for falling over.'

'That's great!' Carys says, relief overriding any personal sense of having been usurped by these memories of Alice.

'A textbook first session,' Ajay says. 'I feel I know Alice really well already.'

'Join the club,' Carys says.

'She sounds like a great lady.'

'I never actually met her,' Carys says, her fingers crossed behind her back. 'But the reports are excellent.'

'She was the best mum in the world,' Lucy says.

Ajay looks apologetically at Carys like he can see her smarting behind her smile, then he turns to Lucy.

'You may feel a little sleepy, so do be careful tonight. Don't drive or operate any heavy machinery.'

'I can smelt iron ore, though, yeah?' Lucy says.

'Not for at least twenty-four hours,' Ajay says. 'Then smelt away to your heart's content.'

'When can I come back?' Lucy looks from Ajay to Carys.

Ajay moves past a black leather sofa to a desk at the far end of the room and sits at an iMac, the only item on its surface. He jiggles the mouse with his long fingers and concentrates on the screen, his eyes hypnotic even as he reads his calendar. Carys hopes he only ever uses his powers for good, because he could clearly get anyone to do anything he wanted. Without warning, he turns his gaze on her, making her blush. 'Is it possible not to bring the little one next time?'

'Why?'

He smiles. 'As we go deeper, it would be good for Lucy to have your undivided attention after the session.'

His implication that Lucy might get upset tightens Carys's chest. 'Not unless it's during the day.'

Ajay frowns at the screen again. 'Her dad can't have her? Bill, isn't it?'

'How did you know...?'

Ajay smiles over at Lucy, who rolls her eyes. 'I told him all about Dad, of course. Can't leave *Dad* out of it.'

'I do Binnie,' Carys says.

This is partly down to Bill's back, which makes being with Binnie a challenge for him. Also, he works more on the creative side of their business, and needs long, uninterrupted dreaming time. But mostly it's because Carys just loves being with Binnie. With her own sister dying aged just six, she has an acute awareness of how precious the childhood years are – even more so since her failure so far to conceive again means this could be her one shot at being a full mother.

'I can do ten next Monday morning,' Ajay says.

Carys brings up her own calendar. Binnie is on summer holiday then, but she is booked into the local play scheme. As project manager, Carys needs to be on site at Five Oaks as much as possible during the coming few weeks. But Lucy is way more important than any building project – even this one, where she and Bill have not only their life savings but also their considerable reputations as eco-architects at stake.

'Cool.' She notes the appointment in her diary.

'It's going to be a great ride,' Ajay says as he moves over to shake Lucy's hand. 'Fantastic to meet you.'

As Carys unlocks the car for Binnie and Lucy, she runs over Ajay's parting shot. She can't help feeling there was an implied 'at last'. And 'a great ride'? Isn't that an odd way of looking at a course of treatment?

But whatever. Lucy is blissed out on the ride back to Muswell Hill. So much so that she declares she is happy enough to go back to Stoke Newington that night.

During the discussion that follows this – he has no idea of course about the hypnotherapist visit – Bill supports Lucy's choice and reminds Carys that she is an adult whose wishes must be respected.

Powerless then to stop it, Carys even finds herself driving her stepdaughter back to the flat.

EIGHT

Weary from sleepless hours worrying about Lucy alone in the flat and Sara's arrival from Australia tonight – she's planning to surprise her at the airport – Carys runs a final check over the set-up for the presentation. At least the weather is lovely and they haven't had to go to the contingency plan expense of putting up the marquee.

Elsa's PR company have done a great job. The canapés are laid out on the trestle table and the Sussex white wine chills in a zinc ice bath. They're just finishing setting out folding chairs facing the podium where she and Bill – Earthstrong Architects – will present their vision for Five Oaks and take questions from the neighbours.

Despite all the costly preparation, this is not going to be easy.

Carys turns to look at the site. It used to be Bill and Alice's back garden. It was briefly hers too, until she and Bill built their new home just north of here, a house free of ghosts and a prototype for the carbon-neutral homes Earthstrong plan to raise right here.

The old Georgian house still stands at the top, although its former incarnation of rambling boho family home has been erased. It's now sleek apartments, the sale of which has partly funded Five Oaks. Like the homes to be built behind it, inside their grand shell the flats have impeccable environmental credentials.

Bill and Alice bought the house with its huge garden twenty-seven years ago. They got it for a song – it was a wreck, and this was long before the area became fashionable. The garden occupies almost an entire block, with those on the enclosing roads backing onto it. There's a nice story about a former owner of the big house winning portions of his neighbours' back gardens at backgammon. Sadly, Bill's research uncovered that it was in fact the first building in the area and the other houses were built around it in the mid-1800s.

Given that, the opposition the current owners of those houses have put up to the new development is a little ironic. Carys suspects that a big part of the problem is that a full 60 per cent of these homes will be affordable, thereby threatening the tone of the area.

Affordable is of course a relative term in north London, so it's hardly going to become the kind of place she grew up in. But today is not going to be a lesson in history or politics. All the legal and planning battles have been won. Today is all about charm.

And Carys is certain the neighbours will come round in the end. Five Oaks will be low-level and visually unobtrusive and there will be an urban village green for everyone to use around the five old oak trees the site is named after.

Bill strides past the podium, charm personified. He is looking particularly good today, in his usual minimalist style – a blue linen ensemble that manages to not look like a suit and a beautiful shirt with a subtle leaf motif that Carys bought him specially for today. His best walking cane – vintage ebony with a nice silver knob – sets the look off extremely well, making a virtue of its necessity.

'Hey.' He puts his arm round her waist and kisses her. 'All good?'

She nods. 'Ready to meet the beasts.'

A woman in a pink dress asks the first question. 'What about the trees?'

'I'm so glad you asked that,' Carys says, even though she has just covered the trees in great detail in her presentation. She looks up at the thirty or so wealthy neighbours sitting in front of her, drinking their free wine. Elsa and her team stand behind them, ready to refill any glass threatening emptiness.

'If you look around you' – the mostly grey heads of the neighbours turn to where Carys is pointing – 'you will see that we have many great old trees on the site. We have designed the development around them, and are also reinstating other plants to fit around the buildings. We have potted up some of the spares for you to take home today for your own gardens.'

The anticipated murmur of appreciation reaches everywhere except the corner where Mr and Mrs Bullock sit. Mr B, who has long established himself as a thorn in Carys and Bill's side, puts up his hand. 'What about the wildlife area?'

Although most of the neighbours here weren't in residence during Bill and Alice's time, the Bullocks – Alastair and Claire, but never anything but Mr and Mrs to Carys – actually pre-date them. During the costly and lengthy planning process, they objected on every possible ground. Earthstrong resolved each point through the design process, but yet here they are, still hoping they can somehow stop things.

It's too late now, though. Bill and Carys have it watertight.

Bill steps forward. He and Bullock have never seen eye to eye. There were always complaints about the noise of the children, the parties he and Alice used to throw in the garden. Indeed, Mr B kicked up a stink about the very wildlife area he now seems so keen to protect, claiming that it could spread weeds into his manicured patch.

Bill is too much of a pro to allow any of this to intrude. 'That's a very good point, Alastair,' he says.

Carys watches Bullock bristle at the first-name use, as if Bill, five or so years his junior, should show deference.

'We will have to dig up the wildlife area, which as you know came about through an absence of gardening on our part!' A ripple of laughter runs through the audience, although yet again the Bullocks remain stony and silent.

'But we have engaged an environmental archivist who will collect seeds and rehome any native species, and we will establish a small wildflower meadow on the village green, complete with a pond where we hope to encourage frogs and newts. If anything, there will be more rather than less wildlife and wild flowers here when we're finished.'

Bullock stands and waves his *Telegraph* in the air. 'And when will that be? We've already suffered weeks of disruption, sawing, lorries, diggers moving in.'

'If you look at your brochure, page twenty,' Carys says, and the assembled neighbours bend their heads to the beautiful booklet Elsa's graphics people put together, 'you'll see a full schedule of works, with dates and what to expect. We've designed it to keep any inconvenience to you to the minimum.'

'This isn't worth the fancy paper it's printed on.' Bullock's face, already full of broken veins, is turning quite purple. 'All these projects overrun. Over time and over budget. It's the same old story everywhere.' His lip is lifted in a snarl as he speaks with what appears to be complete authority.

Although Bill's voice remains level, Carys can see his exasperation in the way he clenches his cane. 'As I hope we have demonstrated,' he says, 'in both this meeting today and our actions up until now, we are a different sort of developer.'

'Oh, they all say that.' Still standing, Bullock tries to engage his neighbours, but nearly everyone here has been at one time or another the butt of his complaints, and they all receive his passive-aggressive round robins about DIY noise, dog mess and swearing in the street.

Even Mrs B, sitting meekly beside him, is looking at her feet as if she wishes the ground beneath her would swallow her up.

Carys gives Elsa a surreptitious thumbs-up.

The Bullocks can make all the noise they like: they're not going to bring Bill and Carys down.

Carys waves off Elsa's team, who have done a great job clearing up, then kisses Bill goodbye. He's heading back to the studio to think about plywood detailing for the kitchens.

Back in the site office, she kicks off her heels and slips on her bright red Hunters. She wishes she could build houses without mud or environmental disruption, but you can't make an omelette without breaking eggs.

The builders are just starting up again after the presentation, so she grabs the platter of canapés she has saved for them and the flask of coffee she brought in earlier. With Nonna trotting beside her, she heads off to find Artur, the site manager.

He's with Stanislaw, his chief ground worker, discussing the plan for digging up what the Bullocks referred to as the wildlife area – 'The Wilderness', as Alice dubbed it. The name stuck with the family, and now the builders use it too.

Greeting both men, Carys hands Stanislaw the canapés to pass on to what Artur calls 'the boys'. Her entire professional life she has sworn by the skills and work ethic of Polish builders, and she is delighted that with the post-Brexit shortage of construction workers, Artur has managed to negotiate visas for his workers.

'Well, that went well,' she tells him as she pours him a coffee. They sit at one of the picnic tables she installed for breaks for the builders. 'And the site's looking great.'

'We have speedy first week. My boys are hard workers.' Artur's big hands make the mug look absurdly tiny. She and Bill have worked with him for years. He's tall, fair, capable and strong, with extraordinary forearms.

'I thought you'd not be moving on to this area until the end of next week,' she says. 'But here we are.' She's delighted, because time is, after all, money, and she and Bill have a lot riding on this – everything, in fact. They are, not to put too fine a point on it, in hock up to their eyeballs. If they go over the year they have scheduled for completion, they are in trouble.

Artur and Carys check through some paperwork then, coffees in hand, take a tour of the site. Meanwhile, over by The Wilderness, the boys make a hell of a racket with a couple of chainsaws. When the work's noisy like this, Carys can't help feeling sorry for the Bullocks and their fellow neighbours backing onto The Wilderness end of the garden.

After a while, the chainsaw stops. But the respite is short-lived, because shortly afterwards, the boys fire up their digger.

The noise continues, and as Carys nears the end of her muddy walkabout with Artur, she starts thinking about how soon she can get back to the nice cool, clean and quiet Earth-strong studio a short cycle ride from here.

But just as they are sharing a satisfied farewell handshake, there's a lot of Polish shouting. Carys and Artur rush towards the commotion to find the digger bucket suspended in mid-air with something dangling from it.

It looks like a tartan blanket and a disembowelled spotted cushion. Tangled up in all that is a… She can't quite believe it.

A sleeve with a toy skeleton hand dangling from it?

The boys are in a high-vis huddle around the hole they have just dug. Stanislaw hurries over to Carys and Artur.

'We got to stop,' he says.

They follow him to the newly dug earth.

'Oh damn,' Artur says.

'Get back,' Carys tells Nonna, who is all ready to leap in.

In the ground, curled up like a large dormouse, is the body – no, skeleton – that the sleeve and hand belong to. From its size, and from the remains of the clothes that still cling to it – a gold-adorned princess dress that Carys instantly, chillingly recognises – the skeleton is that of a child. A young girl about Binnie's age.

To do Carys credit, *Poor thing* is the first thought that comes to her mind. It is a good minute or so before she echoes Artur's *Oh damn*.

Because Stanislaw is right. They are going to have to stop.

NINE

Non-stop sounded like such a great idea, but as Sara gathers her cabin baggage and stumbles off the plane at Heathrow, she realises how much the Singapore stopover on her original journey to Australia had helped her body cope.

She wonders if she can upgrade her return flight, which she has already booked for six months' time, or at least change it so she can break the journey. But that's for the future, and this moment, when she finally shuffles off the jetway and onto the airport floor, is the first time she has stepped on British ground for a whole third of her life.

When she left, she was a broken girl quitting a mess of an existence. Her father was useless to her, destroyed as he was by grief, alcohol and his motorbike crash. At least neither she nor Lucy was in the sidecar, she thinks as she trundles her carry-on along the moving walkway, and since all he smashed into was a large sycamore, no one else was hurt. Also back then, her clingy ex Tom was in denial about her wanting to finish with him. And worst of all, Carys had just moved in: so sweet and kind and so keen to mend everyone that Sara couldn't help but mistrust her.

But all of this was trivial beside the yawning space left by losing Alice just a year earlier. It hollowed Sara out, and there is still a Mum-sized gap inside her. Her new discovery about Alice's body not being found has only expanded it.

Her big regret is that in the year leading up to her mother's death – or disappearance – she doesn't think they exchanged a civil word. At the time, she thought it was Alice's fault, but now she sees that she was just being a typical impossible, irrationally angry teenage girl.

It didn't help of course that her mum was stretched in all directions with her GP centre, her art and her family. There were a lot of fights between Bill and Alice around that time too, which Sara blamed entirely on her volatile, stressed, sometimes unstable mother.

But Sara herself was out of control back then – boys, drugs, alcohol, all the usual teenage rebellions. She thought she was such a bad girl, but her police career has shown her what an amateur she actually was in that respect.

Poor Alice. If she did die, she didn't deserve to, even though Sara, in her most awful, dark and grief-stricken moments, has sometimes tried out that thought.

But if she didn't die? If she's still around somewhere, a new life, a new family...

Well, then she really does deserve to die.

She shakes that idea out of her head. Spotting a toilet, she slips inside to see if she can find drinking water.

There is none.

The last Tube leaves just before midnight, and the queue at passport control is snaking so slowly round the hall that it takes an hour for her to get through. Her backup plan to get to Lucy's flat is a very expensive cab, and although she isn't exactly broke, she could do without that.

When she finally gets past the hatchet-faced border official – it's so nice to feel welcomed – the icing on the shit cake hits the fan when the luggage from her flight hasn't even arrived in the baggage hall, 'due to a shortage of handlers'. Another twenty-minute wait – not even alleviated by a coffee, because the machine is out of order – and the conveyor belt farts into action; finally Sara's two hefty suitcases sail into view.

Her heart pounding in a body that has no idea where it is in time, she rushes through the Nothing to Declare channel and out into the arrivals hall, scanning the ceiling for any indication as to which direction she should take to get to the Tube station before it closes.

'Sara! Sara!'

She stops, suddenly. Someone in an equal hurry for no doubt the exact same reason bowls straight into the back of her, curses, then slides past, rolling his suitcase over her toe.

'Ow!' she cries.

'Sorry,' he says, offering a perfect example of the British passive aggression she had almost forgotten.

She returns her attention to the voice, which calls her name once more.

There she is, a small, slim figure in a tasteful, no doubt organic and expensive linen dress, waving a slender brown arm. Her other hand is curled tightly around an astoundingly pretty bunch of wild flowers and foliage that look hand-picked rather than bought from the M&S concession behind her.

Bloody, bloody Carys.

Against Sara's express instructions not to do so, she has come to meet her at the airport.

And now Sara is going to have to pretend to be all glad to see the woman she sometimes thinks had more to do with her mother's death – disappearance – than anyone yet knows.

Despite all that, and despite the fact that she just wants to lie down and go to sleep on her suitcases, she paints a smile on her face and steps forward to hug her stepmother for the first time ever.

Carys looks older. Sara, who is turning thirty in October, wonders if that's what happens on the way to forty. Also, being married to Bill must be pretty hard work – not the easy cash cow Carys probably thought it was.

She feels like a fragile little bird in Sara's arms, all tense and held together by worry. Something is wrong, and Sara thinks of all the arguments and shouting and fighting that went on between her mother and her father. Is it happening again? Is Bill going to end up full-on Ted Hughes? To lose one wife to suicide may be regarded as a misfortune; to lose two looks downright suspicious.

'Oh, you poor thing,' Carys tells her. 'You look exhausted.'

Here we go, thinks Sara. Let the stepmummy gaslighting commence. And pot kettle black, of course, although she is too polite to return the comment.

'I'm actually OK, thanks. Just a long flight, you know. You didn't have to come and pick me up.'

Carys hands her the flowers and takes one of the suitcases from her. 'I wouldn't have it any other way. Now, let's get you home. I'm in the short-stay.' She starts pulling the case past a row of shops, one of which is a Starbucks.

'I need a coffee,' Sara says.

'Sure.' Is there a tiny hint of exasperation in the way Carys turns and smiles? In any case, there's no suggestion that Sara should sit and drink her flat white at the tables outside the concession. So there's a walk to the car park balancing bags and coffee, while Carys flutters on about how pleased they are to be having her back, and how Lucy is dying to see her, and how Bill is beside himself with excitement – an emotional state that is beyond Sara's powers of imagination to picture on her father.

Carys puts the suitcases in the back of the Volvo, then opens the passenger door for her, like she's her chauffeur. Sara experienced this pathological looking-after when Carys first moved in with/on Bill. It hurt her teeth even back then, when she arguably needed it.

Now it really boils her piss.

'I've got the spare room ready for you,' Carys says as she fastens her own seat belt. 'I found your old duvet cover and that lovely Irish blanket you had on your bed. It's not as big as your room in the old house, but it's got a fantastic view out over the trees, and there's a little sofa in there too.'

Sara should have been more explicit earlier, as soon as she made the decision, but, because she knew how much opposition she would have to put up with, she wasn't. So now she needs to put Carys right before they get too far along the journey. As the expensive, silent electric car swings out of the short-stay car park, she sips her coffee for fortitude and turns to her stepmother.

'I'm actually staying with Lucy,' she says. 'She's expecting me tonight.'

Carys turns, shocked, to look at her, and Sara wants to yell at her to keep her eyes on the damn road, which is all bends and roundabouts and lanes to change. But of course sensible Carys breathes in and turns back to do exactly that.

'OK,' she says, smiling just a touch too brightly. 'That will make Lucy very happy.'

'It's just we have so much catching-up to do, and I'd like to be there for her, you know. After all this time.'

'That will be good for her.'

Is there an unspoken *about time too* in there? Or is Sara just projecting?

'Bill was so looking forward to seeing you, though,' Carys says after a few moments.

'I'll come round as soon as I've caught up.'

'Why don't you both come over on Friday? I'll cook a welcome dinner. It's two days away, so you'll have plenty of

time to get over your jet lag and spend some time with Lucy.'
Carys puts her hand on Sara's knee. 'He's desperate to see you,
Sara.'

Sara isn't sure how much she believes that, let alone how
much the feeling is reciprocated. Her father hardly ever instigated contact when she was away, and she's certain that he
viewed her departure as a desertion. After Alice, he lost the
ability to see things from his daughters' point of view. It pains
Sara even to think it, but in many ways it was a good thing that
Carys came along. If it weren't for her, would she even still be
in touch with him?

'Sure,' she says. 'That'll be lovely.'

They head on, along the almost empty late-night Parkway
towards the North Circular, and Sara stares out at suburban
London. Even at this hour, everything looks somehow defeated,
as if this is a country that has given up.

As she sits beside her fidgety, fake-smiling stepmother, she
wonders how long she can bear it here.

Any of it.

TEN

'You said Sara was going to walk me to school,' Binnie says.

'I'm sorry,' Carys replies as they wait for Nonna to pee.

Yesterday was a total disaster. After that poor child's body was discovered, Artur called the police, the whole site was closed down and everyone was sent home. She imagines it silent and surrounded with police tape, the Bullocks smiling smugly down from their bedroom window.

Then she had to console Bill. Lucy and Sara had played on that grave; the family ate blackberries from bushes growing over the poor girl's bones.

'Who could do that to a child?' he asked Carys.

Not once did he worry about how it will put them back, about how they'll lose money. Carys feels quite hard-hearted that this is rising in her own concerns.

What she hasn't yet brought herself to tell him is that the little girl was buried in the garden while he and Alice were living in the house. She knows this because she bought the dress she saw on her body for her sister Emily's sixth birthday present, which was over ten years after Bill and Alice moved in. It was a special edition H&M Kids princess dress, and Carys had been lucky to get hold of one before they all sold out that summer. Like the girl in the ground, Emily had been buried in it. Her little grave is in the cemetery in Hull, just a mile away from their parents' house, but even so, it was too much for Carys to see that yesterday.

Having had enough of thinking of the poor little girl as the body, the victim, the discovery, she has named her Emma, in memory of Emily.

Because she was so busy preparing for Sara's arrival, Carys hasn't had a chance to look into all the possible ramifications for Five Oaks. Tina, the Earthstrong office manager, is on the case, but after she's dropped Binnie off, Carys really needs to crack on. First thing she needs to find out is if their insurance covers it, because a delay that goes beyond their contingencies could be disastrous. Bill, who she made take a sleeping pill before she set off to pick up Sara last night, will probably be out of action this morning, but she's happy to get on alone.

Why couldn't Sara have said she was going to stay with Lucy earlier? And why did Lucy keep it secret from her and Bill?

Is this what it is going to be like from now on, the two girls ganging up against her?

As they turn the corner at the school gates, the mum chatter dims. Carys feels like Clint Eastwood walking into a bar in an old Western.

'Hey!' Trailing Hetty and Milo, Elsa loops through the crowd to join her. Hetty and Binnie lock heads and start talking about best-friend things, and Milo bends to hug Nonna.

'I heard about the body,' Elsa says in a voice the children would be hard pushed to hear.

Carys blinks and frowns. 'What? How?'

'Fiona's blog.'

'Jesus.'

Elsa hands Carys her phone. 'Her cop bloke tipped her off, and she's blogged and tweeted the hell out of it. It's all over the parents' WhatsApps now, too.'

Carys skims the offending article, feeling for the first time in years like she could punch someone.

Fiona – who lolls about six mothers away – is a local shit-stirrer who takes stances purely because they are controversial and dramatic. Opposed to Five Oaks since the start, she's even interviewed the bloody Bullocks. And now she's spreading nasty insinuations about how long Bill has owned the land, and how his first wife killed herself after 'severe mental health issues'.

'Isn't this libel?'

Elsa, who knows about these things, shakes her head. 'She's not making any direct accusations, merely collating and repeating material already in the public domain.'

'Hold this.' Carys hands Elsa the dog lead and steps towards Fiona.

'She's got her gang on her side,' Elsa warns. 'It'll go all *Mean Girls*.'

Carys takes back Nonna's lead.

Louise, a younger mum, sashays up with her gaggle behind her, yoga bags slung over their shoulders. 'That poor little girl,' she says.

'What poor little girl?' Binnie asks.

'Just something in the news,' Carys tells her. She angles her head so Binnie can't see her. 'Please don't talk about it in front of the children,' she whispers.

Someone else speaks up from behind Louise. 'Why do you want to keep it secret?'

The bell goes and the Year 1 teacher opens the school door. Carys turns her back on the women and bends to kiss Binnie, who runs off hand in hand with Hetty.

She turns back. 'I don't want my six-year-old daughter to know about it, because it's horrible. I hope you are treating your own children with the same respect.'

'Better split, girls,' Louise says. 'Asana Stevie don't wait.' They strut off towards the strategically placed yoga studio at the end of the road.

'I hate all this school-gates bollocks,' Carys says to Elsa.

'Only another five years to go. Uh-oh.' Elsa nods over at Fiona, who is hurrying towards them.

'I'm so sorry to hear about you-know-what.' Fiona homes straight in on Carys, giving her a hairspray hug.

'It was a shock.' Carys extricates herself, aiming for a civilised rather than murderous response.

'Is it true they think the body's been there for twenty years?' Fiona asks.

'Far too early to tell.' Carys is saying nothing about the dress.

'It must have been a total shock to you. And to Bill.'

'It is.' Carys doesn't like the placing of her husband's name. It feels like an accusation.

'You've closed the site down?'

That's enough for Carys. 'Fiona. I really don't want to talk about it at the moment.'

'Of course. It must be devastating for you.'

'It is, actually.' She leans in. 'And it's not just a body, a good story, a great bit of gossip. It's a young girl who lost her life, possibly violently and illegally, and who instead of a proper grave has been buried in the garden where Bill brought up his daughters.'

'Bill and poor Alice,' Fiona says.

Carys looks at her, her mouth slightly open.

'I remember her from when I was at school with Sara,' Fiona goes on. 'Lovely lady. Such a pity.'

Carys can't speak.

Elsa steps in and pulls herself up to her full six-foot-plus-heels. 'Stop speculating, Fiona. And tell your husband to stop leaking confidential information.'

'Wow,' Fiona says.

'Yes. Wow.'

'What Elsa is saying,' Carys says, 'is can you please just have a bit of empathy for the poor girl, and possibly even for us. Like you say, our family has had its challenges. We can do without gossip.'

Fiona puts a hand on her arm, her voice more sickeningly sympathetic than Carys can actually bear. 'Of course, Carys. And if you need support, I'm here.'

Elsa picks up her rucksack and slings it over her shoulder. 'Carys. Shall we go? Asana Stevie don't wait.'

'You're taking the dog to yoga?' Fiona calls as they head off.

'Dog yoga,' Carys throws back over her shoulder. 'You should do a piece on it.'

'Coffee?' Elsa says once they're out of earshot.

'I wish, but I've got a heap of stuff to sort out.'

However much they might like each other, Elsa and Carys never manage to meet up socially. Such is the lot of women like them, working full-time and doing all the child and family work as well.

Carys pushes open the front door to a silent house. Bill is still upstairs in bed.

She makes two cups of tea, texts Tina to let her know that she'll be in late, then heads upstairs.

The soft darkness of the room smells of Bill in the morning. Even today, it's reassuring, like coming home. She puts his mug on his bedside table, then tiptoes round to her side and lies down next to him.

'Wake up, Billy.' She kisses his eyebrows.

His eyes flutter open, and for a moment it's as if nothing has happened and it's just another day. But then she sees him remember, and his pupils contract as if a filter has dropped in front of them.

'At least I was having a good dream.' He props himself up on his elbows and takes his tea. 'Is she asleep?'

For a horrible moment she thinks he means poor Emma. But of course he's referring to Sara, who he thinks came back with her last night. She tells him she is staying with Lucy and she can see his spirit sink lower.

'It'll be good for Lucy to be with her,' she says. 'They can reconnect after all this time.'

'I made so many mistakes,' Bill says. 'So many things I shouldn't have done, or should have done better.'

She puts down her mug and curls up against him, cradling his cheek in her hand. 'You were grieving. Alice had turned your whole world inside out.'

'It wasn't her fault. She was ill.'

'For the millionth time: if you can forgive her, then you have to forgive yourself.' Carys says this gently, but behind it lies an almost violent wish for it to happen.

'I should have been there for my daughters.'

'You did what you could. And it wasn't your fault that Sara was an angry, grieving teen.'

'I should have helped her.'

'We did our best. But she found happiness in Australia, Billy. She did it by herself, without us, but that's a good thing. She's built a life.'

'While my remaining daughter wants to go the same way as her mother.'

Carys gently puts her finger on his lips. 'That's not true. You know it was an accident.'

He drains his mug, puts it down on the sisal rug at the side of the bed and takes her hand. 'You are my saviour.'

'Don't get carried away.'

'How was she?'

'Sara? Good. Looked like she'd been on a plane for twenty-four hours, but apart from that...'

'Did she talk about what happened with that tosser Pete?'

Carys shakes her head. 'We'll find out in time.'

'I hope she really is happy.' He shifts in the bed and winces.

'Have you taken your painkillers?' she asks.

He shakes his head, so she fetches his Tramadol from the dresser and hands him two capsules and the remains of her tea to wash them down.

'I'm going to cook a welcome supper for her tomorrow night. It'll be great. Everything's going to be fine.'

'Positivity prize to Ms Carys Jones.'

'And you'll make a killer dessert.'

He smiles and nods. 'I've been wanting to try a croquembouche.'

'Sounds delicious, whatever it is.'

Carys's phone rings. It's not a number she recognises. She tries to answer it with more composure than she feels.

'Carys Jones?'

It's a male voice at the other end.

'Who is this?' she asks.

'DS Jackson, Tottenham police station. I was wondering if it would be OK if I came to have a chat about the discovery at your building site?'

Bill can hear, and puts his hand across his eyes.

'Of course,' Carys says.

'I'd like also to talk to your business partner, William Anderton. Is he available this morning?'

Carys looks across at her husband, who has now curled over onto his side. She gives their home address. Bill isn't going to get in to the office this morning.

'I should be with you in an hour or so,' DS Jackson says.

When Carys hangs up, Bill turns to her. 'I don't think I can face this.'

'Of course you can,' she tells him. 'You can do anything. And I'll be with you all the way.'

She slips through to the en suite and runs him a bath.

ELEVEN

They're just stacking their breakfast plates in the dishwasher when the doorbell rings, the ridiculously retro seventies *bing-bong* she selected for kitsch value.

'That'll be the pigs,' Carys says, checking on the app and seeing a pleasant-faced man peering straight into the camera.

Bill licks a buttery knife before sliding it into the cutlery basket. 'Show a bit more respect, commoner, or you'll be nicked.'

Carys is grateful for the playfulness. It's sorely needed.

DS Jackson is a lanky white man in a pale baggy linen suit that lends him the air of a watered-down David Bowie. His soft features are given edge by a nose that has at some point in his thirty or so years been broken.

'Come on in,' Carys says, feeling like a character in a TV cop drama. 'Can I get you a cup of tea?'

He declines, so she ushers him towards the sofas. Bill seems to have vanished.

'Nice place,' DS Jackson says as he takes a seat. He's looking around like a burglar casing the joint. 'Very unusual.'

'We designed and built it ourselves. It's a prototype for the buildings at Five Oaks.'

Driven by the oddness of the situation, she witters on about sustainable materials and zero-carbon homes. She is mightily glad when Bill, not having got the no-refreshments memo, backs in through the door carrying a tray with tea and a plate of his milk chocolate chip cookies.

'Good morning,' he says, placing it on the coffee table.

'This is my husband and business partner, Bill Anderton,' Carys says.

'Please, don't get up,' Bill says as he leans over to shake the detective's hand. He busies himself handing out the refreshments. DS Jackson is too polite to decline twice.

'So.' Bill sits down. 'How can we help you?'

'Have you found out anything about the little girl?' Carys asks.

DS Jackson frowns. 'How do you know it was a girl?' It sounds ever so slightly like an accusation.

'I was there when the builders found her,' Carys says. 'She looked about five or six. Same age as my sister when she died. Same age as my daughter.' Her eyes smart. Is this really the time for her grief about Emily to resurface?

She tells the police officer about the dress, but it's hard.

'I'm sorry,' Jackson says. 'It must have been horrible for you.'

'I'm sure you've seen worse.' She pulls out the tissue she had up her sleeve for Binnie's nose and dabs at her eyes.

Bill takes her hand. 'We're both very upset about this whole business. I don't know if you are aware, but I've owned that land for twenty-seven years. My children grew up in the old house.'

'I know, Mr Anderton.'

'I'm sorry?' Bill says.

'I'm Tom. Tom Jackson,' the policeman says.

Bill frowns. 'Tom?' He looks like he is flicking a Rolodex in his brain. Clearly the right card comes up, because he opens his eyes wide with surprise. 'Tom who went out with Sara?'

Tom – he so looks like a Tom – blushes. 'Yup.'

'Isn't there some sort of conflict of interest, you working on this case?'

Detecting a touch of hostility in Bill's tone, Carys shifts in her seat. Being rude to the police is never a good idea – although perhaps it's different if you're a white middle-aged man.

Tom smiles. 'Not if your only link is that you own the land.'

'Of course that's my only damn link.'

'What is this?' Carys asks Bill.

'Tom here was Sara's boyfriend around the time Alice died.' Bill laughs. 'Quite tenaciously so, I seem to remember.'

Tom smiles apologetically. 'It was a long time ago.'

'I don't think we ever met, did we?' Carys says.

He looks awkward. 'Sara kept me out of the way.'

'He was probably the last person Alice saw before she died,' Bill says.

Tom fiddles with his pen and notepad.

'It's so tough, teenage love,' Carys says, trying to smooth things out. 'And small world and all that, guys, but how long do we have to stay away from our site?'

'You'll have to suspend all work while we do the forensics. We need to preserve the crime scene.'

'How do you know it's a crime scene?' Bill asks. Carys hopes he isn't going to be difficult for the entire morning.

'Mystery body turning up is a crime scene, I'm afraid,' Tom says. 'Until we can prove otherwise.'

'So you don't know who she is?' Carys asks.

He shakes his head. 'Doesn't match a description of any missing person. Your comments about the dress will be very useful, and the labs are working to get an accurate date and more details – age, cause of death. We should find out more in a week or so.'

'I thought it would be quicker than that.'

'That's only on the telly, I'm afraid. And we still won't know who she is.'

'What about DNA?'

'Only if we can get something to match it against.'

'Poor girl,' Bill says. 'Poor little girl.'

They all fall silent. Tom's connection to the family makes everything feel less formal, more personal.

To break the spell, Carys offers him another cookie. 'So days? Weeks? What's usual in these circumstances?'

'Nothing's usual, I'm afraid. Every case is unique.'

'But we need to move on with the build,' Bill says.

'Mr Anderton—' Tom says.

'Please, Tom. Call us Carys and Bill.'

'Bill. Can you tell me about the spot where she was found?'

'We call it The Wilderness. When we lived in the house – in fact you'll remember this, Tom – we just let it run wild down there. The garden was massive, and Alice and I were far too busy to do it justice, yet we felt too guilty to employ a gardener. So it was brambles, wild roses, a couple of hawthorns.'

'It was very pretty,' Carys says, reminding them that she too was part of that story; that she too lived in the big house.

'So it was never cultivated or dug up?'

Bill shakes his head. 'The only time Alice or I ever went down there was to pick the blackberries.'

'And you never saw anything suspicious going on?'

'Like someone burying a dead child in my back garden? No.'

Carys takes his hand. 'Bill.'

'You never found anything had been disturbed, or saw any intruders?'

'The garden is entirely enclosed by terraced houses,' Carys says. 'The only practical way into it – until we knocked the garage down for site access – was through the house.'

'The girls could play out there as much as they liked and we never worried,' Bill says.

Carys remembers Lucy spending hours out there, setting her dolls up for tea parties, disappearing with a book, coming back for supper covered in bramble scratches, like a country child. She was so self-sufficient that, ironically, everyone thought she would be the surest survivor of Alice's death.

If Carys's theory about the dress is right, Lucy would have been toddling around the garden as a two-year-old when Emma was put there. Or perhaps the dress was a hand-me-down, so she would have been older. In any case, she was playing in the garden at the time Emma's grave was dug.

Perhaps it was seeing something back then that's at the root of her trouble now.

'There was a spate of break-ins, about ten or so years ago,' she says to Tom. 'But we kept an eye out and you got the guy. A career burglar.'

'So you'd say the neighbours in the houses around the garden were quite observant?'

'Still are,' Carys says. 'Which is a mixed blessing for us.'

'There's local opposition to what you are doing?'

'I don't see why that's relevant—' Bill starts, but Carys squeezes his hand.

'People are always resistant to change,' she says, 'particularly on their own doorstep —'

'Or at the end of their sizeable back gardens,' Bill adds.

'—but we have worked really hard to deal with the objections. Most people are on board now.'

'Except the bloody Bullocks,' Bill says.

'The Bullocks live on the far side of the land and have been consistently difficult—'

'Most unpleasant people.'

'—but we have full planning permission now, so all they've got to hold on to is bad feeling.'

'Still, must be hard though,' Tom says.

Carys smiles. 'It is.'

Bill slaps the tops of his knees. 'Well, this is all very nice, but we've got to get into the office. There's a lot of juggling to be done given the circs.'

'Of course.' Tom reaches into his jacket pocket and hands over his card. 'If you remember anything, just contact me. Any suspicious behaviour in the street. Anything odd in the house or garden – things going missing, being moved. Perhaps strange noises or smells.'

'We had all of that, all the time.' Bill gets up to stack the tray. 'This was a London house full of teenagers and young children.'

'Well then. Anything out of the ordinary.' Tom stands too.

Carys gives him an apologetic smile. 'Please bear in mind that every day we wait is losing us money.'

'I will.'

'But of course, you must do your job. We all want to give that poor child the justice she deserves.'

Tom looks at her as if he is seeing her in a different light.

Bill takes the tray through into the kitchen.

'How's Sara doing?' Tom asks as Carys shows him to the door.

'Really well. She's just come home, in fact, for an extended stay.'

'Give her my regards when you see her,' he says.

'You could have been a bit more civil,' Carys says as she joins Bill in the kitchen. He is washing the mugs by hand, one of his ways of resettling himself after an upset.

'That boy was a complete nightmare,' he says as she picks up a tea towel. 'He made Sara's life a misery with his doggish devotion. She told him she wanted to finish it, and he went to poor Alice on the morning of the day she killed herself, barged into her consulting room and begged her to intervene for him.'

'But that doesn't mean—'

'I hold him partly responsible. And, by the way, wholly responsible for Sara going to Australia.'

'Oh, come on. Alice didn't need a love-struck teenager to help her make up her mind about killing herself.'

Bill winces at this brutal truth. But they have developed the ability to talk about Alice's suicide without euphemism.

'And,' she goes on, 'I'm sure you, I and Alice are more to blame for Sara leaving.'

He concentrates on scrubbing a tea stain from a mug and literally harrumphs.

'What are we going to do?' Carys says. 'Poor little girl. And what about the project? All that planning, all that money...'

He shakes the water from his hands and puts his arms around her. 'We just have to keep moving on with whatever we can.'

He looks at her in that way that reminds her of George Clooney, and she melts. 'Perhaps we could leave any decisions for a bit,' she says, moving into his embrace. 'Perhaps I could just text Tina and tell her we won't be in until after lunch. Perhaps we need a break.'

'Perhaps we do,' he says. 'Perhaps that's exactly what we need.'

She takes him by the hand and leads him upstairs.

Sometimes sex and death, two of the few givens of human existence, sit very close to one another.

There are few couples better placed to know this than Bill and Carys.

TWELVE

As she sits next to Lucy in the back of the Uber to Muswell Hill, Sara wonders how Carys, who paints herself as the perfect stepmother, allowed her sweet, chirpy little sister to grow into this blurry, depressed young woman.

She wants to find out, and stop it.

Poor Lucy.

Sara's teeth itch with anger.

The cab pulls up outside Carys and Bill's house. The odd one out in a row of Edwardian terraces and semis, it's a super-modern box with metal windows set in vertical cedar slats.

'Where's the damn door?' Sara says.

Lucy opens a small box on the wall and holds her finger up to a screen. A door pops out of the cedar. Everything about this house spells wanker to Sara.

'It's super eco,' Lucy says.

As they step through, they are met by the smell of cooking.

Lucy smiles. 'Yum.'

Sara nods. It's all garlic, tomato, herbs. Familiar.

And there he is, standing on the polished concrete floor: her father, for the first time in the flesh in over a decade. He's still handsome, and his walking cane just adds to his elegance.

'Oh, Sara. My love.' He holds out his free arm and she runs towards him like a child lost in the supermarket finding her parent.

'Dad. Oh, Dad.'

As she folds herself into his embrace, the dog bounds up and starts trying to get in on the act, and it's the dog she chose from the litter with her mum all those years ago, and the anger in her is just swept away by an immense feeling of love and relief and the knowledge that she is home.

She even forgets the lies Bill has told her about her mother's death.

Temporarily.

Massive Attack's 'Protection' – Alice's favourite track – is playing in the kitchen. Lucy comes up behind and joins the hug. It's almost like it always was, but then Sara looks up and there's Carys, Alice's gingham pinny over her smart work dress. She's even got a tea towel flung over her shoulder, just like Alice used to.

Interloper.

At least she has the decency to hang back a bit while Sara connects with her real people.

The family bundle untangles and Carys comes forward and kisses her on the cheek. She smells of food and a sort of incense perfume. It's not Alice's vintage Je Reviens, which is a relief. Back home, when she sleeps alone – as she has for the past six months – Sara sprays her pillow with it.

As she steps back, she notices Binnie, the little half-sister she has never met, hanging behind her mother's legs.

'Hey.' Sara squats and holds out her arms. 'Give your big sis a hug.'

'Thank you for my birthday present,' Binnie says as she puts her arms round Sara's neck. Not shy, this one. Brought up in a stable, loving family home.

Lucky girl.

'No worries.' Careful not to allow her feelings about Carys to get in the way – and particularly the ease with which she got pregnant while Sara and Pete exhausted all their options trying – Sara has remembered every birthday and Christmas. She reaches into her bag and hands over the stuffed toy koala she bought ready gift-wrapped at Sydney airport.

Lucy gives Carys a long, tight hug and they all move into a large open-plan living space. The floor is cool underfoot, and despite the cooking chaos in the kitchen area, the space feels light and clear.

'Welcome to our home, Sara,' Carys says. 'Can I get you a drink?'

'Big gin, please,' Sara says.

They sit on two sofas set at right angles to each other, sipping their drinks while Carys asks endless questions about Sara's life in Australia.

Using a tortilla chip, Sara scoops up some bland home-made hummus. Carys wasn't much of a cook when she moved in at twenty-four, and it seems nothing much has changed there. Twenty-four, though. What balls it must have taken to join up with Bill, the state he was in, and with her and Lucy being so royally fucked up.

A song about someone being nothing but a gold-digger comes into her head.

Lucy turns to her. 'Hey – want to come to the tree on Sunday?'

'Tree?'

'Carys and I are doing Mum's tree book.'

'Oh yeah. I saw it on your Insta.'

'You overshare, Luce,' Carys says.

'Documenting,' Lucy says.

'Damn art students.' Bill smiles.

Lucy puts her head on Sara's shoulder. 'Please say you'll come. Pleeeease!'

Compared to how she has been in the flat, Lucy is so animated. Like she's putting on the Lucy's All Right Show.

'I'd love to,' Sara says.

Nonna, who has Binnie leaning against one of her flanks, snuggles her other side up against Sara's leg.

'She remembers you,' Carys says.

'Dogs know everything about us,' Binnie says.

'And we know everything about Nonna,' Lucy says, swiping her phone and showing it to Sara, who squints at the screen. 'It's a dog tracker. Wherever I am, I know where Nonna is.' She smiles like she's in some kind of religious ecstasy.

'Dinner's up.' Carys stands. 'Come this way, family.'

'How's the back?' Sara says, watching Bill use his cane to get up. His nails are clean and short as he grasps the silver handle – perhaps Carys has got him seeing some manicurist.

He smiles. 'Hardly ever think about it.' There's a hint, though, of 'so brave' and she wants to slap him for it.

'We've worked with all sorts of treatments for the pain,' Carys says as she hustles them to the dining table. 'But the current prescription backed up with Pilates is really working, isn't it, Bill?'

Bill nods.

He's so under her thumb. That's what's gone wrong. Carys calls all the shots.

'Look! Mum's tablecloth,' Lucy says, stroking the linen Sara watched her mother embroider every evening one long winter, 'to keep the black dog away', as she put it.

'Ta-da!' Carys says, ferrying a familiar earthenware pot full of steaming stew to the table.

'It's Bops!' Lucy says, smiling at Sara.

Sara looks at the paprika bean stew, which, as Carys ladles it up, stuffs the air with its rich smell.

'Bops because they're beans of art, bops because they make you fart,' Binnie sings.

The sweat springs to Sara's face. This is Alice's recipe in Alice's pot. This is her name for it. That is her serving-up song.

Sara takes half a spoonful and puts it in her mouth, and bam, she is back in the big house kitchen, aged ten. Her mother, not yet pregnant with Lucy, is busy, half-present, a wine glass in one hand as she eats. She and Bill are into their second bottle of red. There may well be a third, and the night will end with one of their loud 'discussions', which Sara will try not to hear, hiding under her Disney princess duvet cover.

Carys, Sara can't help noticing, has made her one small glass of red last from the sofa to the table, and it's still half full. Bill is ostentatiously on fizzy water. He is truly tamed.

'This is great,' she says of the stew. It isn't, though. There's not enough salt, and it just isn't as rich as she remembers.

'So we met your friend Tom the other day,' Carys says, trying to perk up some conversation.

It's the wrong thing to say. For just one second Sara thinks she might tip the beautifully laid table over on its side.

'We don't need to talk about him,' Bill says.

'Tom?' Lucy leans in towards Sara, like she has a big secret.

'My ex.'

'Oh. That Tom.'

Sara doesn't want to think about Tom, about how when Alice died he used her grief as an excuse to cling on to her. She even lied to him about when she was leaving so she could get away without any of his histrionics.

'He's a policeman now,' Carys says. 'He's working on—'

'Carys,' Bill says, holding up his hand.

'They need to know,' Carys says. 'It's bound to get out

beyond our local news, and the girls are big enough to know the truth.'

Carys always bangs on about telling the truth. Which is ironic, given that this family has been living a lie all these years. And *the girls are big enough*? Sara is so incensed that, were it not so shocking, she might have missed what Carys says next.

'On Wednesday, the contractors at Five Oaks found a body buried in The Wilderness.'

'A little girl,' Binnie adds helpfully, looking remarkably calm, considering.

'There was gossip at the school,' Carys says. 'Binnie's got big ears.'

Lucy drops her spoon into her bowl, splattering Alice's tablecloth with red sauce. 'What?'

'It's OK.' Carys takes her hand. 'She's been there for a while, and it's a good thing we found her because now she can be laid properly to rest.'

But this is no comfort to Lucy, who is hyperventilating.

Bill tuts. 'I told you not to say anything.'

Binnie gets up and runs to the kitchen sink. Standing on tiptoes, she pours a glass of water for Lucy.

'How long has she been there?' Lucy says, between gasps.

'We don't know. Perhaps fifteen years,' Carys says.

'Someone buried a little girl while I was there?'

'It's horrible, I know,' Carys says. 'But you didn't know anything about it, did you?'

'It was my special place. My safe place.' Lucy's breath is short and shallow. Sara reaches for her, trying to take her from Carys.

'Some things are better left unsaid, Carys,' Bill says.

'You would say that,' Sara says, and instantly regrets it.

Carys and Bill turn to look at her, but then Lucy collapses, her head ricocheting against the back of her chair.

. . .

'She's been in a bad way,' Carys whispers to Sara as they tiptoe away from the bedroom that Bill and Carys call Lucy's room. After Carys had given Lucy a pill that the shrink had prescribed to calm her down, Sara wanted to take her back to the flat. But Bill completely stonewalled her, saying Lucy needed her parents to be there for her when she woke up.

Carys turns to Sara and takes her hand. 'Please be kind to Bill,' she says. 'He loves you very much and has been desperate to see you all these years.'

Like it's Sara's fault. Like he couldn't afford to lie his bad back down on a first-class flight to Australia. She pulls her hand away. Bill should have looked out for his daughters rather than imploding into his own grief. After all, he got another wife: she and Lucy can never get another mother.

'I'm so sorry,' Carys says to Bill when they return downstairs. Suddenly some hands-on dad, he has put Binnie to bed.

'You weren't to know she was going to kick off like that.' Bill puts his arm round her as she sits next to him on the sofa.

'How long has Lucy been like this?' Sara says.

'Too long. We don't know what's at the root of it—' Carys starts.

'Thinking Mum topped herself probably.' It comes out as bitter as Sara feels it. And has she given the game away about what she knows?

'Don't talk to Carys like that,' Bill says.

Clearly not, then. Sara prickles. She is not going to get upset. She wants to be here as a sane grown-up, not the damaged, grieving teen she once was. She wants to be the one to save Lucy. Not Carys, not Bill, but her, the returning big sister hero.

'So do you think you're going to give Tom a call?' Carys says, all jolly. 'He gave me his number.'

Sara looks up, shocked.

'She won't want to speak to that nitwit ever again,' Bill says.

Sara won't have him speaking for her, so she turns to Carys. 'Can you send it to me?'

Bill yawns. 'It's nearly midnight.'

How time flies when you're having fun. 'I'll head then,' she says, standing up. 'I'll come by to pick Lucy up in the morning.'

'Why don't you stay?' Carys says. 'The spare room's all made up.'

'Nah, thanks.'

Bill hauls himself up off the sofa. Even though Sara would far rather leave on her own, he and Carys accompany her to the front door.

'Come back at ten tomorrow,' Carys says. 'We can have a lovely Saturday breakfast together.'

'I'm not really a breakfast person.'

'Make an effort, Sara, please?' Bill says.

That's too much for Sara. 'Why the fuck should I?'

He sighs, like she has broken his heart. 'We just can't win with you, can we?'

'Bill...' Carys puts her hand on his arm.

A cab swings round the corner, its light on, and gratefully Sara runs towards it.

THIRTEEN

Carys, Binnie, Lucy, Sara and Nonna get off the bus on the Lower Clapton Road carrying picnic, cushions and a blanket. An elderly man leans against a lamp post outside the Sainsbury's Local. Strings of unseasonal tinsel hang around his neck and his dreadlocks bulge in an oversized red, gold and green tam. As they approach, his face cracks into the warmest smile Carys has seen all year, one that reminds her of her dad back in Hull.

'Hail up, lovely ladies,' he sings.

While Sara eyes him with suspicion and Lucy avoids eye contact, Carys gives him her best smile and Binnie joins her.

'Sweet lil pickney,' the man says, winking at Bins.

Carys hears Sara's scandalised sharp intake of breath. It's too much to explain to her right now that this term, racist and horrible in a white mouth, is perfectly fine for a Jamaican. It is, in fact, exactly what Carys's dad called her and her sister when they were little.

This moment reminds her, not for the first time, that these two young women are not her daughters. How could they be? Sara is just five years younger than her, Lucy sixteen. More

sister ages. When Lucy was younger, everyone assumed that
Carys was her nanny. It wasn't all about the age thing, either. In
too many eyes, a black woman looking after a white child
couldn't possibly be anything other than an employee.
Annoying as it was, Carys used to enjoy watching the white
faces resetting their prejudices and assumptions. Still does, now
Lucy insists on introducing her as her mother – the step bit got
dropped years ago.

They reach the corner of Clapton Square. Spotting the
grass, Nonna tugs them through the rusted gates and onto the
tarmac path that winds through municipally planted beds and
trees. Although Carys has never been here before, the girls
know exactly where to go. They used to come to the children's
play area while Alice was working at her health centre just
around the corner.

Bill didn't want Carys to take the girls out today. He said
that with the way Sara had behaved at the dinner, she hadn't
earned Carys's kindness. Her hostility bewildered and hurt
him. 'I know I shouldn't order her around like she's a child,' he
said. 'But it's hard not to when she behaves like she's fourteen.'

'You both need some time,' Carys told him. 'It will come.'

She's glad she decided to come anyway, even if she had to
make Binnie swear to keep the trip quiet from him. In fact she's
hoping to use today to mend the ill-feeling Sara still bears
towards her father.

'The picnics we had here,' Sara says as the five of them
come to a halt on the far side of the play park, underneath
Alice's favourite tree in all of London.

'Can I play, Mum?' Binnie is eyeing a tyre dangling from a
wooden playhouse that looks like a giraffe, and a little girl about
her age who is playing on it under the watchful eye of her
mother. Carys does a quick recce. A group of four older men sit
drinking, smoking weed and shouting on a park bench on the
other side of the playground. But the noise they are making is

good-natured. One of them has a speaker blaring out lovers rock: sweet, romantic tunes, her dad's favourites.

She leaves Sara and Lucy looking up at the tree and checks the playhouse in case anyone has made use of the privacy it offers for, say, injecting or defecating.

'Sure,' she tells Binnie, seeing it's clean. 'But don't go out of my sight.'

Sweetly eyeing the other little girl, Binnie clambers into the playhouse. Carys heads back towards Lucy and Sara, who, with Alice's book open on her knees, looks like the little girl in the family photographs.

'Why's it called a true service tree?' she asks as she joins them on the bench underneath the canopy, where tiny green fruit nestle among the last of the blossom.

'I wish it was something to do with Mum,' Lucy says, 'giving the community round here true service, but she says in the book that "service" is a bastardisation of *sorbus*, the Latin for rowan. "True" differentiates it from the wild service tree, *Sorbus torminalis*.'

'Still, we can think what we want,' Sara says.

Lucy positions everyone and takes pictures for her Instagram story about the visit. 'Hashtag majestic, I think. Don't you?'

'It's a lovely tree,' Carys says, looking up at the leaves rustling in the hot wind. In all honesty, though, had it not been for Alice's book, she wouldn't have given it a second look. It's just a rather big tree on the edge of a scruffy Hackney square.

'Shall we have our picnic over there?' She points to a grassed area on the other side of a low metal fence.

'No dogs,' Lucy says.

'No one need know,' Carys says. 'And Nonna will behave herself.'

'Mum was very strict about that,' Sara says. 'We went over

there.' She points to the grass at the south end of the square. 'You can still see the tree.'

'But not the playground,' Carys says.

Sara picks up the cool bag Carys has brought along. 'Binnie will have to come and sit with us over there, then.' She takes Lucy by the hand and leads her to the old picnic spot.

Very briefly, Carys bristles, then she reminds herself that this trip is for Lucy and Sara, not her and Binnie. It is not for her to assert herself over how they remember Alice.

She calls Binnie over.

'Your father really loves you, you know, Sara,' Carys says as they finish the grilled vegan halloumi sandwiches she ordered in from her favourite local deli. Binnie, who said she wasn't particularly hungry, is running with Nonna, round and round a circular flower bed.

'What was it like growing up in Hull?' Sara asks her in a blunt swerve away from the subject.

It makes no sense to rub up against her spiky stepdaughter, so Carys plays along. 'Very different to London. We had more space, being on an estate set around a green, and it wasn't too hard to get out of town. And you always know the river is there. Unlike the Thames, which you only really get a sense of if you're close by.'

'I wish we could visit Mam-Gu and Grampa more,' Binnie says. 'I like their house and their chickens.'

Carys smiles. 'I know. But it's a long way.'

'Mam-Gu?' Sara says.

'Welsh for Granny,' Lucy says. 'Because Mam-Gu's from Swansea originally.'

'We'll go soon. It's just we've been a bit tied up with work and life.' Carys doesn't add how guilty she feels at not having visited her ailing parents for over a year. And even then it was just her and Binnie. She pays for their carers and gets them a weekly Tesco delivery, but it's not the same.

Lucy turns to Sara. 'And Dad hates Hull,' she tells her. 'Calls it Hell.'

'Not surprised,' Sara says. 'After what happened to Mum.'

'What do you mean?' Lucy says.

Carys tries to signal to Sara to be quiet, but either she doesn't see or she chooses once again to ignore her.

'When she went through that case about the baby when she was training to be an obstetrician? The birth injury, and the General Medical Council hearing that nearly got her struck off?' Sara goes on. 'That was in Hull.'

'What?' Lucy says.

'The reason she retrained to become a GP,' Sara says.

'I didn't know about this,' Lucy says, looking at Carys, who is willing Sara not to go on with the next part of the story.

'Mum had been working for nearly forty-eight hours,' Sara says. 'She made a bad decision during a birth that meant a baby got brain damage from being starved of oxygen.'

'Sara...' Carys puts out a warning hand.

'I can't believe Lucy doesn't know this,' Sara says. 'How can she get better if you just bullshit her?' She turns back to Lucy and softens her tone. 'Mum always blamed what happened to Danny on it, like it was bad karma, repayment time.'

'Danny?'

'No—' Carys says.

'Our brother.'

'What brother?'

Sara turns to Carys, who wants to scoop Lucy up and take her far away from here, to insulate her from this explosion of truth. 'You mean she doesn't even know about Danny?'

Lucy looks at Carys, her mouth open. 'I have a brother?'

Carys takes her hand. 'Had, Luce. Your mum had another baby, a year and a bit before you were born. Danny. He lived less than a month. He had a poorly heart, it turned out, but it hadn't been detected at his birth.'

Lucy tears herself away and scoots back on the grass, away from the picnic. 'Why didn't anyone tell me this?'

'With everything that happened—' Carys begins, but Sara speaks over her.

'Mum didn't want anyone to talk about it,' she says. 'So we didn't.'

'So why didn't you tell me when I got older?' Lucy says.

'It wasn't my place,' Sara says. 'I just assumed Dad and Carys had dealt with it, and that if you wanted to talk about it with me, you would.'

'But it should be you and me together,' Lucy says. 'Where were you?'

'Lucy...' Carys says.

'Poor Mum.' Lucy speaks through her tears. 'Poor Mum, to get all that blame and then to lose her baby. How did she cope?'

'She didn't,' Sara says. 'Or that's what we're supposed to believe.'

'What does that mean?' Carys says.

Sara turns away. 'I'm sure you know.'

Carys wonders who the anger in Sara's voice is directed at. Is it her and Bill? Or Alice? Or is it everyone? She also marvels at the compassion poor, troubled Lucy is showing towards her mother.

If only she, Carys, had managed to find the same empathy for her predecessor, perhaps things would have turned out differently for everyone.

But then she wouldn't be where she is today. And all things told, this is where she wants to be.

She tiptoes across this minefield every day, holding her secret like an unexploded device. Never before has it come so close to detonation.

'What's the matter with Lucy?' Binnie asks. She has run up to them, all out of breath from her games with Nonna.

Lucy scrubs the back of her hand across her face, sniffs heartily and sits up straight. 'Nothing, little sis. Just thinking about the poor little girl again.'

'Emma,' Binnie says. 'Mum and Dad have called her Emma.'

'Fucked up,' Sara mutters under her breath.

'We needed to give her a name. To honour her,' Carys says, trying not to let it sound like a rebuke.

'It's very sad.' Binnie goes up to Lucy and puts her arms around her neck. 'But she'll be laid to rest soon.'

This is something Carys has told her, but it never fails to astound her how level-headed Binnie is. She is the proof that she is a good parent, that Lucy's mental health challenges are not of her doing.

Lucy puts her arms around Binnie. Carys gets some paper napkins out of her picnic bag and delicately places one in front of each of her daughters. Then she goes back to the bag, pulls out the brownies she bought at the same time as the sandwiches and lays one on each of the napkins.

Sara sighs. But she picks at her brownie, as does Lucy. Binnie greedily scoffs hers in four mouthfuls.

'So anyway, that's why Bill don't like Hull and calls it Hell,' Sara says.

Her timing is spot on. Lucy sniggers.

Carys can't understand this dark humour. Surely it's not healthy.

'Got your appetite back, then?' Sara says to Binnie.

Binnie grins at her with brownie-gummed teeth.

Carys's little bomb-disposal expert.

. . .

After Carys has cleared everything away, they go back to the true service tree.

'Mum must have stood here so many times, looking up,' Lucy says. 'She says on the true service page that trees have a permanence and a wisdom we can only dream of, that we can all learn from standing under them.'

They gaze up, like they are looking for truth. Or in Nonna's case, squirrels.

'Oh!' Sara gasps.

'What?' Lucy says.

'Over there.' Sara points to the other side of the park, where, just beyond where the men are still sitting and chatting, a short white woman in a light olive parka and sunglasses is just going through the gate to the street. 'That could be Mum,' she says.

Lucy sighs. 'She had a coat like that. But her hair was shorter and redder.'

'Hair grows. And fades.'

'Wouldn't that be nice?' Lucy says. 'If it was her, come back to see us?'

Carys isn't so sure.

Lucy sighs again.

'I'm sorry, Lucy.' Carys takes her hand. 'We thought we were protecting you over Danny and all that, but we should have told you.'

'Damn straight,' Sara says.

'Good job they didn't, though, really,' Lucy tells her sister. 'Just look at how I reacted. Gaga.' She twirls the index finger of her free hand at her temple.

A breeze shakes the leaves of the tree, and petals fall on them, like hot-weather snow.

FOURTEEN

With Binnie at her summer play scheme, Carys sits alone in Ajay's waiting room, trying to read a novel. But her mind is elsewhere, worrying about secrets and poor Lucy's face when Sara told her so brutally about Hull and Danny.

She tries to calm herself by watching Nonna and Fig sleeping in a spot of sunlight on the floor. It's impossible to tell which dog is which.

Artur calls, and she is glad of the excuse to stop pretending to herself that she is reading.

'I've taken the boys off the job for two weeks,' he tells her.

'Are they OK with that?' Carys says.

'Sure,' he says. 'We have small job to do on a flat in Elephant. Put in kitchen, lay parquet floor.'

He pronounces it *parkwet* and she wants to hug him for his resourcefulness. This new arrangement will save them thousands of pounds.

It doesn't solve everything, though. There is thousands more pounds' worth of plant hire lying around the site. If she returned it, there would be no guarantee when it would be available again, so she has taken the gamble of holding onto it.

And then even if the police clear out quickly, there is the danger that the whole Five Oaks project will be forever tainted by the fact that a child lay there for years in an unmarked grave.

Neither Bill nor Carys feels noble for listing this among their concerns, but there it is.

She thanks Artur and hangs up, and is just about to turn back to her book when a horrible wailing comes from Ajay's treatment room. Before she can react, the door bursts open and Lucy streaks across the waiting room, hitting the air around her head like she is swatting flies.

'I saw them!' she says to Carys as she bowls into her and buries her head in her chest, just like she did when she was little and having nightmares. It still pricks Carys's pride that this girl chooses her arms for shelter.

'Who?' She looks over the top of Lucy's head at Ajay, who is standing on the other side of the waiting room, shifting from foot to foot. The half-smile on his face is unreadable – he could be scared, he could be amused, he could be embarrassed.

Carys puts her mouth against Lucy's hair. 'Who did you see, Lucy?'

Lucy pulls away and looks at her with eyes that don't seem to be quite focused on the present.

'They had a knife...'

'Who, Lucy? Who had a knife? When?'

Lucy pushes herself to her feet, closes her eyes and holds her hands up in the air like she's speaking in tongues. 'I don't know! I have no idea who they are.' She turns to face Ajay. 'Tell her!' she says. 'Tell her what happened.'

He sighs and looks at the reclaimed station clock on the white wall. There's fifteen minutes left of Lucy's session. 'I think you'd better come into the treatment room, Carys.' He is putting out an almost aggressive level of calm, but then perhaps this is his way of keeping a lid on a freaking-out patient.

. . .

Lucy throws herself across the room at the expensive Danish chair and curls up on her side, her thumb in her mouth.

Ajay ushers Carys to the leather sofa. She sits at one end and he takes the other.

'So,' he says, 'we were in a deep state of relaxation – where we'd got to last time. Lucy was really enjoying it. We were exploring the happy days, her childhood before her mother died.'

Carys winces at this, at the truth it contains.

Lucy wriggles into the sheepskin and clamps her hands over her ears. 'I don't want to hear this.'

'Shall I stop?' Ajay says. Lucy lifts her hands away. 'I can only speak to Carys with your permission.'

'Go on,' Lucy says, then once more covers her ears. She is shaking, Carys notices. This is not good.

'I took her out into the garden of her childhood and we explored the grass, the flower beds, The Wilderness.'

Carys, who can see what is coming, is kicking herself for not briefing Ajay about Emma. She can't tell him about her now, not with Lucy in this state. But a thought does strike her.

'How do you know about The Wilderness?'

Ajay stops and frowns. 'We talk through the geography during the session. I ask Lucy what she sees.'

'Sorry,' Carys says, hearing the defensiveness in his voice. 'I wasn't trying to catch you out or anything.'

'Lucy seemed happy at first, telling me about the book she had in her hand, the birds, naming the trees – she knows a lot about trees because of her mother?'

Carys nods. Ajay's voice is gentle and low, and she wonders if he is trying to hypnotise her too.

'Then she went down to the very bottom of the garden. It's massive, right?'

'It was. Is,' Carys says.

'And there was a little den she had there, in among the brambles, inside a hawthorn.'

'I didn't know about the den.'

Lucy, whose hands are clearly not fully stopping her ears, looks over her shoulder. 'No one knew about my den. When I was little, I nicked a tartan blanket and some cushions from the house, big cushions with spots on them, and I made a bed where I could read.'

'How old were you when you did this?' Carys says.

'Little.'

'Before your mum died?'

Lucy shakes her head and curls over onto her side once more. 'I don't know. I don't know.'

Ajay gets up and squats beside her, taking her hand in his long, spidery fingers. 'It's OK, Lucy, it's not a test. Our memories are our own stories.' He leans over and speaks into her ear. 'Tell us what you saw. Like you told me.'

Lucy lies back in the chair and closes her eyes.

'I'm in my den, lying with my head on my pillow, and I'm reading a pile of my Dr Seuss books.'

Carys remembers those books. They still have them, and like Lucy at her age, Binnie is obsessed with *The Cat in the Hat*.

'It's summer. It's getting dark and I know I should be going in, but no one has called me. Mum and Dad are busy with work and supper and drinking wine, and Sara's out with Tom. I like Tom.'

'Tell us more, Lucy,' Ajay says, his voice slow, almost a whisper.

'I'm really cosy with a little torch, and I've got a bag of sweets. Haribo cherry sweets. Sour.'

'And...'

'There's a little girl crying, a lady making sounds, and there's someone else telling them to be quiet. I turn off my torch so they can't see me and I peek through the bushes and someone is pushing the girl and the lady and they're gagged with their hands tied behind their backs and he shoves them right over so they are lying face down on the ground, just a few feet away from me. The little girl sees me and I see her and I scream, but nothing comes out and then the other person's got a knife and then there's blood and the little girl isn't looking at me any more.'

Lucy's voice has become tiny, childlike. It's like watching a possession.

'And then what?' Ajay lowers his voice. It rumbles, like a whisper.

Lucy shakes her head and lies still for a few moments. She takes a big breath. 'The person who had the knife is putting earth back into a hole in the ground and the little girl isn't there any more. And then they're dragging the lady away, and I hear digging going on again but it's too far away, so I quietly take my shoes off so I don't make a noise and I run as fast as I can back up to the house, where the lights are all on. But I can't find Mum and Dad.'

Lucy stops. It's almost as if she has gone to sleep.

'Good girl,' Ajay tells her, stroking her arm. He looks over at Carys, who realises she is holding one of the patterned sofa cushions against her belly like it's a shield against Lucy's testimony.

'You mustn't be alarmed,' he tells her. 'Very often, at this stage, these sorts of memories are metaphors – stories that we put together out of other things we have seen or heard or read, to try to help us make sense of our actual narrative.'

'There's something you need to know.' Twisting the cushion, Carys tells him about Emma.

'So that explains it,' Ajay says. 'Lucy has absorbed a current event and is trying to make sense of it by combining it with her childhood memories.'

'It happened,' Lucy whispers from the chair. 'It really did.'

Carys wants to drag her away from here.

'For you, this is very real, very alarming.' Ajay strokes Lucy's hand. Is he allowed to touch his patients like that? 'But we have to unpick it, work out which strands come from which experience.' He's still stroking, but Lucy pulls herself away, stumbles to Carys and grabs her hands.

'It's real, Mum. It really happened.'

She hasn't called Carys Mum for years, not since her troubles started. Carys loves it, but not coming out of this distress.

'What are you going to do about this?' she asks Ajay.

'Work through it. Very often this process can open up some painful areas, like stirring up mud in the bottom of a river. It's important that we continue, let it settle in the right places.'

Lucy breaks away from Carys and looks at him. 'Why are you talking like it didn't happen? It really, really happened!'

Ajay picks up her bag and hands it to her. 'It's very real to you at the moment, and lots of the detail is true.'

But what if Lucy is right? Carys thinks. What if she actually did witness a murder? Emma had to have got there somehow.

She shakes her head. The woman being killed is too much. Lucy's life has a lot of darkness around it, but it's just too wild to be true. This needs to be resolved. 'Can you see her sooner than next week?'

Ajay goes to his computer and takes a look. 'I have a slot free at one p.m. on Wednesday?'

Carys notes it in her diary.

Lucy is silent as they make their way to the car.

'Do you want to come back with me and Dad?' Carys asks. 'Stay the night? I could get a What the Pitta.' Lucy's favourite takeaway can often entice her home.

'Sara's taking me out for a kebab.' Lucy stops and faces her. 'You won't tell Dad about this, will you?'

Carys smiles. 'How could I when he doesn't know about Ajay at all? We'll keep it between ourselves. Like Ajay says, it's part of a process, not fact.'

Lucy glares at her.

Carys pats her hand. 'Not necessarily fact. Perhaps don't talk to Sara about it just yet?'

As she drives Lucy home, Carys tries to put away the idea that things would be so much easier if Sara wasn't around.

Last time she thought that about someone, it actually happened.

FIFTEEN

The police station smells of stale urine and strong tea. Although perhaps the stink is coming from the man sitting on the plastic chairs opposite Sara and Lucy, who looks like he hasn't had a shower since all this was fields.

The receptionist behind the thick Plexiglas screen is laughing at something on the phone, a sound that seems horribly out of place. Sara rubs the back of her neck. It's unbearably hot.

'How much longer?' Lucy says through gritted teeth.

In an interesting twist to the secrets and lies in the Anderton-Jones-Herman family, this morning, behind Bill's back, Carys took Lucy to a hypnotherapist. But when she got home – Carys dropped her off then had to get back to work – Lucy properly freaked out. She said she wasn't supposed to tell Sara about what had come up in the session, but she went ahead and told her anyway.

And oh. My. God.

And Sara's not supposed to tell Carys she knows about the freak-out, and Bill's not to know anything. What is it with this family?

She's going to see to it that all this lying stops. But it will take time. After lobbing one big truth bomb into the park yesterday, she's going to sit for a while with the one about Alice's death or not-death. Something in her detective bones smells a rat. She has no idea what it is yet, but she's keeping a close eye on Carys.

And in the meantime, she will do whatever it takes to make Lucy happy.

Which is why she is here, at Tottenham police station, where the team dealing with Five Oaks are based, waiting with Lucy so she can tell them what she claims to remember. Sara's feeling is that something needs to change for her little sister to be happy, and if this is the start of it, then so be it.

'You do believe me, don't you?' Lucy asks, for the millionth time.

Sara takes a swig from her water bottle. 'I know you wouldn't lie about something so important.'

'I mean, why is it so unlikely? That poor girl was buried there, and I played in the garden. Perhaps this is the reason I'm such a fuck-up.'

'You're not a fuck-up.'

'Tell that to the shrinks.'

Sara turns to her sister. 'Why do you always joke about it?'

Lucy pulls a face and looks away, a sullen teenager refusing to engage.

A door to the side of the reception desk opens and a tall, thin man in a crumpled linen suit walks out. He doesn't look like a policeman, so Sara barely gives him a second glance. But he comes over and stands in front of her and Lucy.

'Sara,' he says, smiling down at her. 'Wow.'

She looks up, sees familiar eyes. 'Tom!'

She was wondering if this was going to happen.

She gets to her feet, not wanting to be sitting down, beneath him. Even so, she only reaches his chest, where, for a couple of years, before he exhausted her, she used to rest her head.

'What happened to your nose?' she asks him.

A couple of uniforms pass behind him, escorting a sheepish-looking young man.

'Punched by a drunk,' Tom says.

One of the uniforms stops and turns to Sara. 'Being a bloody hero saving a DV victim's life is what he won't tell you.' He hustles the man to the desk to book him in.

She lifts her face to meet Tom's eyes. 'Carys said you were working on the case.'

'I am.' He is smiling so much he looks as if his face is going to burst. 'Wow. Look at you.'

Sara can't hold his gaze. 'My sister has some stuff she wants to talk over with you.'

Nose apart, time has been kind to Tom. He looks like he has grown into his skin. He is more like the boy she fell in love with all those years ago, rather than the limpet he became.

'Hey, Lucy.' Tom speaks to her like she is still the child she was when he last saw her. 'Do you remember me?'

Lucy nods, like she too has been sent back in time. 'You were Sara's boyfriend,' she says. 'I liked you.'

'I liked you too.' Tom's smile is genuine, and briefly a golden filter is dropped in front of a time that was actually a complete nightmare.

'Well,' he says at last, 'would you like to come backstage and have a cuppa?'

Lucy stands, her face so serious it almost feels like a rebuke to Sara for the moment of nostalgia. 'I've come to make a statement. About the body at my parents' building site.'

'I'll sit in as Lucy's appropriate adult,' Sara says. 'If that's OK.'

'My mental health issues,' Lucy adds.

'Best come through then,' Tom says. Sara can tell that beneath his studied cool he's excited.

'So why didn't you remember this before?' Tom says after Lucy has told him about what she supposedly saw when she was small. They're in an anonymous, fluorescent-lit interview room, and the tea is as bad as it is in Australian nicks, a fact Sara finds oddly depressing.

She is enjoying, however, watching Tom's hands as he writes down what Lucy tells him. The beauty of them was the first thing that drew her to him. She wonders if he is as good with them as he used to be. She has a theory that men tend to get better at sex as they age. Unless you're married to them, when – at least in her experience – familiarity breeds a contemptuous lack of foreplay.

But what is she doing sitting here thinking about sex? She should be listening to her little sister.

'I guess I just blocked it out,' Lucy says, eyeing the camera recording her statement.

They decided on their way here that they weren't going to mention the hypnotherapy, because any police officer would probably think the same about that as Sara does.

In fact Sara is wondering why exactly she is humouring Lucy. She suspects it's because her testimony will cause Bill and Carys a whole load of trouble. It's amazing how her teenage anger is resurfacing, like some fossilised seed being brought back to life.

'It happens,' Tom says, gently. 'It's the mind protecting itself from processing a challenging event.'

'It was certainly that,' Lucy says.

'Well, I'm glad you're remembering now.'

Lucy smiles at him.

'And what can you remember about the person you saw with the girl and the woman?'

'The girl and her mother,' Lucy says.

'How do you know she was the mother?' Sara asks.

'I just know.'

'What can you remember about him?' Tom says.

Lucy closes her eyes and thinks for a minute. She shakes her head. 'I can't even remember if it was a him or a her.'

'No age?' Sara says. 'Or size, or colouring?'

Lucy shakes her head again. 'I can't.' Her voice is receding, becoming more childlike. This, Sara realises, is something she does when she is distressed, like she's running away.

'It's OK,' Tom says. 'It may come.' He offers her a biscuit from the plate he brought in with the dishwater teas.

Because of the extreme nature of what Lucy has just told him, Sara can't quite believe how readily Tom believes it. But then why wouldn't he? She is utterly convincing. She's dressed carefully, brushed her hair, is well-spoken, and as she told her story, her voice took on an almost theatrical seriousness.

Fair enough, it all sounds like fact.

Tom switches off the camera. 'Thank you, Lucy. Your evidence is really helpful.'

'What's going to happen now?' she says.

Tom's making moves like he needs to get on. His face, which Sara remembers shows every passing thought and feeling, glows with an excited sense of purpose.

'Can't say until I consult my colleagues. But this is a big development. We can help you with victim support if you need it.'

'I'm not the victim, though. It's the girl and her mother.' Lucy reaches across the table and takes his hand. 'If you dig, you will find the mother. I promise.'

For the first time since Sara arrived, she sees Lucy smile fully and openly.

. . .

'So how's Pete?' Tom asks as he leads them back down the corridors towards reception.

He knows about Pete because when she got married, Sara finally accepted his Facebook friend request, just to let him know she was now completely out of the question. She has not, however, visited or updated her profile since she found out Pete was screwing another officer in her unit.

'History,' she says.

'Huh,' Tom says. 'I'm divorced too.'

'I'm sorry,' Sara says.

'No. It's just as well.'

'Me too.'

They both laugh.

'Fancy both of us ending up coppers,' he says.

'Yeah.'

She doesn't like the way this feels like it's going, so says nothing more until they're through the security door and out on the public side, where piss guy is still stinking the place out.

Tom gives them both his card.

'You won't let Carys and Dad know it's me who said anything?' Lucy says.

'All witness statements are confidential.'

He lingers just a bit too long when he shakes Sara's hand, but she refuses to meet his eyes, which she knows are looking for hers. This makes her so weary, and so sick about how she allowed him to treat her back then. It showed itself in despair and weeping rather than – as she has seen in other men too many times through her work – violence and fury. But his assumption that she was his no matter how much she said she wanted to be free of him was just as controlling and oppressive.

. . .

'Shall we walk?' Lucy says. 'I need to clear my head.'

It's at least an hour back to the flat. Sara would far rather get an Uber, but she nods anyway.

'They'll guess it's me,' Lucy says as they head off into the clogged streets.

Sara dodges a dog turd. 'Not necessarily.'

'Carys will.'

'But she's not going to let on to Bill, is she? Because she doesn't want him to know about your hypnotist.'

They stop at a pelican crossing.

'Hypnotherapist,' Lucy says. 'But Carys hates lying.'

'Does she now?'

The crossing lights turn green, but they have to wait for three speeding cyclists who barrel through the red light.

'Jesus, doesn't anyone in this country ever play by the rules?' Sara shouts after them.

SIXTEEN

'She's turning Lucy away from us too,' Bill says. He and Carys are having supper and he's brought the subject around to Sara, who, he says, is breaking his heart. 'Four days now, no contact. That's unprecedented.'

'They're probably just having fun together. Reconnecting,' Carys says. She knows she's playing a dangerous game hiding the visit to the true service tree from Bill, especially since it involves getting Binnie to lie, but the way she sees it, she's protecting him from unnecessary upset. She still believes things will get better and everything will be all right soon, so long as she keeps working on it.

'We wait for them to make contact, OK? We're in charge, not Sara.'

Carys nods.

The doorbell rings, which is unusual at this time in the evening, so she checks the video on her app. It's Tom, the policeman.

'Oh hell,' Bill says. 'What does he want now?'

Carys has a pretty strong idea, but of course she's not letting on.

. . .

'But how long is this going to take?' Bill says.

Carys puts her hand on his shoulder: he's becoming agitated.

Tom shakes his head. 'I'm afraid I can't say. It's until we have all the information we need from the scene.'

They're sitting at the kitchen table, where Carys, Bill and Binnie's ramen bowls and chopsticks still sit from the supper they were finishing when Tom arrived. Carys pours green tea from a squat teapot.

'And who is this so-called witness?' Bill says.

'Again, I'm afraid I can't tell you.'

'Like you can't tell us about what they've told you that'll have you digging up our entire site and delaying us for who knows how long, losing us yet more time and money and potentially endangering our entire business.'

Carys wants to run away. She knows exactly who has spoken to the police and what they have said. But there is absolutely no way she can let Bill know it's Lucy, or where her story came from.

'Why can't you tell us? It's not as if we're suspects,' Bill says. 'Or, hang on: Are we?'

Tom remains silent.

Carys puts down the teapot. 'You don't think we had anything to do with this?'

Tom looks at his feet. 'I'm afraid we can't rule anything out at this point.'

Bill stands. 'I think that's all we need to hear.' He moves over to the door and opens it. 'Tom.'

Tom takes his cue. But as he passes through to the hall, he stops and turns. 'Bill. Carys. I'm sorry about the disruption to your build, and I know how hard it must be for you. But we now have potentially more than one victim of what is increasingly looking like murder, and I'm sure that if they were your family, you would want us to do our best for them.'

Carys nods. 'Of course. It's just there's a lot to process. And while I appreciate what you're saying about ruling nothing out, I hope you also appreciate how difficult we find that.'

'How *offensive* we find that,' Bill says. He is dangerously close to Tom, and for one terrible second, Carys thinks he might lift his cane and hit him.

'I mean, you know the family,' she says quickly. 'From back when we lived in the house. Surely you know we can't have anything to do with...'

Tom switches into formal cop mode. 'I can only assure you that we will work as efficiently and effectively as we possibly can.'

'So why haven't you come up with any ideas about who this girl is, or exactly how long she's been buried in our garden?' Bill says.

'It's been five days.' Tom spreads his hands. 'I'm afraid these things take time. I can't let you know the exact details, but as you are probably aware, we are severely underfunded at the moment, and because it is clearly a historical case, it's not going to be a priority at our lab.'

'Even though we are being so inconvenienced?'

'Whatever the forensics outcome, we would still have to act on this new information, so we would still be putting you out.'

Bill turns his back on Tom and heads back in to clear the kitchen table.

'I'll see you out,' Carys says.

'Once again, I'm sorry for the disruption,' Tom says as he stands outside the front door.

'I understand you have to do your job,' Carys says. 'Thank

you for not letting Bill know about Lucy and the hypnotherapist.'

Tom blinks. 'Hypnotherapist?'

'She didn't tell you that she saw the girl and the woman being buried during a hypnotherapy session, did she?' Carys says.

'She didn't.'

'Look, Tom. I know you can't give anything away. But I know your witness is Lucy. Just be careful. Even her therapist says these aren't necessarily real memories. And she has a history of mental health issues, including delusional thinking.'

She knows it sounds like she is talking Lucy down. The look Tom gives her shows he thinks she is too. But she knows how Lucy would have presented when she gave her statement, how she would have appeared entirely plausible, entirely together and sane and well. It's a good act she pulls. And Carys can also understand – particularly given Tom's history with the family – that he must think she is some sort of evil stepmother telling him about how mad her stepdaughter is in order to save her business.

But what can she do? Everything she's saying is entirely true.

'You'll give me the details of this therapist, will you?'

'Of course. I'll text them to you right now.'

'Good.' He shakes her hand and leaves.

When she goes back to find Bill, he is sitting at the kitchen table looking into space, a whisky bottle and glass beside him.

'For you,' he says when she looks questioningly at him.

'Thank you.'

'What can we do?' he asks. 'What can we do?'

Shaking her head, she sits beside him. 'There's nothing we can do. We just have to wait.'

'Who's gone to the police? And what did they say?'

'I don't know.' Carys puts her arms around herself to contain the lie.

'I hope to God there's not another poor child buried there.' Bill pours the whisky and hands the glass to Carys. 'I don't want more bodies turning up in my old back garden. It's bad enough that Emma's in the papers, but who'd want to buy a flat built on a mass grave?'

Carys drains the whisky and pours another. 'I'm sure it's not that bad.'

'We could lose our life savings, all our capital and our professional reputation,' Bill says. 'This could be ruinous.'

'We have to remember the poor little girl,' Carys says.

'I wish I could forget her. She's in my dreams. It's a nightmare, the whole thing. What the hell did we do to deserve it?'

Carys shivers. She knows exactly what she did.

What was that her Bible-bashing Jamaican grandma used to say all the time, whenever she played up?

Those who plow iniquity and sow trouble reap the same.

SEVENTEEN

'Lucy. Sara. Let me IN.'

Carys bangs on the street door, feeling the effects of last night's whisky. No answer. Driven by memories of the last time she stood here, she lets herself into the communal entrance and shouts at the flat door.

'All right, all right, I'm coming.' Sara's footsteps thunder downstairs and she opens the door. 'Ah,' she says when she sees Carys.

She leads her up and through into the living room, which looks, as ever since Lucy's occupation, like a glitter bomb has hit it. Kitsch little trinkets cover every surface. Her massive, brightly coloured canvases crowd the walls. Netted fairy lights hang from Lurex lampshades; metallic embroidered cushions smother the old, tasteful sofa.

'Tea?' Sara asks, disappearing into the little kitchen.

Carys sits on one of the two matching chairs she and Edina bought one argumentative Saturday in IKEA. So much history in this room, underneath Lucy's layers.

'Where is she?' she asks, glancing over at the mantelpiece,

where Lucy's eighteenth birthday cards are still on display, nine months on.

'Corner shop,' Sara says as she carries two mugs of tea through. 'We're out of biscuits.'

'You know what she's told the police, don't you?'

'Yup.' Sara hands Carys one of the teas, then sits on the sofa, cradling the other. 'I went with her.'

'Why the hell didn't you talk to me first?'

'We have to run everything past you?'

'When it's something like this, something that has such massive implications for me and Bill and our business? Yes.'

'Sorry, Carys, but I'm a big girl and can think for myself.'

'But you know it didn't really happen?'

'That's neither here nor there. Lucy believes it, and I'm here to help her in any way she needs, not just those I approve of. I'm not that controlling.'

'This could ruin me and your father.'

'Is that all you really care about? What if there *is* a woman buried there? Wouldn't it be better for "the business" if she were found and her death properly investigated, instead of one of your customers digging her up in their garden three years from now?'

Carys sighs. 'Why are you being so difficult, Sara?'

'Not difficult. Just not doing what you want. Listen, Carys. I'm only five years younger than you. I've lived on my own terms since I was Lucy's age. You are not my mother. You're someone who's had the great fortune to marry my father. That's all. You can't control me like you do Lucy.'

'I don't control her.'

'You do. And anyway, why are you so sure that she's not telling the truth?'

'She's disturbed and highly suggestible, with no sense of proportion. Also, she's vulnerable and damaged.'

'Perhaps by seeing a double murder.'

'It's more likely, though, isn't it, that it was her mother killing herself when she was a small child that messed her up.'

'Hey.' Lucy comes through from the hallway, a pack of chocolate digestives in her hand. 'I'm the only one allowed to say I'm damaged and messed up.'

She is, for once, not joking.

Carys goes to her, her hands out. 'Oh, come on, Luce.'

'No.' Lucy turns away, cradling the biscuits.

'Why did you have to go to the police?' Carys says. 'We'd decided to keep it between ourselves, hadn't we?'

'It was the right thing to do. I saw a *murder*. And you're here, aren't you, because unlike you, they've taken me seriously.'

Carys lets out a long breath, like a puncture slowly going down. 'I take you seriously, Lucy.'

'She's worried about herself and Dad and how they might lose money,' Sara says.

Lucy narrows her eyes at Carys. 'Really? Is that it? Well, listen: however much cash it costs you, it really happened.'

Carys looks at Lucy and then at Sara. She should have listened to Bill and stayed away from the girls. But instead, here she is – behind his back, of course – and she's just made things worse.

'Shouldn't we be together in all this?' she asks them.

'Yes,' Sara says. 'Yes, we should.'

It's more accusation than agreement.

'Could you leave now, please?' Lucy says.

Carys picks up her bag. 'I'll call for you tomorrow, then. For your next Ajay session.'

'Whatever.'

She heads off along the corridor, down the stairs and out of the flat. As she lets herself through the street door, she hears the security chain of her own flat being threaded through its slot.

. . .

With eyes that feel too small for her face, she wheels her bike up to the Five Oaks gates.

An overheated uniformed policewoman stops her. 'Can't go in there, I'm afraid.'

'I need to pick up some papers.'

The policewoman turns her back and radios someone, who sounds through the crackles like Tom. Nodding, she turns back to Carys, an eyebrow raised.

'For some reason he says yes. Half an hour tops. Enter via the marked-out path. Only visit the office,' she says wearily, like Carys is some naughty child bound to play up.

Once inside the gates, Carys sees the site is deserted. Surely they should be working all hours to speed things along? But then of course this isn't an urgent matter. The police probably have their hands full with all the boys stabbing each other and the climate protesters gluing themselves to buildings.

She lets herself into the site office, a Portakabin she and Bill are paying a considerable rental on to stand empty doing nothing.

It is nearly a week since they found poor Emma, and the office has the fetid air of a space locked up in the summer heat. Underneath the site plans pinned on the walls, three unwashed coffee cups moulder away. An apple core left on the draining board fills the room with the stink of decay.

Wanting to cry, she sits at the desk she calls hers, the one with the best view of the site. Right now, all she can see out of the window is three diggers and a small crane sitting motionless in the dust, eating up their cash. Two grand or so a day, all this is costing them.

She has discovered that Bill, who did all the admin on the insurance, didn't take out the expensive optional clause that allowed for payouts in the event of archaeological or forensic finds. Why would he? He thought he knew what was in his own back garden.

She gets up, tidies the office and gathers the paperwork for Tina.

She should leave, but something is nagging at her. Not for the first time in her life, guilt nibbles at her edges.

Because she's worrying about cash while out there a little girl lay in the cold, hard ground, under a tangle of brambles and wild roses, fox turds and spiderwebs. She puts down the bulging wallet file of builder-fingered delivery notes and invoices and checks through the Portakabin window.

Definitely no one there.

She tiptoes out of the site office, slips under the police tape and, sticking to the edge of the site, makes her way down to The Wilderness, where the wild roses are in full bloom and the bramble blossom has fallen early, revealing hard nubs, great-great-grandchildren of the blackberries Alice and Bill used to pick.

A white tent stands over where they found Emma. First looking over her shoulder to check she is still alone, Carys undoes the zip on the door and slips inside.

The hot tang of recently dug earth hits her nostrils, which seem exceptionally sensitive today. She catches her breath, then lets it out slowly as she kneels on the blue tarpaulin covering the earth around poor Emma's grave.

'Emma,' she says, touching the soil. 'Same age as my sister Emily when you died. I hope your death was peaceful like hers and that you found as much happiness in your life as she did in hers.'

She closes her eyes and watches herself aged sixteen whizzing Emily in her wheelchair along Victoria Dock, bombing along as fast as she possibly can. Emily shrieks with laughter, a noise that to non-family sounds like she's screaming.

Once a disapproving old bag had a go at Carys.

'She's my sister, we're having fun,' Carys shouted over the top of Emily's laughter.

'You should show more respect,' the old woman said. 'That's a crippled child.'

'Piss off,' Emily said. Picked up from Carys's mum, who had a bit of a mouth on her, this was the one thing Emily could say that non-family ears could understand.

The racist abuse the woman then yelled at them really showed her colours.

Carys puts her fingers in the earth at the edge of the tarpaulin and smiles like she often does when she thinks of Emily. The joy is undercut, though, by the pain of knowing that her multiple, life-threatening disabilities had been caused by a trainee obstetrician screwing up at her birth.

A trainee obstetrician in Hull.

Carys is pretty level generally. But even with all the work she has put in, all the loving kindness and forgiveness exercises, all the reasoning she has done with herself, she hasn't ever fully mastered her anger about this. It continues to gnaw at her like some vicious little rat.

Even with all the practical steps she's taken, too: tracking down the perpetrator, seeing a sort of justice enacted...

The day she confronted Alice, after all those years of preparation, was nothing short of a disaster. Tears on Alice's part, shouting on Carys's as she accused her of ruining not only her sister's life, but those of her entire family. It all just sort of exploded out of her, after the years of bottling it up. And – although she's never hinted at a memory of it – there was little Lucy, aged six, not quite through the school door, possibly hearing everything.

Even Alice's death didn't bring the closure Carys hoped it would. In fact, it just splayed the whole issue like an open wound. She bandaged it carefully so no one else could see. Her parents, for example, have no idea that her husband, Bill Anderton, is the evil Dr Alice Herman's widower. Carys drummed into them that he doesn't like to talk about his tragic first wife, so on the few occasions they have met him, no mention has been made. He, of course, has not made the connection. He would probably only have known of Emily as Baby W – the name she was given for the hearing – and anyway, like Carys's parents, he and Alice tried to erase that whole episode from their memories.

She can talk to Bill about almost anything except this. If he were to learn how she used him to get at Alice – how she targeted his architecture firm for her Part One practical experience precisely because of who his wife was – it would be the beginning of the end. And whatever path brought her to him, their life together is everything she now holds dear.

She would rather die than jeopardise that.

Emily's short life so shaped Carys's family that when she was gone, their parents collapsed into the hole left behind.

'But her spirit lives on in our hearts,' Carys says to Emma, her thoughts spilling once more into her words. 'And I've got a space for you in here too.' She touches her chest, aware that she sounds like a bad greetings card, but it's true. She saw too much of Emma's remains to stay detached.

'I promise you,' she tells her, 'I will do everything I can to make sure we find out what happened to you, who put you here and, if they are still around, that they are brought to justice.'

A voice outside makes her start.

'Hello? Ms Jones?' It's the policewoman from the gate.

Carys slips out of the tent and tiptoes around the back of the bushes Artur and his boys left half dug up. She slides along the garden wall, then dashes between the oaks, using each one as cover as she watches the policewoman contaminate the crime scene by stepping over the tape and looking inside the tent, just like she did.

She takes that moment to run up the garden, past the site office, out of the gate and onto the street.

Tina will have to wait for the papers, which are still in the Portakabin.

But hey.
There's no rush.

EIGHTEEN

'Luce wants me to take her to Ajay.'

With Lucy cowering behind her, Sara stands on the threshold of the inner door to the flat, her arms folded like Carys imagines she might have done at work back in Australia, perhaps barring an abusive husband from entering his wife's home.

Sweat prickles on Carys's back. 'But I know Ajay, and there were so many issues last time. I just want to see this through, Sara.' She reaches a hand out. 'Please let me take you, Lucy. I just want to be there for you.'

'To keep an eye on her, you mean,' Sara says.

What has Carys done to deserve this from Sara? She has tried so hard over the years to make her feel included, despite the fact that she turned her back on them all.

'I believe you, Lucy,' she says. 'I completely believe that your memories are your truth. And I promise I won't ever get in the way of what you decide to do with them. Promise. No matter how inconvenient it may be for Bill and me, however much it impacts on our business. I'm pulling away from that. Whatever happened to that poor child needs to be put to rights.'

'And her mum,' Lucy says. Her voice has taken on the little-girl tone that makes Carys want to both slap her and hold out a wing for her to creep under.

'And her mother,' Carys says, reaching past Sara and taking her hand.

So once more she sits in Ajay's waiting room while Lucy sees him behind his securely shut treatment room door. She looks out of the window at his glorious garden and wishes she could breathe that level of perfection back into her own life. It was all so good. And now everything is falling to shit. All she really wants to do is to lie down and sleep, but she's had to work her arse off to sort out the financial and practical fallout of all of this.

Bill has been trying hard, but she can see that he is not dealing well with the situation. This hurts her doubly because she knows she is partly responsible for it. She wants to tell him everything is going to be OK, the police will stop searching soon, Lucy will be happy again, Sara will love him and everything will be back to how it was. But she doesn't know if she believes that herself.

She called Ajay yesterday to tell him about Lucy going to the police, adding that she was half-minded to cancel him, the trouble the hypnotherapy was causing. He said that would be disastrous. If he stopped now, Lucy could end up like a half-built house.

Like Five Oaks, she thought when he said this. Part-excavated, with bones and graves and God knows what else still buried.

Nonna and Fig sleep on the dog cushion and sunlight streams through the garden window. The calm so lulls Carys that she nearly gives in to her need to sleep.

But just as she is tipping over into unconsciousness, Ajay's treatment room door bursts open.

'Horrible, Carys. Horrible!' Lucy flies out like a snotty, raging bullet, a blur rather than a person.

The dogs jump up, and for the first time in years, Nonna barks, joining Fig in running in circles around Lucy. It's not clear what they're trying to do: Catch her? Pin her down? In this scribbled moment, Carys can't work anything out.

What's horrible? Has Lucy remembered the time Carys yelled at Alice? Is this it now?

All she knows is that she is on her feet, out in the hallway, her hand over Lucy's as it tries to pull down the handle on the stained-glass front door.

'Stop it, Lucy. Stop it! What are you doing?' She has to shout over the barely human wailing coming from her step-daughter.

'I can't do this,' Lucy yells, turning on her, trying to hit her away. 'Get away from me! Let me out of here. Let me out.'

A low voice comes from behind them. 'Lucy. Stop.'

It's Ajay, of course, who is standing outside his treatment room at the end of the hallway, his hands out like a statue of Jesus. 'When I count to five, you will go to sleep. One.'

He counts through, and indeed, by the time he reaches five, Lucy flops against Carys, all tension flown from her body.

He comes towards them and takes one of Lucy's arms. Together they lead her to the treatment room. She's not asleep exactly, but her body is like a piece of loose rope.

'What has she remembered?' Carys says, once they have settled her on the Danish chair. She notices her own hands are shaking.

Lucy sits bolt upright, like a shot of electricity has gone through her. 'Don't tell her!' she yells at Ajay.

Ajay smiles. 'I'm afraid I can't discuss it then,' he says. 'Patient confidentiality.'

'But I'm paying for this!' Carys wants to run away. 'And you're making her worse, not better.'

Ajay, who perhaps for protection has moved behind his desk, holds up his hands. 'This is, I am afraid, part of the process. It's like peeling back the layers of an onion to find the truth.'

'But if you keep doing that, you end up with nothing.'

He closes his eyes and shakes his head, a tiny smile on his lips, and Carys wants to punch him.

Instead, she turns to Lucy. 'Come home with me.'

'I want Sara.' Lucy flings herself up from the chair. Her nose and eyes are red, and her face is as white as the walls, making her hair look more orange than ever. She stumbles across the room and grabs her phone from her bag.

'Siri, call Sara on loudspeaker,' she yells at it.

Sara answers.

'I'm just round the corner,' she says. 'Give me two minutes.'

'Wait. She followed us here?' Carys's mouth is open.

'She did,' Sara says from the phone. 'Just as well, too, from the sound of it.'

Lucy hangs up and turns to Carys. 'I want to go home with my sister.' She holds out her hand. 'And give me your flat keys.'

'What?'

'I don't want you letting yourself in any more.'

'I don't let myself in. '

'You did.'

'That's because you weren't answering! If I hadn't, you'd be dead, Lucy.'

Carys freezes the room with that. The doorbell chimes in on them like an ice pick.

'The door's open!' Ajay sings, but he heads through to the hallway anyway. He is still bloody smirking!

'What did you see?' Carys hisses at Lucy, the moment he is out of the room.

Lucy looks at her, shaking her head, her eyes almost swirling. 'The keys, please.' She holds out her hand again.

'Why are you being like this?'

With no answer from Lucy, Carys has no choice but to hand over the keys to the flat she owns and which Lucy is living in rent-free.

'What's happened?' Sara bundles into the room like she's on a morning cop raid – all that's missing is the gun. Throwing Carys an accusatory glance, she storms past her and folds her sister in her arms, which Carys notices are almost too muscular for her tight frame.

She would make a fearsome opponent in a fight.

'Ask him.' Carys looks at Ajay, who is standing behind Sara, an air of satisfaction about him, like a party host who has put two strangers together who are getting on like a house on fire.

'Can we go home?' Lucy uses her baby voice on Sara.

'Course we can.' With one strong arm around her sister, Sara scoops up Lucy's bag and sweeps her towards the door.

'Don't forget the tree tomorrow,' Carys says to their departing backs. 'Four o'clock under the Caucasian zelkova in Hyde Park Rose Garden. Binnie is so looking forward to our picnic.'

She winces at the way she inserted that last piece of emotional blackmail.

'We're out of here.' Sara steers Lucy out of the room.

Carys jumps as the front door slams. She looks at Ajay.

'Like I say, Carys, it's a work in progress. Ripples.'

'Bloody tidal waves. Was it something about me that upset Lucy?'

Ajay smiles again. 'Why? Is there something about you?'

Blood heats Carys's face.

He laughs. 'No. It's not about you, Carys. *You* don't have to worry.' He jiggles his mouse like he's back to business. 'I'll see you and Lucy next week, then.'

Carys hangs there and looks at the empty Danish chair. Shouldn't this be the end of Ajay interfering with Lucy's head?

'Remember what I said about the half-built house,' he says, as if he can read her mind.

Carys breathes in and out, then goes to fetch Nonna, who has settled again on the cushion with Fig.

She wishes she could talk to Bill about all this. But of course she can't. It's just another layer on her laminate of lies.

NINETEEN

Lucy is too wrecked to tell Sara what she saw during her session. Sara gets her home, gives her her pills and helps her to bed, where she draws her knees up to her chest and sets stone solid.

Later, Sara slips out to the Sainsbury's Local and buys a couple of bottles of good Australian red and a Taste the Difference ham and cheese macaroni bake. She puts the dinner in the microwave and pours herself a whacking goblet of red.

If Lucy isn't any better in the morning, she will have to contact Carys, find out who her sister's shrink is.

She chews on the tough macaroni and thinks about her stepmother's face when she walked in to rescue Lucy at the hypnotherapist's place. She knows that look from her work.

It's guilt.

Carys is guilty.

But of what?

Sara finishes her meal, cracks her knuckles and paces the living room, trying to imagine Carys living here with Edina, back in the days before she traded up to Bill. She has always wondered if there was an overlap. The thought makes her feel ill. Was Carys screwing Bill while Alice was still around?

And did Alice's death/disappearance suit her?

The public version of the story is that while on placement in his practice, Carys started looking after him after his motorbike crash. They got together – Sara makes a barf gesture – during that winter. Indeed, she remembers the most awful vegan Christmas lunch cooked by Carys that year in the old house. She bought crackers and extravagant presents – far more expensive than the family were used to. As if all the trimmings could smother the one brutal truth: that it was the first Christmas since their mother, their rock, had – apparently – thrown herself off Beachy Head.

Sara still hasn't had that 'apparently' thing out with Bill. Despite her feelings towards Carys souring by the day – and therefore her suspicions growing – she still wants to wait and watch.

She has done a lot of reading-up about Beachy Head. After the Golden Gate Bridge in San Francisco and the Aokigahara forest in Japan, it is the third most popular suicide spot in the world. About twenty people a year choose to end their lives there. A horrible way to go, she thinks. What if you change your mind as you're falling? And does it hurt when you land?

Only about half of all Beachy Head deaths are officially recorded as suicides. The rest are inconclusive. Massively inconclusive presumably if, like Alice's, no body is ever found.

She tries again to imagine Carys living in this flat: a young woman, girl really, fresh down from Hull, starting out on her architecture degree with a usefully acquired older girlfriend so she doesn't have to slum it like her fellow students.

And then to land her professional practice with Bill's firm. How starstruck she must have been. Then as now he was the darling of the eco-architecture community, with his work featured in Sunday colour supplements accompanied by photos of him in all his Clooney handsomeness in front of rough-hewn industrial-looking walls.

How long did Carys have her greedy little eyes on him, the next step up the social and career ladder from Edina? The irony is that Edina has become something of a media star herself recently, with a TV series and several books on what makes criminals tick. Perhaps Carys regrets leaving her now.

All the furniture here, all the cooking stuff, all the white goods, lampshades, everything in this flat dates back to their time here. It's kind of creepy that nothing has changed. It's like Carys just walked out of her old lives – first the one in the council house in Hull with the Welsh mother and Jamaican father Sara imagines as wizened little folk, a bit like hobbits. Then the life of relative comfort and sophistication with Edina, in turn abandoned for a giant leap up to the big old house and garden, the ready-made family and the on-the-rebound widowed handsome older architect.

Oh, what's the point in turning it over and over? Carys has won, and that's it. And she plays the part of Bill's new young wife so brilliantly well. She's too fucking clever, that's what.

Wearily, Sara takes her wine and laptop up to her room, planning to spend the evening under the duvet, watching crap TV and getting drunk.

Annoyingly, her charger cable doesn't stretch across from the socket on the wall opposite, so she looks around for an alternative.

She traces the cable from a lamp on the little table beside her to a socket behind her bed. Sighing at the effort, she tugs the bed away from the wall, uncovering a set of low locked doors where the wall meets the sloping ceiling, giving access to the eaves.

The doors are square and just big enough for an adult to crawl through. The lock looks pretty straightforward, so she runs downstairs, finds a large paper clip on Lucy's art table and uses her police skills to pick it.

Opening the door, she meets a hot blast of dusty air mixed with a faint stale whiff of Carys. She creeps in, shining her phone torch.

Four big blue IKEA bags squat against the rafters. Three are stuffed with clothes. Carys cuts a strong figure in her expensive organic linen tunics, clumpy sandals, cropped hair and big black glasses. Here, though, is a different version: a Carys who shopped at Primark and Top Shop for cheap, bright, tight-fitting instant fashion, the kind she would refuse now on ethical grounds. Clearly far too embarrassing to bring with her when she moved in on Bill.

The fourth bag contains what at a cursory glance looks like bric-a-brac. Sara knows, though, from her detective work, that even the most ordinary bit of junk could be a vital clue in the search for a murderer.

'Not that you're searching for a murderer,' she says out loud into the dusty space. On the other side of the roofing tiles, a pigeon grumbles, making her jump and bang her head on a beam.

Cursing and crawling backwards, she drags the bag out of the eaves cupboard, hitting her head one more time as she levers it through the doorway.

She pours herself another big glass of red, then, crap TV plans forgotten, sits on the floor for a good old rummage.

There's a teddy bear, some old Spice Girls and All Saints CDs, boxes of little trinkets: lone earrings, badges, favourite pencil erasers, that sort of thing. Sara left a plastic box full of similar stuff in the loft in the old house. It's probably gone by now: her childhood has more or less been erased from every living memory except her own, and even that is hazy. Alice's disappearance from her life distorted everything.

Underneath all that, she finds a cardboard box with *Emily*

written on the top in black marker pen. Thinking this must be another ex-girlfriend, she eagerly opens it. But on the top is a photograph of a little girl aged five or six, smiling gappily at the camera. It's a professional portrait – the kind flogged yearly to parents of schoolchildren. At first Sara thinks it's Carys, but the girl's head is at a strange angle, her arm contracted so her hand hangs in front of her chest. Her eyes have a marked squint and her skull, under neat cornrows, is long and thin, depressed above the ears.

She looks so happy.

Sara lifts the photo to reveal a dog-eared scrapbook. She flicks through it, releasing the smell of cow gum.

It is full of newspaper cuttings.

She settles on the floor, opens the cover and gasps.

There on the first page is her mother's graduation photo. The original now lives in a box in Global Self Storage in Sydney, having previously sat framed on the sideboard in the house Sara shared with Pete.

This one is on the front page of the *Hull Daily Mail*.

In it, Alice looks bright, brainy and beautiful, her red hair loose beneath her mortarboard, her capable hands clasping a scroll. She looks rightly pleased with herself for completing five years of gruelling study and junior doctoring while having baby Sara and marrying Bill. For all his baking, Sara imagines her father wasn't exactly a nappy-changer.

The headline sitting above it, however, turns Alice's pride into smug self-satisfaction: *Doctor in tragic Baby W case not guilty says GMC.*

The accompanying article gives the facts Sara already knows about her mother's mistake while attending a birth as an overworked, under-slept trainee obstetrician. It says there were 'red flags' during labour that went unobserved and misunderstood and as a result Baby W suffered serious brain damage. The General Medical Council found though that Alice was acting in an emergency so was not liable and would be allowed to continue to practice.

The article makes this out as horribly unfair. The poor baby is left damaged and disabled, the smug young woman gets to go on with her brilliant career.

It doesn't tell the full story, however, of the damage that young woman also suffered, and the way in which the fallout was ultimately revisited on her own family with her suicide.

If it was suicide.

Sara holds the picture of the happy disabled little girl in one hand and the scrapbook in the other. She's pretty certain she knows where this is going.

As she flicks through the book, the press cuttings document Baby W's parents' campaign to win financial recompense both for the suffering caused and to pay for round-the-clock care. Before they get anywhere, though, the girl dies, aged six, from failure of a birth-damaged heart.

After her death, Baby W is finally identified as Bethan 'Emily' Jones and her picture published – the same one lying on the floor next to Sara. Her family remain anonymous, the report notes, because they are still engaged in legal action against the healthcare trust, and they want to preserve the anonymity of their remaining daughter, aged eighteen.

Sara does the sums, just to be sure. That's Carys, of course.

What follows in the rest of the scrapbook chills Sara. Every bit of press about Alice and her health centre has been collected and stuck in. There's that piece the *Guardian* Saturday magazine ran – 'You *can* have it all' – with a photo featuring Alice, Bill, Sara aged eleven and Lucy as a newborn babe-in-arms. No mention of course of poor baby Danny, who came in between them and broke Alice's heart so badly she couldn't ever sleep again without pills.

Alice's success meant that her own family's anonymity was sold right down the river. The *Guardian* profile is followed by pages and pages of those fluff pieces on Bill in arty architectural and eco-design magazines.

When she reaches an article cut out of the *Ham & High* with a photograph of herself running past the finishing post when she won the Haringey under-18s 100 metres, Sara comes to a horrified halt. That was when Carys was living in this flat, when she was doing her professional practice at Bill's firm.

Underneath where the scrapbook lay in the shoebox, she finds a plait of black curly hair, a tiny silver bracelet and a handful of photos of the little girl – Bethan, Emily or Baby W, whatever – smiling, laughing, being whizzed along in her wheelchair by her big sister.

This box must be so precious to Carys.

So why is it here, locked in this loft?

Because Carys doesn't want anyone to know that she stalked Alice and her family.

Bill surely has no idea about any of this. He probably tried to forget Alice's mistake, but anyway, with the anonymity and it happening up in Hull, it would be nearly impossible to make the connection.

Did Carys turn up at Bill's practice for revenge? And if so, how far did she go?

Sara returns to the thought that made her so itchy earlier this evening.

How Carys had looked so guilty at what might have been dredged up out of Lucy's brain.

TWENTY

'Lucy!'

Carys hammers on the door.

She's left Binnie at home with strict instructions not to tell Bill about the arrangement to meet Lucy and Sara at Hyde Park today. 'They didn't show up, so he doesn't need to know, does he?' she told her.

Binnie nodded. She is an old hand at guarding important secrets – how much Carys's bag really cost, what Fiona's little girl said about Alice at school, how Mam-Gu cried her eyes out last time Carys took her to visit because she reminded her of someone called Emily.

And of course Carys also couldn't tell Bill where she's going tonight, so she has her yoga bag slung over her shoulder, but for all sorts of reasons, she's worried about the no-show at the park.

She bangs and yells again. 'Lucy! Sara!'

Across the road, Constance lifts her net curtain, frowning. Carys needs to tone it down. Soon the less vigilant neighbours will start coming to their windows. She doesn't want to set yet more tongues wagging.

She picks a few pieces of gravel from the tiny front garden

and throws them up at the living room window.

She feels sick now. The image of Lucy bleeding out in her bathroom works at her brain. Should she call the emergency services again? And if so, which one? Police or ambulance?

But Sara is there, she tells herself. Sara is there.

She leans her forehead on the front door, unable to think of what to do next. To calm her brain, she counts to one hundred.

She's reached eighty when a gasp and a scuffle make her swing around.

Behind her, Sara stands at the front gate, her hands on Lucy, stopping her from running away.

Like a mother who has just saved her child after it has run out into the road, Carys's relief at seeing both girls intact flips over into anger. 'Where the hell have you been?'

'I don't want to see her,' Lucy says under her breath to her sister.

'Aziziye,' Sara says. 'For a kebab.'

Carys and Edina's favourite restaurant.

Carys bars their way. 'Why didn't you turn up today?'

Sara laughs. 'Lucy's hardly in a state right now to play your "Mummy cares" games.'

Carys takes a long, slow breath. 'You could have let me know.'

'How deep a state of denial are you actually in?'

Lucy puts her hands over her ears. 'I don't want to hear this. I can't deal with this.'

'Jesus. Don't worry, Luce, you don't have to. I'll take you in, then I'll come out and deal with her.' Sara turns to Carys. 'See you in the White Hart in ten minutes. Now, if you don't mind?'

She ushers Lucy past Carys and through the door. Before she opens the inner door to the flat, she stops and turns to her. 'You always have to stick your oar in, don't you?'

'I'm her mother,' Carys says.

Sara closes the front door in her face.

.   .   .

Carys perches on one of the pub sofas, picking at a supper-replacement bag of crisps and nursing a glass of wine. The rest of the bottle – a good Rioja, not the house red – sits alongside a glass for Sara on the table in front of her. It's a hot night and most of the clientele are out in the beer garden, but Carys is happy to have the window separating her into this corner, where conversation is soaked up by the background music. It's Elvis Costello, a singer both Bill and her mum admire from their teenage years – a pretty sobering fact when she discovered it.

It has been fifteen minutes since Sara said she'd see her in ten.

She tells herself to chill.

Is Sara right? Does she always stick her oar in? She's doing her best as a stepmother, and surely that involves the occasional intervention. True, her attempts at confronting the vile girl who bullied Lucy in Year 9 made things so much worse that they had to change schools. And she got it all wrong at first with Lucy's eating disorders, thinking that leaving delicious titbits lying around would tempt her out of her anorexia, when in fact it acted like a workout for Lucy's psyche, actually strengthening her resistance to food. But then failure can't just be the preserve of too-young stepmothers. All parents get things wrong from time to time.

The pub door swings open and Sara strides in, a large Sports Direct bag on her shoulder. The soft focus in her eyes as she looks around for Carys shows she has already had a few drinks with her kebab.

As she approaches the sofa, Carys pours her a glass of wine. She takes it without thanks and sits down on the low stool opposite, all businesslike and no preamble. 'Lucy has asked that you don't contact her for the time being,' she says.

'What do you mean?'

'Pretty self-explanatory?'

'What's going on, Sara? What did Lucy see at Ajay's?'

Sara shakes her head. 'She still won't say. Other than that she knows who the "evil one" is.' She looks across the table, her blue eyes like ice. 'There's a lot of messed-up shit going on in this family and it needs to stop.'

Carys shivers. 'What does that mean?'

'It means you've got to talk to Bill. Tell him why you decided to work at his practice.'

'It was the leading eco-architecture firm in the country.'

'Sure. But it was also run by the husband of the doctor you held responsible for your sister's disabilities.'

Carys's stomach twists. The crisps she has recently eaten threaten to make a reappearance. Her words form at the back of her throat, on an in-breath. 'It's not what you think.'

'Oh, isn't it.'

Sara reaches into her bag, takes out a familiar cardboard box and puts it on the table between them.

Carys grabs the box and pulls it towards her, like a mother retrieving her baby from a kidnapper. 'You've been snooping!'

'Good job too.' Sara folds her arms, a little smile on her face. 'Found you out at last.'

Carys looks at her open-mouthed.

'You know, of course, that my mother's body was never found,' Sara says.

Carys frowns. 'What?'

'Don't bullshit me.'

'I didn't know that!'

'You did.'

'No! The funeral—'

'Empty casket. I've looked it up. It can be arranged.'

'We buried her ashes.'

'Stop lying, Carys. You know it, I know you do, and I have

all the proof I need. Dad had to declare her presumed dead in the local paper before the High Court could legally confirm it. It's all there on the internet if you know what to look for. No doubt he did it to spare us the pain of not knowing what happened to her. But that doesn't alter the fact that what happened to her is not known. At least not known by everyone.'

'What does that mean?' Carys's voice comes out of her like she has hands round her throat, throttling her.

'What do you think it means?'

She wants to go back in time to when she moved out of the flat after the bust-up with Edina, when she sat there with that shoebox wondering whether to burn it or tuck it away into the eaves cupboard with the rest of the life she was leaving behind.

'That cupboard was locked!' she says.

'I've got crim skills.'

'It was my private stuff.'

'Hey.' Sara hunkers down, her elbows on her knees, and gives Carys a good, hard stare. 'Did you ever actually love Bill?'

'Of course I did! Of course I do!'

'Or is he still your revenge? Move in, spend his money, take his daughters' inheritance away.'

'You have to believe me, Sara!' Carys reaches across the table and tries, without success, to take Sara's hand. 'Yes, I went into it with thoughts about my sister. OK, that's true. But then I met Bill and saw how hard Alice found life, and...'

She folds in on herself, unable to speak any more.

'And you thought you'd move in on him.'

She shakes her head. 'No. That's not what I thought.'

'Yeah, right.'

She closes her eyes.

The two women sit there in silence, shielding under the sounds of people shouting and laughing and having a blast on the other side of the window.

'How is Lucy?' Carys asks in the end, like running up a white flag.

'She slept it off last night. Woke up quite calm. Like, I dunno, like a storm had passed right through her. Look. Let me deal with it, yeah? I'm going to care for my sister from now on. I want you to send me all her medical details.'

'But—'

'You have to tell my dad the truth. About how you stalked him and Mum. And what you know about Mum's death.'

Carys shakes her head. 'I don't know anything, like I said. Nothing.'

'We'll see about that.'

'Why are you turning over all these old stones, Sara? What do you want?'

Sara leans forward and holds Carys's gaze so that she can't look away. 'The truth. You could have got another sister. But a mum? Lucy and me, we can't ever replace our mother. So I'm not stopping until I find out every last detail about what happened to her. I've had enough with all the lies in this family. It's what's getting in the way of Lucy's recovery. It's probably what *caused* it, growing up in your toxic false front of "oh, isn't everyone lovely". She needs to know the truth.'

'She's too ill. Too fragile. It's not the right time.'

Sara gets up and looks down at Carys, who feels like an insect caught in an observation jar.

'Yeah, but it'll never be the right time, will it? Look. Bottom line: you and Bill need to sort out your shit and stop lying to each other and to us. And if you don't dare tell him the truth, then you've really got a problem. Because when I've finished digging, I will make sure it all comes out, Carys. However bad it is. And whatever it is, it will be better for you if you own up to it first.'

'Don't tell Lucy anything, please.' Carys never thought she

would find herself in this position, a beggar to her stepdaughter. 'It could send her right over the edge.'

'That particular horse has already bolted, Carys.'

Sara picks up her empty Sports Direct bag and heads across the bar and towards the door. Then, like a bloody tornado, stirring everything up then disappearing, she is gone, the door swinging behind her.

Carys puts her face in her hands and shakes her head.

She drains her glass, finishes Sara's, then, leaning against the buttoned leather sofa back, steadily downs the rest of the bottle, telling herself she hates waste when actually, here she is, like Bill when he was at his most addicted, boozing away her problems.

Is this yet another thing to worry about?

Her brain burns with shame.

As she drinks, she watches the people having fun outside like they are on a different planet. A nice-looking man about her own age – nose ring, lovely soft 'fro, dark blue tats – catches her eye through the window as he makes his way back into the bar. He gives her that raised eyebrow that asks her if she's interested. She smiles back and gently shakes her head. He is well enough behaved not to pursue it, but as she feels the muzzle of the empty-stomach wine closing in on her, she wishes she could just run outside and take his hand. She should be out there having fun, not in here doing all this.

Her phone buzzes. It's a text from Bill.

Where are you? I miss you.

Using the warmth of his message to arm her against the ice field Sara left in her wake, she slings her yoga bag across her shoulder and wobbles across the floor towards the pub door.

If Sara tells him everything, then Carys is well and truly done for.

TWENTY-ONE

'A few of us went to the pub,' she says, to explain the red-wine smile Bill has just pointed out on her.

'Doesn't sound very om namaste to me,' he says, placing a bowl of rice and dhal on the table.

'I'll just wash my hands.' She ducks into the downstairs loo and hides the box, which she left in the hallway, at the back of the winter-coat cupboard.

Carys runs a piece of naan around the bowl to get the last bits. Emboldened by the wine, she decides there's no time like the present. 'So,' she says. 'Sara said something the other day about Alice.'

Bill looks up sharply. 'What? What other day?'

'Um, when she came to pick Lucy up, the morning after the dinner? When you were at Pilates?'

'And you're only telling me now?'

'It was hard, with all the Five Oaks stuff, to find the right moment.'

It's plausible enough. She always has to work up to talk to him about Alice. They both know that if she, the love of his life, weren't dead, he wouldn't be with Carys, and he thinks she finds this difficult.

The truth is that she feels pretty robust about the situation. Even though their twelve years together is not all that far off the twenty of his first marriage, Carys really does understand why Sara particularly, who has been away for almost all that time, might think of her as the upstart newcomer.

But she has to address what Sara said about Alice. Not least because she hopes it will buy time so she doesn't have to bring up the other thing Sara demanded she talk to Bill about.

The thing about Emily.

Carys started tracking Alice a couple of years after Emily's birth, when she was fourteen. An exceptionally bright student, championed by her teachers, who knew her challenging family circumstances, she was already dreaming of becoming an architect. She was also passionate about the environment. When she found out that Alice's husband ran a celebrated eco-architecture firm, it seemed like fate. She designed her whole career plan, through GCSEs and on to A levels, around doing her professional practice with him.

She had no idea through all this what she would actually do when she finally confronted Alice, but the goal-setting meant that at least she was doing *something*. And when Emily died, this sense of purpose stopped her ending up like her parents, sunk with loss.

What she also couldn't foresee was how she would fall in love with Bill.

She hadn't gone in with a plan to seduce him away from his wife – and despite Sara's suspicions, nothing happened until after Alice's death. After all, up to then, she had only ever slept with women. And Bill was old enough to be her dad.

How life turns out.

How life turns out.

Bill picks up Carys's empty bowl and plate and carries them to the dishwasher. 'So what was it that Sara said?'

'She has this idea that Alice's body was never found,' she tells him.

'Ah.' He drops the cutlery into the dishwasher basket with a clatter. 'How did she find out?'

Carys shrugs. 'The internet? Some police search thing? She's quite good at all that, it seems.'

Bill rinses out a cloth and starts wiping down the kitchen surfaces, which are already operating-theatre clean. 'She's always been clever.' He sighs so deeply that Carys is surprised the floor doesn't rumble.

'So she's right, then?'

He looks down at his hands and nods. 'Yep.'

'OK.' Carys folds her hands in her lap and frowns at the table.

'Can you imagine how that felt?' he says. 'To not know what really happened to the woman you love.'

Carys shivers.

'They scoured the coast for weeks. No part of her ever turned up. The currents there, they normally drag jumpers towards the east; usually people are recovered. But sometimes they just get pulled out to sea and that's that.'

'Jumpers.'

Bill twists his mouth. 'I'm sorry. I sound blasé about it. But believe me, I'm not. I was desperate. She left her car at the west car park—'

'I know,' Carys says. It's where she and Lucy park when they visit the spot, not that Bill knows that.

'And her note.'

'Yes.'

'"I'm Sorry."'

'I know.'

'So, given her history of depression and two previous suicide attempts, the police thought it was pretty conclusive.'

Carys nods.

'And I didn't tell the girls because it was horrific enough for me, but for them? Enough to damage them for life.' He lets out a brief, bitter laugh. 'And yet here we are, with Lucy damaged for life and Sara hating me. And, I suppose, hating me even more now she knows how I lied.'

Carys reaches a hand across the table to take his. 'Why didn't you tell me, though?'

He shakes his head. She can see there are tears in his eyes. 'We'd only just met properly. I mean, you'd only just become something more than the professional practice placement.'

Carys nods.

'And I'd gone through the whole fake funeral rigmarole, to help the girls, give them a focus for their grief.'

'I see that.'

'And if you knew, perhaps you'd have felt compromised keeping it from Lucy.'

'I've kept baby Danny secret from her. And the Hull business.'

'I know you have. I mean, it's not because I don't trust you.'

And while it was technically Sara who instigated telling Lucy about Danny and Hull, Carys still feels like she's going to choke on this lie.

'I kept Alice's missing body totally quiet,' Bill goes on. 'I was supposed legally to inform her mum about it before I could get her death registered, but I didn't.'

'Didn't anyone notice?'

He shakes his head. 'It's amazing how easy it is to just not do stuff when it comes to admin like that. No one checks, not when you're respectable like me.'

'And white and a man.'

'Yeah. Sorry about that.'

Carys strokes his fingers.

'It was just best,' he goes on. 'To protect everyone. Her poor mum, out there in Australia. The one blessing is that she died not knowing that Alice's death was something of a mystery.'

'Suicide was a comfort for her?'

'It's the second worst to not knowing.'

'If she even died.'

Bill frowns. 'I've never allowed myself to think that. The idea that she would walk away from us... that would imply a rational choice.'

'And suicide is never a rational choice.'

'It's something you have to do because you're so sick – either mind or body – that you can't see another way out.' This is the mantra they have repeated to each other over the years, and usually it provides comfort.

But today, Bill stops and puts his hand over his eyes. 'I should have helped Alice more.'

'Hey.' Carys gets up, moves round to his side of the table and stands behind him, her arms around his shoulders. 'No should-haves, remember?' This thought formed the backbone of their conversations about his grief as she helped him after the motorbike crash, when they were falling in love. 'It was just something she had to do, yes?'

'Yes. It was nothing I did, nothing I didn't.'

'That's it.' She kisses the top of his head.

He turns to her and presses his face up against her belly. 'You have saved me, Carys.'

She closes her eyes and drinks in the moment.

'We won't tell Lucy just now?' he says, his voice muffled by her linen top.

'No. She's not ready.'

'Thank you.'

But she knows it's no longer fully in her gift to keep things quiet from Lucy.

As if summoned by a dark angel to prove this, a text arrives on her phone. It's from Sara, with a Google map pin.

Lucy has spoken. Meet you here tomorrow, 10 a.m

.

TWENTY-TWO

Carys stands on the pavement, her back to the derelict school building. She's on the exact spot Sara sent her, but she can't work out why she has been asked to come here. It's a fairly ordinary road in Clerkenwell, traffic fumes lingering from the morning rush hour, and there's no bench or green space or coffee shop in sight where they could possibly sit and talk.

She leans back against the railings and waits, her eyes tight with a hangover but the rest of her body alive. Perhaps it was the relief at releasing his secret to her, but Bill lit up in a way he hadn't done for some time, and they had a night like the early days when they first got together, when, even though he was mending from his motorbike crash, they couldn't keep their hands off each other. Her nerve ends still fizz with it.

Sex also allowed her to put off telling him about how she actually found her way to his arms. She hopes she'll find a way of swinging it with Sara so she never has to own up to that one.

And speak of the devil, here is Sara, half an hour late. She offers no apology, so Carys offers no greeting.

'Why did you want to meet here?' she asks instead.

'Turn around,' Sara tells her.

Carys turns. Behind her is a massive fig tree, twice as wide as it is tall. A series of rusty poles support its sprawling branches, which almost entirely hide the building behind it.

'Oldest fig tree in the country. It's in Mum's book, of course.'

'It doesn't look very well,' Carys says. Half the branches are bare, and there's not a single fruit on it.

'Kind of fitting, no?' Sara says.

A truck thunders past, trailing a fog of diesel fumes and showering them in dust from its open-topped container.

'We can't talk here,' Carys says.

'There's a square nearby.' Sara holds her phone up to take a photo of the tree. 'For Lucy's Insta. She asked me.'

They find a tree-shaded bench in the square, which is actually quite a sizeable park, surprisingly quiet for such a built-up area.

As they sit, a flock of bright green parakeets squawk into the sky from the branches above them.

'What did Lucy say about her session with Ajay then?' Carys asks. It's the first time either of them has spoken since they left the fig tree.

Sara looks out over the empty square. 'She says the woman killed in The Wilderness was Bill's lover.'

'*What?*'

'The child was her daughter, who she claimed was his. She was going to blackmail him and spoil things between him and Alice and he couldn't bear it.' Sara turns to look at Carys. 'Lucy saw Bill kill the woman and the child.'

Carys surprises both herself and Sara by bursting into laughter. Partly because of the release of tension, partly at the absolute ridiculousness of the accusation, she laughs and laughs until her ribs hurt. When she stops, she sees that Sara is watching her, her face hard and unsmiling.

'It's not funny, Carys,' she says. 'It's tragic. Tragic if it's untrue, because Lucy believes it. Even worse if it's true.'

'I know,' Carys says, wiping the tears from her eyes. 'But Bill? Kill someone? That's just absurd.'

Sara breathes slowly in and out. 'He lied about my mother never being found. Why not lie about this?'

'That's completely different!' Carys shakes her head wildly, her earrings rattling. 'He lied to spare us the pain!'

'Us!'

'I mean you.'

'No. You're right. It would suit you well if everyone thought she was dead by her own hand.'

'What do you mean by that?'

'You stalked my mother. What was your intention?'

'I'm not doing this again.'

'It would be a real problem for you if there were any question marks over her death, wouldn't it? If she were still alive, for example. Or if she had been found and there was evidence that she had been murdered.'

'So you're saying that both Bill and I are murderers?' Carys is once again on the edge of laughter.

'My parents didn't get on.'

'Bill *adored* Alice. He was heartbroken when she died. I saw it, remember?'

'When she very conveniently died.'

'We're not going to get anywhere if you use everything I say as a reason to attack me.'

'That adoration is just a myth he's invented to make himself feel better. They argued all the time. Shouting and fighting.'

'He would never hurt anyone. He's gentle.'

'I heard it when they thought we were asleep, or when they were in the garden. She wasn't happy. She wanted out. Bill wanted her to stay.'

'This isn't true.'

'Oh, it is.'

'So if it is, why would Bill have a lover? A lover he killed, along with his own child?'

'I'm not saying I believe Lucy. I'm just saying what I saw when I was younger. *My* truth.'

'And what Lucy saw?'

'That's *her* truth. And who's to say that Bill didn't have a lover? Perhaps that's why Mum wanted to leave.'

'He wouldn't do that. He's faithful.'

'Is he? For example, we've only got his and your word about when you got together. Perhaps *you* were the cause of the arguments. Perhaps you were lovers before she disappeared.'

'She died.'

'Did she? What makes you so sure, Carys?'

Carys picks up her bag and stands, ready to leave. 'This is too much, Sara. I don't have to listen to this.'

Sara moves in front of her, her face right up close. 'Yeah, stay in denial. Keep lying to us, to yourself. Tell yourself everything's all peachy, when in fact it's very, very far from that. You need to wake up, Carys. Perhaps you and Bill were lovers while Alice was still around and Lucy picked up on that and that's what's coming out in these "memories". Perhaps *you're* why she's so fucked in the head.'

'Don't talk about Lucy like that.'

'The only way to start mending things is to tell the truth. By the way: Have you told Bill yet about how you stalked Alice, and how you used him to get at her?'

'I—'

'Of course you haven't. I'm giving you one more week, and if you don't tell him, I'm going to do it myself.'

Sara is almost shouting. A middle-aged red-haired woman walking a dog on the other side of the square stops and looks over at them, her face shaded by a wide-brimmed sunhat.

Perhaps she's considering intervening in this fight between two young women.

Carys gives her a little wave, to let her know she need not worry. She moves on.

'That's right,' Sara hisses at her. 'Make out everything's hunky-dory.'

Carys shifts her feet and looks up at her stepdaughter, adopting the stance she uses on site when she has to confront a large man who thinks he knows better than her.

'The big problem here,' she says, 'the one you are burying in all the issues you clearly have with me, is that Lucy thinks her own father murdered a woman and a child. A child she believes to be her half-sister. It's absurd beyond words, utterly untrue. So what are we going to do about it?'

'We?' Sara smiles and shakes her head. 'You can't control everything, Carys.'

'What do you mean by that?'

'Let it come down, little wicked stepmother.'

Still smiling, she strolls away.

TWENTY-THREE

Thirty minutes later, clogged in a stationary traffic jam up in Belsize Park, Carys leans forward in the black cab and hands the driver a twenty.

'I'll take it from here on foot,' she tells him. She jumps out, slams the door and runs.

By the time she arrives at Ajay's treatment room, she is sweating, and the fury that powered her out of the square and away from Sara has reached the point where it cannot be contained, even by her normally screwed-down lid of hard-won calm.

As usual, his front door is open so patients can just let themselves in to the treatment part of the house. As she storms into the hallway, Carys wonders what goes on behind the second, locked door at the end of the corridor, which presumably leads to the living quarters.

It's one o'clock, lunchtime, so, as she charges into Ajay's treatment room, she's assuming he's not got anyone in. But there he is, standing over a young woman stretched out on his fancy sheepskin chair.

Instantly she realises what a fool she has been sending Lucy here. The power dynamic is so obvious – the patient prostrated, him looming over them as they give him all their trust, him feeding them all sorts of lines about what they 'see', what they 'remember'. It's all power games, all suggestion, all hocus-pocus.

Before she can say anything, he is across the room, his hand over her mouth, steering her back out through the door and into the empty waiting room.

'I can't let you wake her,' he whispers to her. 'It would be dangerous.'

'Such crap,' she hisses at him.

'I know what you want to talk about, but you have to wait.'

He goes back into the treatment room and she hears a key being turned in the door. Her first instinct is to smash her way back in, warn the woman on the recliner that she is putting her trust in an abusive charlatan, but the way Ajay said the word 'dangerous' stops her.

How could she have taken Lucy to a complete stranger, a man she met on a dog walk, whose only credentials she really looked at were the letters after his name on his business card and the fact that he had a dog of the same rare breed as her own.

Madness.

Or desperation.

And now all this. Any hope of Sara's return being a completion of her family is lost. All Sara wants to do is create chaos, and Ajay's work with Lucy has weaponised that.

This thing with Ajay has to stop.

He lets his patient out fifteen minutes later. Expensively dressed in a lawn smock that Carys reckons is a vintage Liberty print, she looks relieved, happy, liberated. Such a different picture to poor Lucy last time she was here.

'I have forty minutes,' Ajay says as he calmly shows her into his treatment room.

Carys speaks over him. 'What the hell do you think you're playing at?'

He motions to her to sit on the sofa, and takes the armchair next to it. 'I'm sorry, Carys,' he says in that voice that makes her want to tear him up, 'that the process Lucy is going through is causing her difficulty.'

'It's not just causing her difficulty. It's ripping my family apart.'

Ajay nods in his irritatingly sage-like way. 'Sometimes the troubles of a young person lie very close to home,' he says, his eyes open and clear, as if he hasn't a single toxin in his entire temple of a body.

Carys cuts him off and stands up. She doesn't want to share the air with him. 'You've turned her against both me and her father. You've filled her head with disgusting obscenities about Bill, and instead of getting better, she's worse than she ever was.'

Ajay continues to smile like some bloody Buddha. 'She's actually doing really well. She said just yesterday that she was calmer than she has been for years.'

'Wait: yesterday?'

Again the smile. 'I called her. I am aware that she is in a liminal state—'

'What the hell is that supposed to mean?'

'—that she could be troubled by the process. It would be irresponsible not to stay in touch.'

Carys backs away, towards the door. A wild part of her wants to stay and take that damn pointed crystal and smash it over his head. But the more rational part of her smells danger. She wants out.

'Who even are you?' she says, her hand on the door handle, ready to escape.

'A qualified medical doctor and certified hypnotherapist

with twenty years' clinical experience.' He gestures at the framed diplomas that line the wall behind his desk.

'Yeah, right.' She rubs her fingers together and mimics his voice. '"It's a long process. Could take many sessions." Yeah, at a hundred and fifty quid a pop.'

'Like all therapy, it can take a while.'

'Well, that's it. I'm not giving you any more hundred and fifty quids. You are sacked, Ajay. You've done enough damage.'

'I'm sorry, but I can't leave Lucy's treatment now.'

'I'm not paying.'

'I'll carry on pro bono if necessary.'

'No. I'm her parent. She won't be coming.'

'She's an adult. She can do what she wants.'

Carys looks at him open-mouthed. 'Who are you? Why are you doing this?'

'Because I want Lucy to get better,' he says.

He is still infuriatingly calm, like he's dangling her rage in her face to show her how irrational she is, how low-bred.

Blind with fury, she flies across the room to slap him. But without even getting up, he catches her hand and holds it, still smiling. His hands are hot, though; she feels the sweat on her wrist.

'I'm just looking after Lucy,' he says,

'You're not, though! You're acting like you've got it in for us.'

'What makes you think that?'

She snatches her hand away, steps back and lifts her lip like Nonna when she doesn't want to be touched. 'I'm going to set the police on you, tell them you're abusing the trust of young women.' Somewhere inside her she is telling herself that this is an unfair accusation, but the harm he is actually doing is even worse than that. His abuse reaches right into people's souls.

'I'm going to ask you to leave,' he says, his voice too calm now, like he has smoothed a plastic coating over it.

'"Look into my eyes"? You're going to count to ten and ask

me to leave?' Carys says. 'I'm wide awake. You can't get to me like that.'

'I don't think you're in the right space for any sort of discussion.'

'Tell you what. Fuck you, Ajay. I'm calling the police.'

She gets her phone out and starts calling the number Tom gave her. He needs to know about all this. She realises now that she has to own up to Bill about the hypnotherapy, because Ajay needs to be factored into the investigations. Perhaps if they can discredit him, they can lay Emma to proper rest and get back to the building work.

'I want you to leave now,' Ajay says.

Carys puts her phone to her ear, waiting for a reply.

'You are now trespassing,' he says. 'And you've been threatening me. If the police arrive, I'm going to tell them that. And who do you think they'll believe? The qualified therapist or the wife of a man whose daughter accuses him of murder.'

Carys stabs at her phone to stop the call. 'What?'

'Lucy has told me she intends to go to the police.'

'What? Is that a threat?'

Ajay has found his smile again. 'It's what she intends to do.'

'And you didn't try to talk her out of it? Tell her it's just "the process"?' She claws the air, describing the quotation marks. 'That it can't possibly be true?'

Finally Ajay stands. 'Who's to say that?'

'I'm his wife!' Carys says. 'I know him!'

'Be careful, Carys,' Ajay says. 'Bad things happen to Bill's wives.' He moves towards her.

She steps back, a wave of ice passing down her spine. 'Are you threatening me?'

Before she is even conscious of it, she is heading out of the treatment room and towards the front door.

As she leaves, she bumps into a skeletal teenage girl and her mother on the way in.

'Don't go in there,' she tells them, aware of how her voice, squeezed through her tightened throat, must make her sound. 'He's evil.'

Ajay's next client backs off, like Carys is a madwoman, or a witch, or both.

TWENTY-FOUR

'Lucy has been seeing a hypnotherapist.'

From where she has sat him on the sofa and told him to brace for bad news, Bill blinks and shies, like she has just thrown acid at him. 'What?'

Carys sighs and screws up her face. 'I'm sorry. You hate hypnotherapists, I know. I couldn't tell you. I took Lucy to him as a way of getting her to take her meds.'

'Great job.'

Bristling at his sarcasm, Carys checks her phone again to see if there have been any replies to the seventeen voicemails and forty-two WhatsApp messages she has sent over the course of the afternoon to Lucy, to try to talk her out of going to the police. Her continuing silence fills her with dread. She has also left four messages for Tom and he hasn't yet replied. His silence is even more ominous than Lucy's.

She wants to creep upstairs, throw the duvet over her head and hide.

'Which hypnotherapist?' Bill grabs her hand. On the other side of the bifold doors to the courtyard garden, Binnie is playing in the paddling pool with Nonna. Carys closed the doors before she made her confession, and despite the eco air-cooling system, the room is now almost unbearably hot. He wipes the sweat from his top lip. 'What's his name?'

'Why?'

'Just tell me.' Something in his voice makes Carys want to retch. This is all too much, and it's looking like it's her fault. Like it was her fault with Lucy's bully and her anorexia...

'Ajay. Ajay Gupta.'

'What?' Bill says, his voice a whisper.

Carys repeats the name.

Bill stands up, walks over to the exposed brick wall where the checking-yourself-before-you-go-out mirror hangs. Before Carys can stop him, he yells and smashes his fist into it, punching it right in the middle of the glass, so that it splinters and cracks, showering silver pieces onto the ground beneath it.

Carys runs to him. 'What? What is it?'

Red-faced, his hand bleeding, he turns to her, takes her by the shoulders. 'Do you know what you've done? Why didn't you tell me? If you'd told me, I would have warned you off him from the very start.'

Carys is on the edge of a panic attack and she hasn't even told Bill the worst of it yet. 'I don't understand. What? What is it?'

'That man is an unpleasant creep. An utter weasel. He worked at Alice's centre. He was obsessed with her. If anything, he was the one who drove her to her death. Stalking her, turning up at the house, texting endlessly, cornering her in her treatment room. She was too kind, gave him too much rope.'

Carys's knees feel weak. She reaches over to the sofa, levers herself down onto the cushions and cups her hands over her face. What has she done?

'But I just bumped into him.'

'Where did you "just bump into him"?'

'In Coldfall Wood. When I was walking Nonna. When Lucy was in hospital. I was upset...'

'Let me guess, he just happened to be there and you just got talking and he just happened to get out of you what was troubling you and he just happened to mention that he could help with Lucy?'

'Yes, I—'

'Don't you realise how dangerous he is with those skills? He can get anyone to do anything he wants, just by using the right sort of words in the right sort of way.'

'I didn't—'

'Except Alice. She stood firm against him.'

'He has a dog just like Nonna. A Lagotto.'

Bill looks at her, his lips twisting. 'His dog is just like Nonna because it's one of Nonna's puppies. Alice gave him one to try to keep him away. She felt sorry for him, but I saw him for what he is.'

Carys winces. 'What is he?'

'A dangerous fantasist. What do you think, Carys, are the odds of you just bumping into the man who stalked my late wife, eh?'

She takes a sharp in-breath. As she lets it out, she realises she is shaking. 'You mean he's been stalking me too?'

'I mean exactly that.'

'But why?'

'To get back at me for the fact that Alice loved me and not him.'

Carys can't bring herself to tell him what she has to say next.

'And it's his work that's got the police digging up Five Oaks, isn't it?' Bill nurses the hand that punched the wall.

She nods.

'You know, I sometimes even wonder if that head-fucker did more than drive Alice to her death.'

'What do you mean?'

'Do you know what a stalker can do?'

Carys shakes her head.

'If the object of his attention doesn't give him what he wants, he can end up killing her.'

'Bill—' she starts.

'I should have pushed it. I just wanted closure, though, for me and the girls. Just wanted to say goodbye to her. Didn't want to dwell on the fact that it might not have been as simple as it appeared. It wasn't going to bring her back, was it?'

'Bill—'

'But perhaps it would have been better knowing it hadn't been her decision...'

'Please, Bill, I've got something else to tell you.'

But Bill is chewing his lip, heading for the kitchen surface where he has left flour, eggs and sugar out from the baking session he was about to start when Carys came in.

'I'm an idiot.' He flings the eggs onto the floor, where they smash and splatter over the polished concrete. 'I should have made sure that creep couldn't do any more harm. Creep.' He picks up the full bag of flour and slams it against the wall. It explodes, sending a dusty whiteness over the broken mirror and the plants, the chair, the rug that surrounds it. He turns to her so fiercely that she shrinks into the sofa. 'I want him out of our lives for good.'

Carys has never seen him like this. Never. She doesn't want to tell him the next bit. Not at all. A powdery coating on his hair and shoulders, he leans on the kitchen island and shakes, great man-sobs heaving his shoulders.

'Bill, I—'

The doorbell rings, the jaunty *bing-bong* grating right across the tight air.

Carys tries to stand up, but her legs don't work. 'Leave it,' she tells him.

But what right does she have to tell Bill what to do? Ignoring her, he looks at himself in the flour-coated remains of the mirror. With a bloody hand he swipes some of the dust from his face and sweeps his hair back. The cut on his hand smears blood over his efforts, but still he walks out of the room and towards the front door.

Carys puts her hands over her ears.

Her worst fears are confirmed when Bill tears back into the room and heads straight for her, all blood and flour and wild confusion, like a wounded hunted animal looking for somewhere to hide.

'What the hell, Carys?' He has pulled her up and is shaking her by the shoulders. 'What the hell?'

But then two uniformed police officers are on him, yanking her brilliant, gentle, grieving, cake-making husband away from her. Tom rises up behind them, looming like a bad smell. He swings round in front of Bill, who, now handcuffed, is only able to stay upright with the support of the officers, who have him by the arms.

As he turns, Tom clocks the broken mirror, the floured, bloodstained wall, the mess on Bill. He turns to Carys. 'Are you all right?' he says. 'Has he hurt you?'

Carys shakes her head wildly. 'Of course not!'

She stands there powerless, her elbows tucked tight in at her sides, her hands flapping like dying birds, the fingertips tapping over her face. 'Please...' But her voice has stopped working.

'William Anderton, I am arresting you on suspicion of the murder of two females, date unknown.'

'What the hell?' Bill says as Tom continues to read him his rights. 'What the hell is this?'

'Do you understand me?' Tom says once he's finished.

Carys has no idea what Tom is thinking, what he is feeling as he does this. Is it victory? Is it that he knew it all along? There certainly doesn't seem to be any doubt in him. Lucy must have been extremely convincing.

'Yes! No. I don't...' Bill turns to Carys. 'Is this Lucy, Carys? Is this what Ajay told Lucy to say? I'll fucking kill him if that's—'

'Lucy's lying,' Carys says to Tom. 'She's making it up, I've told you before. She has a history of—'

But she is stopped just before she really gets stuck in on discrediting her stepdaughter by a sound from the corner of the room. She looks round and sees to her horror that Binnie is leaning on the bifold door, using her body weight to slide it open. Nonna is at her side, as keen as Binnie is to get inside.

The moment she sees her father weeping, pinned between the two uniformed officers, the other strange, tall man leaning over him, Binnie stops on the threshold. Carys knows this is a scene her daughter will never, ever forget.

'What's happening, Mum?' She has one foot in the house, the other on the terrace, the dog leaning up against her as if she is propping her up. 'Dad?'

Bill shies away like a carthorse. 'Take me out of here,' he hisses at his captors – for that's what it must look like to Binnie. As they hustle him out of the room, he turns to Carys.

'Get me a lawyer,' he says.

Torn about what to do first – should she go with him, should she stay with Binnie and make out everything is going to be OK, should she call Suki, the firm's solicitor, to see who she recommends? – Carys ends up doing something completely other.

She sits and puts her face in her hands and she roars.

'Mum, Mum.' Binnie runs to her and pulls at her arms even harder than she tugged at the bifold doors. 'Stop it, Mum. You're frightening me.'

TWENTY-FIVE

Carys spends the evening trying to find out where Bill has been taken, trying to contact a solicitor and trying to calm Binnie. She fails on all counts. Lucy and Sara are not answering messages or phone calls. Even though she never wants to speak to Tom again, she calls him several times, also with no luck. She imagines him in a dark room, aiming his crooked nose into Bill's spotlit, terrified face, interrogating him as he struggles against the two police officers who are still holding him down...

At gone midnight, her phone rings, number withheld.

'It's me,' Bill says, his voice echoing like it's in an empty hall on the other side of the world. 'I haven't got long. I'm in Wood Green Custody Centre. I need a solicitor. Go with whoever Suki recommends.' His voice breaks. 'This is all a big mistake, Carys.'

'I know, love. I know.'

'I wouldn't... I couldn't...'

'I know. Lucy is making it up, it's horrible. We'll work it out. I'm trying to contact Suki.'

And she carries on, until seven in the morning, when Suki finally picks up.

'They *what?*' she says. Outraged, she promises to get her best criminal colleague down to the station, 'sooner than is humanly possible'.

'We're having a few family issues,' Carys whispers to Liz, the play worker, as she drops off a strung-out, reluctant Binnie at the local leisure centre where her play scheme is holding a Saturday sports day. 'If you could just give her a bit of extra attention, that would be great.' When she leaves, Binnie is crying, but Liz waves her off, saying she will be fine. Carys isn't so sure about that, and leaving her daughter physically hurts her, but she has stuff she needs to do.

She pedals furiously to Wood Green Custody Centre, an Edwardian red-brick building with a modern extension so unsympathetic that, despite her situation, it makes Carys wince when she sees it.

The reception is full – drunk people, crying people, people who look almost as desperate as Carys feels. A sign Blu-tacked to the wall says: *Take a ticket and wait until you are called.*

When Carys's number comes up, she runs to the desk and asks for Bill. The bald white receptionist, contained behind safety glass, scrolls slowly through something on his computer. She feels herself growing itchy.

'And you are?' he asks. Carys can read the racism in the way his mouth sets as he looks at her.

'I'm his wife and I want to see him.'

The receptionist folds his hands on the desk and smiles, but not with his eyes. 'Not possible.'

'But he needs me.'

The man looks over his shoulder, then leans forward and whispers to her, 'Hubby has been arrested for something very, very serious, love. All his needs beyond eating and shitting are put on hold right now. So piss off.'

Carys wants to swear at him, but she has just enough sense left to walk away. She uses the public toilet, then outside on the main road she tries calling Tom again, and this time, finally, he picks up. She tells him she is at the station.

'I'm just breaking. Meet me at Enjoy Café, two blocks down on the left.'

Enjoy.

Carys sits with a mug of thick tea and waits, looking out at the last dregs of morning traffic. The only other patron, a small, ramrod woman with a faded red and grey plait down her back, sits with a coffee on the other side of the café, apparently staring at the wall. Eventually Tom turns up, looking as though, like Carys, he has had a sleepless night. Which of course he has: interrogating her husband.

'What the hell is going on?' Her jaw is so tense she can hardly open her mouth to speak.

Tom greets the café owner by name, orders to take out and looks around before he speaks to her. 'I'm not supposed to be talking to you. But Bill's got his solicitor now. He's no-comment-ing, so it's going to take some time.'

'Then you'll let him out.'

Tom shakes his head. 'It's serious. We have an excellent witness statement—'

'From Lucy.'

'I'm not at liberty to say.'

'You need to talk to Ajay Gupta, a so-called hypnotherapist. He's the one who started all this.'

'We've already been in contact with Dr Gupta.' Tom folds his arms. 'You should know that he has worked with us on several witness cases in the past. We rate him highly.'

'But he stalked Alice! He may have even been responsible for her death.'

'Bill told you this, yes? He's made those allegations to us, too. Dr Gupta says they're completely false.'

'Lucy's the one making the false allegations!'

Tom sits down opposite her and leans across the Formica table. 'I'm sorry, Carys, but we now have evidence to back up Lucy's statement.'

'What?'

'We've found other human remains at the site. Adult bones. They're with the lab right now.'

Tinny Capital Radio covers up their words, but when Carys, who has been sipping tea, splutters and chokes, the woman with the plait wriggles her shoulders and shakes her head.

'You need to know,' Tom goes on, 'that this is serious. Bill may not be the man you think he is.'

'You've always had it in for him, haven't you? Ever since Sara—'

'Has he ever hurt you?'

'No! Bill is the gentlest man. He's been through a lot.'

'I know he's been through a lot.'

'Cappuccino and bacon sarnie, Tom love.' The woman behind the counter reaches over a cup and a greasy paper bag. 'Enjoy!' she sings.

'Cheers, Sam.' Tom takes his breakfast and turns back to Carys. 'I've got to get back. I'm stepping out of line here. This is serious, Carys.'

'How long will you keep him?'

He shakes his head. 'Can't say. I'm sorry. Just be prepared, OK?'

'For what?'

But he is out of the door.

. . .

The day passes in a ghosted blur, with silence from the police and the solicitor, and no one else returning her calls. She feels put back in her place as a scrappy Hull council house girl who thought she could pass as an elegant London architect.

At some point she sleeps on the sofa, clutching her phone, afraid to switch it off but ignoring the calls coming in from Tina in the office, who is probably tearing her hair out with unanswered questions about suppliers and contractors.

Knowing that word will have got out, she has switched off Wi-Fi and data. She doesn't want to see or hear any news.

They started the year so full of hope, breaking ground on the construction site. Lucy seemed happy and it felt like Carys had finally mended the family; that at last the ghost of Alice had been laid to rest.

But of course Lucy was hiding her distress. And Sara was riding in on the clouds, an angel of fury, waiting for her moment to descend and disrupt.

This family will never mend.

And now Bill, her poor Bill.

Bloody Ajay. The creep, the weasel, the stalker, the cause of all this.

She wants to kill him.

She starts to text Sara, outlining the reasons she should keep Ajay away from Lucy. But then she stops herself. What's the point? It's only going to further alienate her stepdaughters. She has other things to deal with right now.

At 3 p.m., she drags herself from the sofa and puts on a bit of brave-face eyeliner and perfume. Her first thought as she steps out of the door with Nonna is that the street is particularly busy today. Then she realises that all the people are looking at her. A camera clicks, a woman runs up to her with a microphone.

Someone shouts out, 'Carys! Carys! Did you know your husband was a murderer?'

She tightens her hold on Nonna's lead and hurries off to pick Binnie up from Saturday Sports.

As she walks into the reception area, the other mums – basically the school playground crowd – fall silent and look at her.

'What?' Carys says to them, her voice too loud. 'What then?'

Elsa comes towards her, hands out. 'What's happened, Carys? How's Bill?'

Carys shakes her head. 'I don't know and I don't bloody know.'

Elsa guides her towards two empty chairs. The women nearby draw themselves away, like Carys has some murderer husband virus.

'Fiona's put it on her blog, I suppose?' Carys says.

Elsa nods. 'And "someone" has told the press who the sixty-year-old man arrested on suspicion of a double murder is. It's already on the *Daily Mail* website, I'm afraid, photos of him, you, Alice, everyone.'

Carys glares over at Fiona, who is sitting surrounded by the yoga mums, and adds her to her list of people she wants to kill. 'Show me,' she says.

'You sure?'

She nods.

Elsa holds up her phone. There on the home page is a snap of Bill and Carys, taken by someone – from the camera angle it could well be the Bullocks – while they were doing the Five Oaks presentation. Bill has red-eye and looks exactly the kind of man who might have murdered his mistress and child. And Carys, captured pre-sneeze, looks like a haughty, sneering cow.

'He didn't do it,' Carys says.

Elsa puts her hand over hers. 'Of course he didn't.'

She's a good friend. But something in her voice suggests she's not as convinced of Bill's innocence as her words suggest.

'I don't know what to do,' Carys tells her. 'What do I do?'

'If I were you? I'd keep a low profile until it all blows over.'

All blows over. How lovely that sounds.

Carys prays for a strong wind.

When the children come out to their mothers, they are swept away from Binnie as if she too has the virus. Indeed, after the night she and Carys had, she looks quite possessed.

'We've got to go,' Elsa says as she gathers up Hetty and Milo. 'I'm cooking dinner for eight. Imagine.'

She's out of the door with everyone else before Carys can even say goodbye.

'Sit,' Carys says to Binnie.

Binnie flops herself down, her face grim.

'How was it?' Carys asks as she hands her a muesli bar. Even at the best of times, Binnie needs fuel to pick her up mid-afternoon.

Binnie bypasses the food – never a good sign – and flings her arms around her mother's waist. 'I don't want to go any more. Not here, not play scheme, not school.'

After lunch, it seems, one of the play workers, who must have looked at their phone during their break, asked Binnie about her dad.

'You don't have to,' Carys says. 'We'll have fun by ourselves instead.'

She takes Binnie for a treat rarer than diamonds, pearls or gold – a McDonald's vegan burger.

Full of acceptable junk food, they turn the corner onto their street. It's thick with people all wanting a piece of the guilty-before-proven man's wife and child. Not only press, but gawpers with their iPhones, filming the house, their car, Carys's bike chained up in the cycle cage.

And there's bloody Alastair Bullock, smiling like he's at the circus. This must be making his day. Just behind him, a slight, pale woman – not Mrs B – stares at Carys and Binnie through thick dark sunglasses.

A whirring sound makes Carys look up. Someone is flying a drone over her house, spying into her garden.

'Bitch!' someone cries out. An egg flies through the air, just missing her shoulder. 'Murdering scum.'

The crowd swarms towards them, cameras clicking, microphones thrusting, voices clamouring for a word from the wife of the man they have already decided is definitely a double murderer.

Carys takes off her linen scarf and uses it to shield their faces. 'No comment,' she shouts as she stabs the fingerprint entry pad and pushes into the house with Binnie and Nonna, slamming the door behind them.

The doormat is littered with scrawled notes and messages. She squats to take a closer look. Some are from journalists offering money for interviews; others are abusive, with words she doesn't want Binnie to see. As she stands and shuffles her feet to hide them, she steps on something soft. An unmistakable disgusting smell hits her nostrils and makes her retch. Someone has posted a bagged turd through the door.

Herding dog and child into the living room and away from the stink – which she will clear up later – she moves from window to window, shutting out the sunlight and the electronic and human eyes.

As she pulls down the final blind, her phone plays the incongruously riotous intro to Desmond Dekker's 'Get Up Edina', the happy-go-lucky ringtone she never got round to changing, the sound that indicates a text from her ex, who is still listed on her phone as *Edinadingadingdong*.

Juggling bags, child and dog, her heart suddenly and strangely lurching, she picks up her phone.

Hey doll. Long time no see. I see ur in a bit of trouble. Maybe I can help. Coffee? Exxx

TWENTY-SIX

Sara walks into the George in Borough High Street and Tom stands to greet her like an old-fashioned gentleman. You wouldn't know he was the policeman who has spent the past twenty-two hours interrogating her father for double murder. She is grateful for this.

'What are you having?' he asks.

She accepts his offer without argument and asks for a double gin and tonic.

'Sorry it's such a schlep,' he says, returning with her drink and two packets of crisps – he's remembered that salt and vinegar is her favourite. 'It's just I shouldn't really be talking to you at the moment, what with you-know.'

'Sure. Appreciate it.'

'How's Lucy?' he asks.

'Broken,' Sara says. 'But also kind of relieved that she's said something and something's being done.'

Tom nods.

'You totally believe her?' she asks, because she doesn't think she does, but she's not sure. She thought Lucy was bonkers first off, but her utter conviction that she saw what she saw and the fact that Tom and all his colleagues believe it are in danger of swaying her. The thing stopping her going for it 100 per cent is that however compromised she feels about her father, however much she thinks he's a moral weakling and a controlling bully cloaked in an ooze of charm, she just can't see him killing someone. Certainly not his own child. Who, for God's sake, could do that?

Not that it's a good thing, but the only violence she witnessed when she was growing up was emotional. She heard the fights between him and Alice, but she thought that was what all adults did – indeed, her experience with Pete has somewhat borne that out. And to give Bill credit, however brilliant Alice was, however high achieving in the outside world, she, like Lucy after her, had a long history of challenging behaviour, manic episodes and irrational impulses.

At least that's what she's been told.

Perhaps Alice couldn't give him the devotion he needed. Whereas Carys is wedded not only to him, but also to his work. His acolyte in every way.

Sara has always sought out solid ground. But with what she's discovered about Alice never being found, Carys consciously seeking the family out to the point of stalking, and now this Bill-possibly-murdering-a-lover-and-child shitshow, all she has is quicksand.

And now here she is in this clandestine meeting with the boy who caused her so much grief in her late teens. They're sharing a strong drink and snacks and he's looking at her in a way that, even with all this going on, stirs something inside her.

'I do believe Lucy.' He taps his nose. 'Spidey sense says she's telling the truth.'

Sara wishes she could share his conviction.

She really wants Bill to suffer for lying to her about her mother, for falling apart when she needed his support, for marrying a woman almost the same age as her, for supplanting her and Lucy with a new child.

In fact, in her eyes, his failure to stand up after whatever happened to Alice *is* a sort of double murder – of the Sara and Lucy who could have been, had he been there for them.

So while the more rational side of her knows it's unfair, her loud, shouty teenage self is yelling for him to squirm.

But then Tom tells her that the digging team have found some more human bones.

Her mouth drops open. 'So this could be proof that Lucy's right?'

He nods. 'We're just waiting for the forensic anthropologist to report back to the PolSA. God, sorry. Acronym alert: that's police search adviser—'

'I know. Remember I'm a cop too?'

'Oh yeah.' He smiles. 'Funny how we both ended up as filth.'

'We're both surprising people.'

There is a look, and she thinks, oh no. Not again. She reminds herself of the tears, the hysterics, the time he even threatened her with killing himself if she left him.

Far too much for a seventeen-year-old to deal with. But then he was so good to her after that, after Alice died, a rock amid all the grieving chaos. Though it quickly got too suffocating again. Even when they were asleep, if she extricated herself from his grasp he would shimmy across the bed and latch onto her. She woke up most mornings half hanging off the bed.

'I was once part of a team that didn't believe a witness,' Tom says. 'Let's call her Hannah. She was about the same age as Lucy and claimed to have been sexually abused by her father. It surfaced in memories her therapist said she had buried in order to protect herself.

'When we investigated the therapist, we found she had done some weird things, like taking part in Twitter pile-ons during MeToo. She had agendas. And at the time, Hannah's testimony just didn't add up. The father in question was a professional man too, like Bill. Respectable. We believed him over her and what we thought was her whack-nut therapist, so we didn't pursue it.

'But Hannah had a little half-sister, about seven years old. Her teacher red-flagged her, we got involved and a medical examination showed that exactly what Hannah said had happened to her was happening to this poor kid. So we nicked him and he's inside now where he can do no more harm. But it was too late for Hannah.'

'You mean...?'

Tom nods. He blinks like his eyes are stinging. 'Overdose.'

'That must have been shit.'

'It was. Look, I shouldn't bring what I know about Bill from the past into it—'

'You shouldn't even be on this case.'

'Shh.' He isn't smiling when he puts his fingers to his lips. Both he and Sara know that, at best, he would be taken off the case immediately if his personal link to the accused were found out.

'Hasn't he let on?'

'I don't think he knows it's a problem. And he's no-commenting, so no, not yet.'

'But you're not going to get away with it forever.'

'I can't let it go, Sara. I fell into this case and it's potentially the biggest of my career. I was involved by chance, and now I'm in it, I can't step out. That poor little girl, and her poor mother. I want him brought to justice.'

'A man who made your life hell when you were younger.'

Tom looks down. 'He never liked me.'

'He never liked any of my boyfriends. He wanted us all to himself. Me, Mum, Lucy. Are you sure you can be impartial?'

'Absolutely. I'm a professional, Sara.'

'He could be a dick sometimes. To all of us. I don't know why Mum put up with it.'

'She didn't, did she, in the end? Oh God. I'm sorry.'

Sara wanted to tell him about Alice's body not being found, but this crass remark makes her change her mind. Indeed, Tom might know more than he lets on. She takes a drink of her gin and tonic and looks him in the eye.

'When you saw her, how did she seem?'

'Who, Lucy?'

'No. Mum. You were the last person to speak to her.'

Tom goes bright red. Something shifts in his eyes. 'So Bill claims.'

'What does that mean?'

'He had it in for me. I was his whipping boy. He blames me for pushing her over the edge.' He starts fiddling with a beer mat. 'Not literally, of course. At least, I don't think so.'

'What did you actually say to her?'

'I told you this.' He tears a strip from the beer mat. 'I told you it all at the time.'

'Tell me again.'

The beer mat loses another strip. 'I was desperate. I can't claim I covered myself in glory. I was a stupid boy.'

'So do you think Bill's got a point? After all, it worked for you, didn't it?'

'What does that mean?'

'You got me back after Mum died.'

He lowers his brow and swipes the heap of shredded cardboard that was once a beer mat onto the floor. 'Not for long.'

'Bloody hell, Tom.'

Without warning, he reaches across the table and grabs her hand.

'I'm so, so sorry about the shit I put you through, Sara. I made the same mistakes with Hayley.'

'Hayley?'

'My ex. After she threw me out, I did so much therapy. I've learned my lesson at last.'

'OK.'

He squeezes her fingers. 'I've changed,' he says. 'I really have.'

Sara pulls her hand away and looks at him. 'I have to go,' she says. 'Lucy.'

She doesn't want this. Not now.

TWENTY-SEVEN

'Hey.'

It's 9 p.m. Binnie is finally asleep and Edina is standing on Carys's doorstep. Behind her, the press pack snap and bay.

'Don't like your mates,' she says.

Carys hustles her in, slams the door shut and kisses her on the cheek.

She smells exactly the same.

It's the first time they have met since Carys bought her out of the flat ten years ago. Edina is looking good for nearly forty-three. A little grey at the temples, but the cheekbones are holding out, and her skin hasn't changed at all. Not a line. If Carys didn't know her so well, she'd suspect her of having work done.

Body's in good nick, too, she can't help but notice. Edina is in her unchanged off-duty summer uniform of battered Levi's and a sleeveless linen top. Her arms, with the entwined female symbols tattoo on her right bicep, show that she is still at the yoga and weights.

Carys feels a rush of desire, a need to slip into those arms, to go home, to retreat from all this.

Was leaving Edina the worst decision she ever made?

'Nice place,' Edina says, following her down the hallway to the living room, looking around at the walls, the furniture, the artwork. 'You landed on your feet, girl.'

'Well, y'know.'

'Always were ambitious.'

'That's not a bad thing.'

'I didn't mean it as a bad thing.' Without waiting for Carys to invite her, Edina moves across the living space and sits on the sofa overlooking the back courtyard. 'Very nice.'

'Until now.'

'Yeah. You're going through it, aren't you.'

'Tea?' Carys says.

'You got anything stronger?'

Carys goes to fetch the whisky, but is stopped by Binnie, who is standing at the bottom of the stairs like a little ghost girl.

'Who's that?' she says.

'Ah, Bins. This is my friend Edina. She's come round to help us get Daddy back.'

Binnie runs down the stairs and throws her arms around Edina. 'Please do it,' she says. 'We love Daddy and we need him back home.'

Edina, who was never a maternal sort, surprises Carys by taking Binnie's hands and looking solemnly at her. 'I promise you, Bins, that I will do my very best.'

Binnie eyes her for a moment, then nods her head. 'Thank you.' She turns to Carys. 'I won't come down again, Mum, promise.' She kisses her and goes upstairs. This is the first time she has ever taken herself to bed, and Carys is speechless with shock.

Edina looks at her, impressed. 'Smart kid.'

Proud of her girl, Carys continues on her Scotch quest. She also finds a bowl and fills it with peanuts.

· · ·

'Peaty.' Edina sips her whisky and settles back onto the sofa. 'So we're working from the assumption that Bill didn't murder his lover and their child.'

'Of course!' Carys tells her about Ajay.

'He sounds like an absolute creep,' Edina says. 'Exactly the kind of therapist I see in court all the time, but this guy's got proper history and an agenda.'

'The police rate him, though.'

'They always do. Blinded by the qualifications.'

Carys nods. 'He's a medical doctor turned hypnotherapist. And he's worked for them before in helping with witness statements.'

Edina makes a face. 'That's a bore.'

'Makes it harder for Bill, yes?'

'I can't believe they still allow hypnotism on witnesses.' She takes a handful of nuts. 'The other issue is that the police have been given such a hard time about not believing victims and survivors that they're tending to go too far in giving them the benefit of the doubt.'

'But Bill is the victim here.'

'And that's what we've got to let them know.'

'We?'

Edina puts her hand on Carys's knee. 'Babe, I don't want this to happen to you.'

Carys shivers. 'I—'

Edina laughs. 'Hey! I'm not after old times.' She flashes a slim gold band on the third finger of her left hand. 'The missus wouldn't be happy about that.'

Carys flushes. Embarrassment, yes, but also the thought that she would have liked to be invited to the wedding, which she instantly knows is ridiculous because she didn't even consider inviting Edina to her own.

'So,' Edina says. 'The memory works in peculiar ways. A colleague of mine did this experiment where she interviewed the parents of her student volunteers for salient, concrete facts about their children when they were growing up. Then she met the students in a therapeutic setting and, by focusing on those facts, managed to convince over half of them that they had been in an entirely fictional physical fight with their best friend when they were nine years old.'

'No way!'

'We like to complete our stories, round them off. So we'll take a detail from column A, add it to one from column B, then create a whole new column C to make sense of the combination.'

Carys pours them both another whisky.

Edina takes a slug. 'So, assuming Bill is innocent—'

'Which he most definitely is.'

'—two things could have happened with Lucy. The first, more benign candidate is that she has put the fact of that poor child's body turning up together with her childhood memories of being in the garden and another time when she was scared or really upset—'

'Any time?'

'Yes.'

'Perhaps grief at her mum's death?'

'Exactly that. Add a couple more details, and during her sessions with this Ajay, he allows her to knit them together into a story that is utterly fictional but that she completely believes to be true.'

'That's so frightening.'

'We all do it, all the time. It's called confabulation. I'd even go so far as to say that none of our memories are exactly entirely accurate.'

Carys looks at her. 'None of them?'

Edina shakes her head. 'We're always selecting, putting disparate things together. Editing out the bad bits.' She smiles. 'Which is why I can face seeing you tonight.'

Carys is shamefaced. 'Sorry.'

'We live and learn,' Edina says. 'You taught me a lot.'

'I'm not sure how to take that.'

She smiles again. 'Let's not get into that right now.'

'Good idea.' Carys offers her the nuts. 'So what's the second thing?'

'The second thing is that Ajay has consciously planted the memory in Lucy. An unscrupulous therapist can do that. I've not seen it happen, but if he has some beef with Bill...'

'Which Bill says he absolutely has.'

'...then why not?'

'Ajay did talk about metaphors, about how this memory could symbolise something else, that she's working down through layers to get to the absolute truth.'

Edina frowns. 'Could be. But he's basing that on an assumption that something deeply traumatic has actually happened to Lucy.'

'Well, again: her mum killing herself.'

'No. If this were working as a metaphor, it would be something even worse. Something she has actually witnessed. Anything likely?'

Carys shakes her head. 'Not as far as I know.'

'There's a school of thought that nearly all young people experiencing severe mental health challenges have gone through some sort of physical or emotional abuse in their past. Perhaps that's what Ajay is aiming at – either consciously or unconsciously.'

'Because he hates Bill.'

'Could be. But the main thing is, and I want you to really take this on board: Lucy completely and utterly believes that what she saw is an actual fact.'

'OK.'

'However tempted you may be to believe it, she is not lying. She is as much a victim of all this as Bill.'

Carys flops back into the sofa and closes her eyes. 'My brain hurts.'

'Listen, I've been expert witness in two other cases where hypnosis has been involved, and both times I've got the defendant off.'

'Got the defendant off?' Carys remembers the arguments she and Edina used to have about her work, and she feels sick, because how much of a hypocrite is she now, turning to her for help? But this is different. She knows Bill is innocent.

'Exonerated, then. The Crown Prosecution Service say that information obtained under hypnosis should always be treated with great caution, and that a person who has been hypnotised should only be called as witness in exceptional circumstances. But they still do it, and people still get convicted on the word of a hypnotised witness.'

'There's one problem...' Carys rolls her glass in her fingers. She doesn't want to tell Edina this bit, but it's only fair that she does so. 'They've found more bones. Not child bones.'

Edina nods, sips her whisky, thinks. 'Do they know the age of these other bones yet? The sex? How long they've been there?'

'They're at the lab.'

She puts down her glass and takes Carys's hands in hers. 'Babe. Do you know how many plague pits and graveyards lie beneath our feet in London? We are literally standing on layers of skeletons. These bones could be from anyone, from any time. Are they whole? Fragments? Do they even know they're human?'

Carys takes her hands back and covers her face. 'I don't know. I didn't ask.'

Edina touches her knee again. 'We'll get that information. If it's a woman and her date of death is the same as the poor child's, Bill is in deeper than not, but it still isn't an irretrievable situation.'

'What are you going to do?' Carys looks at her ex, whose eyes are glowing in the way she remembers from so many times in the past when she decided to get her teeth into something. Edina has always been a bit of a Rottweiler.

'I need the details for Bill's brief. And any police contacts you can get me. Plus I'd like to have a chat with this Dr Gupta.'

'Be careful!' Carys says.

'I'm a big girl.' Edina drains her whisky and looks at her watch. 'Jesus, is that the time? I've got to get back by eleven for a glass of champagne or Marcie will kill me. It's our anniversary.'

'You came to help me on your anniversary?'

'She understands how I am. Listen. They can keep Bill four days max before they charge him. The sooner we can head this off at the pass, the better. Time is of the essence.' She stands. 'Ping me those contacts and I'll get on it as soon as I've downed the bubbly and kissed the wife.'

TWENTY-EIGHT

Carys knocks back another whisky then manages to crawl upstairs. Before she undresses, she peeps through the crack between the blind and the window. The press pack have also retired. They'll no doubt be back tomorrow, but she has decided that she and Binnie aren't going out of the house until this is all over. Now Edina's on board, she is certain that will be a matter of days.

Emboldened, she cranes her head out of the window, breathing in the cooler night air and checking the rest of the street. Someone sits on the dimly lit bench on the corner at the end – she can't make out age or sex. She's not overly concerned, though. It's a good distance from the house and, much to the annoyance of her neighbours, a regular dealers' spot.

She climbs into bed and closes her eyes, imagining a doorman showing the thoughts and events of the past thirty hours the exit from her mind. As they leave, she notices a small, previously unacknowledged extra worry among them. It's that her period is nearly two weeks late.

She's too tired to deal with that right now, and anyway, it's hardly surprising, given the stress she's been experiencing. So she lets it go. In the absence of conscious thought, every atom of her body whirrs, and she falls into the sleep of the dead.

She's walking through a forest. The tall red trees smell of sap. It's so strong she can almost see it in the air. There's a crackling, like twigs underfoot, like someone is following her. In a panic, she turns and sees with relief that instead of a malevolent stranger, the noise is coming from a single tree, in a clearing, that stands in flames, its branches cracking, smoke pouring into the air...

A round of coughing wakes her up. She sits up spluttering, marvelling at how the dream has come with her into consciousness, because her room is full of smoke. And then, too late, the smoke alarm starts its shrill wail, and she realises that something very real is very wrong.

Grabbing her phone, she jumps out of bed and, pulling her dressing gown over her nakedness, stumbles out of her bedroom, mindful only of Binnie.

Nonna, who is barking downstairs from where she is shut in the utility room, is second on her list.

She bundles her sleepy daughter out of bed, making sure she grabs Barney, her can't-live-without bedtime cuddly. Before Binnie can even ask what's going on, Carys has child and dog safe out on the street and is calling the fire brigade. Only then does she notice how she has just herded what remains of her family through a doorway of flames, and how, miraculously, they passed through unscathed.

As she calls 999, she feels like she has forgotten someone.

'Daddy!' Binnie wails.

'He's not there, remember?' Carys tells her. 'He's helping the police.'

Significantly, in their formerly friendly street, not a single neighbour comes out to help them. Carys has to wait for the fire brigade and, ironically, the police to arrive before she can finally give over and collapse into the attending officer's car, holding her child and her dog to her.

And then the horror hits her: if she hadn't woken up when she did, they would all be dead. It's a hot night, but she starts to shake, like she has frostbite.

A little while later, a small, plump uniformed policewoman slides in next to her on the back seat of the car and introduces herself as PC Okenedo. 'Is there anyone you can call, my dear?'

Still shaking, Carys has been sitting hugging her dear ones – who somehow, both girl and dog, have managed to go back to sleep – watching numbly as the firefighters beat back the flames, pouring gallons and gallons of water into the beautiful home she and Bill spent years dreaming about then building. It seems like they have been at it for hours. Smoke, steam and charred bits of Carys and Bill's lives fill the air.

Weirdly, the front door is untouched by the flames. Which means that the *MURDERING SCUM* that someone has spray-painted across its flame-retardant surface is entirely visible, as is the racist slur about mixed-race families underneath it.

The press are rushing back, one by one, in their cars and motorbikes. At least the police are keeping them well back from the fire, and therefore from Carys. A few neighbours are now out on the street – not offering help, but gawking. One couple are even sitting on their front garden wall with mugs of tea.

'Carys?' PC Okenedo asks. Pity greases her voice.

Of course the police know who she is. They will have entered the address on some computer somewhere and worked it out about Bill and everything.

Carys shakes her head. It's 4 a.m. and she has no one she can comfortably call at this hour. She used to have lots of friends, but over the years, with work, with Bill, with Binnie, with Lucy, she gradually let them all slide.

It's OK, though. She can look after herself.

A firefighter squats at the open door on the other side of the car and introduces himself as the crew manager. 'Call me Drew,' he says, his big, kind face covered in soot and sweat.

'I'm sorry,' Carys says.

'Shh now, love. No need to apologise. We've put it out.'

'Can we go back in?'

PC Okenedo shakes her head, and Carys flinches as she puts a hand on her shoulder. 'It's a crime scene, I'm afraid.'

Not another one. Carys frowns. 'What?'

'The fire was started deliberately,' Drew tells her. 'A bottle of petrol was posted through the letter box.'

'How?' Carys says. Her architect's spatial sense can't imagine it.

'One of those small, flat gin bottles?' he says. 'Seen it before. Catches on post or papers on the doormat, and boom.'

Carys cleared up the dog shit from the hallway last night but she couldn't face touching all the messages posted through the door.

'Can you think of anyone who might have done this?' PC Okenedo asks her. 'Perhaps in view of your husband's situation?'

Carys feels like laughing. Where does she start?

In fact, she has a couple of good ideas. One of them is Lucy. While the Lucy she knows and loves would never do anything like this, perhaps this new Ajay-crazed version might. Even with that in mind, though, even after everything she has put her and Bill through, Carys can't bring herself to point the finger at her stepdaughter.

'We're not exactly flavour of the month,' she says.

'Have a think, dear, and we'll have a chat in the morning, once you've got yourself sorted, yes?' PC Okenedo hands over a card with her number on it for Carys to add to her police business card collection.

'Can I go in and get some things at least?' she asks.

Drew shakes his head. 'We can't allow it. The building's structurally unsound.'

Carys thinks back to the design. It's a timber-framed house. Despite the fire-retardant insulation underneath it, the cedar cladding took off, well, like a house on fire.

'But the fire pockets,' she said. 'We designed zones, to stop flames spreading...'

'Some of the doors were propped open,' Drew says. 'And the fire just took so intensely that even if they hadn't been, you'd have been in trouble. I'm sorry, love. There's smoke in everything, but we can go in and see what we can pick up for you if you want to write a list.'

'What do I do now?'

'Call your insurance company. They'll sort it out. Let me know when you've worked out what you need. We'll be here at least another hour.'

Carys nods.

'Good news is,' the policewoman says as Drew strides away to join his colleagues, 'that as it's a crime scene, we'll be around for at least the next twelve hours, so you've got a bit of breathing space before you have to secure the building.'

'Good news.' Carys does laugh at this.

The policewoman gets out of the car, leans into the passenger side and opens the glove compartment. 'Here,' she says, handing over a notepad and a pen.

Carys writes a list of the essentials of life for her, Binnie and Nonna for the next few days. 'Can you also get me the telescope from my daughter's bedroom, please?'

In the absence of faith – how she wishes for her Jamaican

granny's certainties – looking up and out is the only way she is going to get through this. She will try to learn about the stars with Binnie, so that when Bill is freed, they can surprise and delight him.

The dog-friendly Premier Inn room that PC Okenedo finds for them in Tottenham is cool, the bed linen crisp. Showered and clean, Binnie sleeps with Nonna curled up next to her on the bed, both clearly enjoying this normally forbidden arrangement. Carys, who is too wired for sleep, drinks coffee from the machine in reception and looks up her insurance on her laptop, which, thankfully, the firefighters managed to save. The woman on the emergency claim line is sympathetic and reassuring. They will liaise with the police to secure the house, and they will pay for emergency accommodation while repairs are carried out and the contents claim is processed.

'We'll take care of everything,' she says in a soothing Cork accent. 'All you have to do is find yourself somewhere to stay within the budget guidelines and look after yourselves.'

In a previous life, the one she inhabited thirty-six hours earlier, Carys would have insisted on organising and overseeing the repairs herself to ensure they met her exacting standards, with the right level of care spent on the details.

But now she is just relieved that she can hand everything over.

Who did this, though? Who burned down their house?

She can't bring herself to think about that tonight. Instead, even though they are booked into the hotel for two nights, she fires up Airbnb.

When Binnie wakes up in the morning, Carys tells her they are going on a little holiday right in the middle of London. She doesn't tell her that it's because they can hide there in plain sight, and that the flat she has chosen, in Earlham Street, near

Covent Garden, is behind a desk where there is a concierge, CCTV and, as the 'other information' section tells her, 'state-of-the-art fire and security systems'.

They gather their smoke-scented belongings and, newly nomadic, take an Uber downtown.

TWENTY-NINE

The flat is bland and corporate, but clean and well equipped. It's ironic, though, that Carys can't take Binnie and Nonna to the flat she owns and knows so well, with all her stuff in it. Unfortunately that is spoken for, occupied by the agents of this very situation. Possibly even the arsonist who has put her here.

But would Lucy – or Sara – really have put what amounted to a Molotov cocktail through the door while she and Binnie slept? And what about that vile graffiti? Surely neither of them is capable of that? But then the past few days have proved that anything is possible with those two.

No, it can't be.

Carys has experienced racism and snobbery – most of it in the form of everyday slights, but sometimes bigger and nastier, scarier and more dangerous. With the internet full of how evil her husband is, it wouldn't be surprising if some trolling scum had got hold of their address and attempted to exert some street-level justice on his guilty-by-association wife and child.

She orders some basic groceries, plus toiletries, a bag of kibble for the dog and takeaway pizza and ice cream for her and Binnie. It arrives and they settle down to a duvet afternoon of

Disney Plus on the massive TV in the bedroom. As she chews her vegan margherita, Carys has one eye on *The Little Mermaid* while the other watches her phone for any news from Edina or the lawyer working for Bill.

Nothing comes. But a text does arrive from Elsa, saying that she has just heard about the house and is there anything she can do? Carys texts back that they are fine, that it's just stuff and that she and Binnie are lying low and waiting for all this to blow over, which she's certain it will in a couple of days.

Certain. Ha.

Could one of the school mums be behind the fire? The poison around yesterday at Saturday Sports... would any of them go that far? She scratches her eyebrow. Of course not. All this is making her paranoid.

Elsa gets back and says that Hetty is desperate to see Binnie, and would she like to come over this afternoon for tea and a sleepover.

When asked, Binnie nods so fiercely she is in danger of her head coming off. While the prospect of letting her go makes Carys feel sick, she knows it will be really good for her poor little girl to do something normal.

To get ready to face the world, Carys takes the bag of courier-delivered toiletries to the bathroom and pulls out the one item she doesn't want Binnie to see.

She unwinds the plastic wrapping, opens the box, takes the plastic wand from its protective packaging and, squatting over the toilet, holds it under her pee.

It's unequivocal. Her period is late not because of stress, but because of pregnancy. Just a few weeks ago, this elusive, longed-for event would have been cause for a massive alcohol-free-champagne celebration.

Right now, it just feels like one more unexpected item in the bagging area.

She looks at herself in the mirror. A ghost of darker pigmentation – a big feature of her pregnancy with Binnie – is already appearing around her face. Of course, of course. She should have known.

'It's a great thing,' she says to Mirror Carys. 'It will make Bill's day when they let him out and he comes home and you tell him.'

And then she remembers that there is no home.

Late afternoon, once she has unpacked and put two loads of smoky clothes through the washing machine, she takes a dog-friendly cab and drops Binnie off at Elsa's, avoiding all of her friend's questions and offers of help.

'We're off to the cottage for a week tomorrow morning,' Elsa tells her, 'so if you could pick up Binnie by nine, that would be great.'

Carys toys with asking if they could bear to take Binnie away with them – their Cornish cottage is certainly big enough to contain another child. But she can't bring herself to do it. She has always stood on her own feet, made her own way, and now is no different. And anyway, she doesn't want to be away from Binnie for that long.

She decides to walk back to Covent Garden through the summer evening, using Google Maps to take her through as many parks and squares as she can manage. She wants to walk underneath as many trees as possible so that, in the spirit of Alice, she can be reminded how small she is in the scheme of things.

But instead of following the route she maps out for herself, she finds herself turning north, towards the Five Oaks site.

It's like Emma is pulling her there to stand where she was buried, to imagine what actually happened. As a sort of dare to herself, Carys has begun to try to picture Lucy's vision: Bill being violent towards a woman and a child. Crazy as she tells herself it is, she needs to be on the ground where it was supposed to have happened to confirm that it's all a sick girl's fantasy.

The same police officer is guarding the only entrance to the site. Carys will never be able to blag her way past her a second time. Cursing, she settles Nonna behind the street bike hangar and sits cross-legged beside her, waiting for her moment. Police officers have to relieve themselves like everyone else.

To her great delight, just fifteen minutes after she arrives, the policewoman looks up and down the pavement then heads off to the pub at the end of the street. Carys unlocks the gate and lets herself in. She doesn't lock it behind her just in case she needs to make a speedy exit.

Like her own world, the landscape has changed so much since she was last here just five days ago. Even in the gathering darkness it is unrecognisable. Emma's grave has now disappeared into a general excavation. Metal posts with numbered markers dot the area, presumably pointing out where various finds have been unearthed. Carys settles Nonna under a bush and tells her to stay. Lagottos are bred for digging truffles in Italy, so she doesn't want her to add holes to what is already here.

She moves to roughly the spot where Emma was found, sinks to her knees, closes her eyes and tries to conjure the ghosts of the past.

She knows that to an objective eye she is behaving like a madwoman. But from her point of view this is a sane response to an insane situation.

She puts her hand on the soil. She has spent the past five years bound up with this ground. She can almost see the lines of the plans she has drawn up for the buildings intersecting under her knees. This was a project born out of her passion for and commitment to fair, affordable housing and sound ecological principles. But it was also going to financially make her and Bill and seal their already considerable reputation.

She tries to stop thinking about it in the past tense. But now, even when Bill is exonerated and set free – which he surely will be – Five Oaks will be forever tainted by the fact that the lead architect was arrested because bones and bodies were found here. Shit sticks. Bill's innocence will be forgotten. Will Artur, a staunch Catholic, and his boys even want to work here any more?

'Please help us,' she asks Emma. 'Please show me what happened.'

She doesn't know how long she kneels there trying to raise shadows, but well after darkness has fully fallen, a twig breaking in the remaining bushes far to her left makes her jump. Nonna, who has fallen asleep over to her right, stirs and growls, which is never a good sign.

She motions to the dog to be still and quiet.

A shape in the darkness scuttles across the desert of blue-black earth, straight towards her.

She fumbles for her phone and switches on the torch, hoping to blind whoever or whatever this is so she and Nonna can get away.

At best she's hoping she will see the policewoman from the gate, at worst a lost soul. But instead the beam catches a thin old woman. Everything about the way she looks – the gummy mouth forming an 'O' of shock in the pale face, the dirty fingers shielding her eyes from the torch, the grubby kitbag slung across her shoulder – says homeless person to Carys.

The stranger shies away and puts up her hands, as if, instead of an iPhone, Carys is aiming a gun at her.

'What do you want?' Carys hisses, mindful that neither of them should be there, and that the wandering policewoman – who must have returned to her post – will hear them.

The woman takes her by surprise by falling to the ground, sobbing.

'Shh, shh.' Carys turns the brutal beam of her phone torch down to its lowest setting and, with Nonna following, alert to protect, kneels in front of the stranger.

She can smell her, a mixture of dirty clothes and hair, sweat, stale wine, tobacco, urine and a hint of ancient sandalwood. She reminds herself to show compassion. Keeping yourself clean is impossible when you have no access to a bathroom, a washing machine, a wardrobe of fresh clothes, all the things she takes for granted. Over the past couple of days she has gone through some of the early stages of falling through the cracks – ending up like this could happen to anyone.

Perhaps this is the ghost of her future, come to get her.

The woman looks up at her, and Carys realises she isn't as old as she initially thought. Yes, her skin is dry and lined beneath the grime, but she can't actually be more than forty.

'Who are you?' she asks Carys. Her voice, through its heroin whine, takes Carys by surprise. It's the accent she sometimes wishes she had herself, so that she could blend in more: the received pronunciation of the southern English middle classes.

'I own this land,' she says. 'How did you get in?'

'Gate was open.' The woman squints at her face. 'Oh. You're the new Mrs Anderton.'

Carys nods, a chill going through her. She doesn't use Bill's surname, but hey, details. 'How do you know that?'

'The paper. Read it in the paper. In Manchester.'

'What?'

'About your old man. William. They've arrested him, yeah?' The woman's voice has relaxed into what must be an adopted street-smart drawl.

Carys says nothing. She's not going to give herself away to a stranger. Even though their names must be on the front page of every newspaper in the land, top hit on every search engine, heading every TV and radio news bulletin, Bill's arrest still seems like her own private business that no one else has a right to talk about.

'They've got the wrong man,' the woman goes on. 'They've got the wrong fucking fucker.' She starts to cry, like someone at the end of a very long journey. As if she is at prayer, she puts her face to the earth and sobs right into it, watering it with her tears.

She says something Carys can't make out, her voice swallowed by the dirt.

Carys takes her by the shoulders and pulls her up so that she is looking at her. Through the worn fabric of the woman's grubby denim jacket, she feels skin sliding on bone, not an ounce of softness anywhere.

'Who are you?' she asks. 'What do you know?'

'Eve,' the woman says. 'I used to live there.'

She points towards the back of the old garden, where a wall separates the property from the people who until a few days ago were the only thorn in Carys and Bill's side.

She spits the way she's pointing. It splats on the turned earth. 'Those bastards used to be my parents.'

'The Bullocks?'

'Yes.' She pulls a face of utter disgust. 'I thought I'd never come back here.'

'Why did you, then?' Carys says.

Eve falls again to her knees and digs her fingers into the earth.

'Because you found Martha.'

'Martha?'

'My daughter. Show me where he buried her.'

THIRTY

The policewoman, who had returned oblivious to the front gate sometime after Eve had snuck in behind Carys, calls a car. It arrives quickly and, with blue lights on, takes the two women and the dog to Tottenham police station.

'I want Carys with me,' Eve tells an exhausted-looking Tom as he greets them.

He frowns, but nevertheless ushers them straight through the reception area and into a room that with its low table and four armchairs looks far more comfortable than the standard interview room Carys was expecting.

Nonna, who clearly feels at home, throws herself down on the floor with a sigh and falls instantly asleep.

'Tea?' Tom says.

'Got any biscuits?' Eve asks. She looks like she knows the police station drill.

He nods and leaves them alone.

As she takes in the box of tissues on the table, the picture of a sunset on the otherwise bare wall, the cheap cushions on the sofa, Carys realises with relief that they are in the place the police put people who are victims rather than suspects.

She wonders if this is where they brought Lucy when she gave what Carys is now 100 per cent sure was a false statement.

'You OK now?' she asks Eve, who didn't want to come here at all. Her intention was to confront her parents. She had, in fact, a detailed, bloody and violent plan in mind. But Carys impressed on her that the most important thing was to see justice properly done.

She didn't mention what is actually most important to her, which is that the sooner this nasty Bullock saga is cleared up, the sooner Bill can walk free.

'It'll get them where it hurts, too. Public shame,' she told Eve. 'Can't beat it. I should know. And from what I know of them, they particularly will hate it.'

She absolutely understands Eve, though. In her position she would climb over their garden wall, smash their windows and stab them with a kitchen knife until they were a stringy mass of pulp.

'I had a baby,' Eve tells Tom and DC Peterson, the kind-faced middle-aged female officer sitting beside him. As she speaks, she showers crumbs of digestive biscuit onto the coffee table. She has agreed to the interview being videoed. 'He put her in me.'

'Who?' Tom says.

'My so-called father.'

Even hearing this for the second time, Carys shudders. She'd always felt that the way Alastair Bullock turned her gut was down to something more than him just being a pain-in-the-arse neighbour.

'You're saying that your father sexually abused you?' DC Peterson asks.

Eve nods. 'For as long as I can remember. My mother knew, but she never did nothing. Just let it go on in the background. Quiet life.'

Tom sighs heavily.

'I had Martha when I was thirteen. When I was expecting, I was shut away from the world. They literally locked me in my bedroom.'

'Didn't the neighbours suspect anything?' Carys says, thinking of Bill and Alice, who had been living across the garden wall for about four years when all this was going on.

'It's big houses in north London,' Eve says. 'No one knows anyone. No one cares. Believe me.'

'Until someone tries to build behind their back gardens,' Carys says. 'Then they start caring.'

'Carys, please,' Tom says. 'You're here to support the witness.'

Carys nods. She knows that the less she says, the sooner Bill gets out. But she is furious now. Her fingers itch. She wants to stamp on her imagined stringy stabbed Bullock pulp until it disappears into the ground for good.

'What about school?' DC Peterson says.

'They "home-schooled" me. No one cared. They're wealthy, look all proper. He's an accountant, she's a bird-brained house-wife. They're white. They speak nice. You lot never suspected them of nothing, did you?'

Tom swallows. Carys knows that this is true. Not once were the Bullocks even considered to be responsible for the poor little girl buried just over the wall from their garden. Nor were any of the other wealthy neighbours.

'So when I had Martha, they took her off me straight away.'

Carys takes Eve's hand. The horror of it makes her insides ache.

'I didn't know what to do. I had to get out. My plan was to escape, then come back once I'd got myself sorted and save Martha.' She swallows and her voice catches. 'I only managed the first bit, though.'

'Take your time, Eve.' DI Peterson slides the box of tissues across the coffee table. Eve is crying now: big fat snotty tears.

'I was only thirteen. I'd literally hardly ever been out of the house. And I was on the streets with no money, no friends, and everything aching from having had a baby too young. I got to King's Cross, thinking I'd get away, but this man came up to me and said he could help me.'

'Bastard,' Carys says, and Tom gives her another look.

'He called himself Spider. I didn't care what happened to me. My body had never been my own, so I didn't care about the drugs and the abuse he pushed on me. And then he put me out to work. It went on for years.'

'What about Martha?'

Eve gulps. 'I went back. I did. I thought I had seven years before he started showing interest in her the way he did me, so I swore to myself that before then I would manage to get away from Spider and back in time to save her. And I did get away. But it was too late. They said she'd been adopted, told me to go away.' She blows her nose and looks up at Tom, her eyes now hard and dry. 'I never believed them.'

'Why didn't you tell us?' Tom asks. 'Why didn't you come to us?'

Eve laughs, but there's no humour in it. 'Word of a junkie prostitute against those two?'

He sits back. 'I'm sorry you felt that. I'm sorry that you feel let down by us.'

There is a knock at the door. A uniformed officer pokes her head into the room and says she needs a word. Tom pauses the interview and steps outside.

'You're doing really well,' Carys says, touching Eve's knee.

'We can help you,' DC Peterson says. 'You're a victim of crime. We can get counselling for you, help you find somewhere safe to stay...'

'I just want that bastard to pay for what he's done,' Eve says.

'And her, for doing fuck all. I want justice done for my daughter. I don't care about me.'

Carys puts her arm around this poor wreck of a woman. She can't quite believe the cruelty that exists in the world.

'OK,' Tom says, coming back in and sitting down. He has several sheets of paper in his hand. 'We've just got DNA results in from Victim A—'

'Martha. Her name's Martha,' Eve says.

DC Peterson reaches a hand out to Eve. 'Let's just make totally sure, shall we?'

'And Victim B.' He scans the paper, frowning. 'Who appears to be at least five hundred years old.'

'Almost a fossil, then, Bill's "murdered lover"?' Carys would laugh if it weren't so desperate, if she weren't so fizzing with anger at the Bullocks, at Lucy, at Tom for being so gullible, at Ajay...

Tom shakes his head. He looks like he has been slapped. 'And it's not Bill's child, either – we fast-tracked a DNA swab from him.'

'She's my child! Take my blood. You'll see!' Eve is on her feet and pulling up her jacket sleeve to reveal an arm threaded with thin white vertical scars – just like Lucy, Carys thinks – and pincushioned with track marks ancient and modern.

'My father Alastair Bullock and my mother Claire Bullock either killed my daughter outright or neglected her until she died, and then they carried her over the wall and buried her in the messy bit at the back of the big garden.'

'Interview concluded.' Tom gets up and turns off the video, then squats down in front of Eve. 'I'm going to leave you with DC Peterson here, Eve,' he says. 'I'm going to arrange a DNA test and bring your parents in for questioning, and we'll take it from there.'

'And Bill?' Carys says.

Tom stands. He can't meet her eye. 'I'm releasing him pending further investigation.'

'And what are you going to do to apologise? To reinstate his reputation? To bring back our firebombed house?'

He has gone bright red. 'We can only proceed on evidence and witness statements. We had to believe Lucy.'

Carys stands and angles her face right up towards his. 'Lucy is delusional. She has mental health issues. I have told you this over and over, and you have chosen to disregard me.'

At her side, Eve mutters something.

Carys turns to her. 'What did you say?'

'No smoke without fire.'

Both Tom and DC Peterson look at Carys. She is outraged to see something like pity on their faces.

'I understand how you can think that, given how you have suffered at your father's hands. But believe me: not in this case, no.' Carys's voice trembles with anger. 'Bill is the kindest, gentlest man you could ever meet. Your father was the worst, Eve. Bill is the best. To *all* his daughters.'

Eve looks at her bitten fingernails, then closes her eyes.

Of course, given her unimaginable experience, she is going to see the possibility for bad in everyone. However old she is, she remains inside a hurt child. Cursing herself for going too far, Carys kneels and puts her hands over those chapped, dry and flaking fingers. Nonna, who woke as soon as Carys moved, joins her and rests a concerned paw on Eve's knee, which makes her dissolve into tears again.

'I'm going to help you,' Carys says. 'I'm going to stand by you and see that you get justice. That's a promise. First of all, I'm going to sort you out with somewhere to stay while your parents are dealt with.'

'I can't afford—'

'I can. Do you have a phone?'

'Yes, but I've not got any credit.'

'I'll sort that out for you too.' She pulls the key card for the Premier Inn room from her wallet. 'You can stay here tonight, and I'll find you somewhere else for tomorrow. Give me your phone number and I'll let you know where.'

She takes down Eve's details, then stands to face Tom, who has been waiting for her.

'Now, can we let my husband out of custody, please?'

THIRTY-ONE

'I wanted to go home.' Bill stands in the middle of the over-lit Airbnb living room, ignoring Nonna, who is lying on her back begging for a tummy rub.

'The insurance company say it'll be six weeks, tops,' Carys says.

He appears not to hear her. The flat is functional but soulless, and she hasn't been in it long enough yet to make it more homey. Tomorrow she'll replace the horrible plastic plants with living, breathing specimens, and while she's at it, she'll visit one of the little shops around the area and find some quirky cushions and throws.

But what is she doing thinking about interior decor when her husband is standing broken in front of her?

She puts her arms around him. His clothes, taken off him when he was arrested and returned for him to wear as he left, smell stale and foreign. She catches a whiff of unwashed body.

'You should never have taken Lucy to see that creep,' he says, unyielding under her touch. 'You should have told me.'

'I know. I'm sorry.'

'You shouldn't have lied to me.'

'It was a crappy, crappy move.' And he doesn't know the half of her lies yet, either. She takes his hands and tries and fails to get him to look into her eyes. 'There's a spa bath in the en suite. And I got some Aesop toiletries in.'

'Great,' he says with no enthusiasm.

'I'll put the kettle on and get you some fresh clothes. I had to wash everything I rescued from the house because it stank of smoke.'

Bill shakes his head and sinks onto the sofa. 'I'm just tired, Carys.'

'You've every right to be mad at me.'

'I know you thought taking Lucy to that creep was for the best.'

'I had no idea you had history.'

'You didn't feel able to talk to me about him. That's partly my fault.'

Carys nods. Here is her reasonable husband back. Thank Christ. Her life partner, her best friend.

He holds out a hand. 'Let's try to put it behind us. With any luck, once they've thrown the book at the Bullocks' – he says the name like it is acid in his mouth – 'we'll be able to get on with the build. We'll tell Artur to put the boys on standby.'

She curls up next to him, puts her head on his shoulder and steels herself. 'I've got some news.'

He tenses. 'What now?'

'Good news.'

'OK...'

She takes his hand and puts it on her belly. 'Baby news!'

He pushes himself up and faces her directly. 'What?'

'I'm two weeks late. I did a test...'

He is smiling. 'Oh, Carys, oh, my love.' He takes her face in his hands and kisses her with what feels like all his heart and soul.

'You're pleased, then?'

'So, so pleased! A new baby. A new beginning.'

She nods. He pulls her towards him, and she knows he wants her.

'There's plenty of hot water for that bath,' she tells him.

He laughs. 'I stink, don't I?'

She smiles at him, neither confirming nor denying it.

'Show me the way,' he says.

While Bill bathes, she sorts out a cheap studio for Eve to stay in from tomorrow. He comes to her fresh from the bath and they have frantic quick sex, which is more satisfying for him than her. She lets it pass this once.

He is now sleeping like a man reborn while she soaks in a freshly drawn tub. It's late, gone midnight, and she's trying to work out how she can carve out a bit more time tomorrow, just him and her, to set out their new normal in this strange environment. She toys once again with the idea of asking Elsa if she could take Binnie to Cornwall, but she knows Bins will be desperate to see her dad.

She decides to call Edina. First to tell her about Bill being freed, but also – and she knows it's audacious, but she has few options – to ask her a favour.

Edina will be awake. Her night-owling was a source of grief when they were together, as Carys normally likes to be tucked up by eleven.

Edina picks up. 'Hey girl.'

Wondering if she still has 'Me and Mrs Jones' as her ring-tone, Carys tells her about the whole Bullock thing.

'What a total bastard,' Edina says.

'You wouldn't work for his defence, then?'

'Not if there's the concrete DNA there, and that poor girl turns out to be his daughter as well as his grandchild. I'd be the first to sign up for the firing squad.'

'What about "needing the process of law or else we'd all be savages"?' Carys says, quoting Edina's favourite defence for her work.

'Yeah, yeah. So what's this favour, then?' Edina says.

Carys skims her hand across the bubbles in her bath and wonders whether Edina's missus is awake too or whether they also have arguments about bedtime.

'Are you busy tomorrow?'

'Not especially.'

It's the answer she was hoping for, with it being the university summer vacation. 'I was wondering if you might be up for getting Binnie from her friend's house in the morning? It's literally round the corner from you. I'd be so grateful. I just think Bill and I need a bit more time...'

'Wow, Carys.'

'Wow what?'

'I'm the only person you can turn to?'

'It's difficult at the moment, with the arrest and so on.'

But Carys knows that's an excuse. It's like how she had no one to call after the fire. What has happened to her friends? Not just the school mums, but the friends she had before she met Bill. One by one they dropped out of her life and now mostly it's just him and her and Binnie.

'Binnie loved you when she met you,' she says instead. 'She's asked about seeing you again. You could take her to the zoo? I can get you tickets online.'

'That could be fun.' Edina studied the London Zoo chimps for her PhD on guilt and remorse, and is an entertaining guide to the primate house. 'OK, I'll do it.'

'Binnie will be so excited.'

'I'll just need to square it with her indoors.'

'Thank you so much.'

'Sleep well, Carys.' Edina's voice turns smoky and deep,

making Carys remember the better times they had, when they weren't arguing.

Edina never left her unsatisfied after sex.

They hang up, and Carys lets the memories and the spa bath bubble jets join her hand in giving her what Bill couldn't manage tonight. She was so horny during her first pregnancy. Looks like, despite everything, it's happening again. She needs to remind him that his isn't the only libido in town.

He was right, though, she thinks as she towels herself dry. This is a new start. Perhaps one day they will be able to have a normal relationship again with Lucy and Sara.

But have they ever really managed normal? She has utterly failed to fill the mother space left by Alice. She doesn't even fill the stepmother gap—

'Stop that, girl,' she tells her reflection in the steamy bathroom mirror. 'Just stop.'

She sits on the toilet, and as she pees, she WhatsApps Sara, telling her about the Bullocks, and Bill getting out. She wants to signal to her that she is across it, in control and kind and big enough to keep her in the loop.

Perhaps, she texts, *we can start to build back some of the bridges that you and Lucy have smashed up.*

She changes *you and Lucy have smashed up* to *have been broken*, then presses send.

Leaving her phone in the bathroom where it can't intrude on her rest, she tiptoes to the bedroom, slips in next to Bill and, under his protecting arm, falls into a deep, dreamless sleep.

'What the hell?'

Carys is wrenched awake to find Bill standing over her. She can't initially figure out where she is and why he's there.

But then she realises he is holding her phone up, and it is showing her call history.

'You've been calling "Edinadingadingdong" in the middle of the night I come back? What is this, Carys?'

'I...'

He swipes over to WhatsApp. 'And you're "reaching out" to Lucy and Sara? After what they did to me? To *us*?'

'They're our daughters.' Carys sits up, swings herself out of bed and brushes past him, taking her dressing gown from the peg on the back of the door. Her Fitbit tells her it's just 6 a.m.

'No daughters of mine.'

'Don't say that.' She shrugs on the dressing gown, ties the sash around her waist and heads for the kitchen. She's not willing to face this without a cup of tea. 'Edina is looking after Binnie this morning so we can have a bit of time to acclimatise,' she says as she fills and switches on the kettle.

'*Edina* is looking after Binnie? How does Edina even know Binnie? Supposedly you haven't seen her since she sold us the flat.'

'Me. She sold it to me.' Carys sets out two mugs and pops a tea bag in each. She's trying to hide her annoyance at his snooping on her. 'And she actually got in touch a couple of days ago because she thought she could help you.'

He is pacing the bland living room beyond the kitchen area. 'Knew I was out of the picture, more like.'

She turns to face him. 'Bill! Stop this!'

His tendency to jealousy has always been a factor in their relationship. It doesn't help that she is bisexual, so he has the whole field of human existence to feel threatened by. When Kelsey, a beautiful lesbian, came to the firm on placement, Carys had to dance around him to convince him that everything was strictly professional and there was no spark whatsoever between the two of them. It's the same with younger men, too, even though, as she tells him frequently, she likes a silver fox. And Bill is a silver fox par excellence. Except when his jealousy turns him into this whining little boy. She virtually pushes him down onto the sofa.

'Despite the fact that I left her for you, when Edina saw you mentioned in the papers, she was woman enough to reach out and offer help. If Eve Bullock hadn't turned up, if the DNA had been inconclusive, she would have been your best and possibly only hope.'

'If, if,' he says. But she sees he's floundering for reasons to remain angry.

She takes his hand in hers. 'William Anderton. I love you. I have always believed in you, in everything you do, everything you say. We have Binnie' – she pulls his hand to her belly – 'and now we have another little bean, growing inside me. Ours.'

'At least I'll have two children who love me.'

'Sara and Lucy love you.'

'Do you really believe that? After all they've done? Look, Carys. We're not going to "reach out" to Sara and Lucy. I know you want to be all stepmotherly and mend everything, but it's not going to work. Not now. I'm exhausted by it all. I've had too much loss. First baby Danny, then Alice, and now my daughters are as good as dead to me. I want no more contact with either of them. Not from you, not from me.'

'But...'

Then Carys remembers Sara's ultimatum about telling Bill the truth of how they actually came to meet. Perhaps right now, amid all this upset, silence is the best policy.

'But what? They've practically ruined us. I'm going to point the police in their direction about the house fire.'

'They wouldn't! Not while Binnie and I were in there. The best bet is Bullock, surely.' This is what Carys plans to tell PC Okenedo this morning.

'I'd put nothing past Lucy and Sara right now. And I'm going to sue the Met too, that incompetent dickhead Tom...'

While Bill goes on to list Tom's shortcomings, Carys tries to focus on the fact that her future lies now with Bill, Binnie and the baby.

Nothing and no one else can matter.

Poor Lucy, though. She's got Sara now, but poor, poor girl. How will she be feeling, knowing that she has been so horribly misled and abused by Ajay? And that Carys brought her to it...

She doesn't know if she can go along with Bill's wishes about not contacting her. But that would mean yet more stuff that she has to hide from him. And wasn't that what caused all the trouble in the first place?

One wish she does capitulate on is cancelling Binnie's day out with Edina. She does it by video call, with Bill looking on, and she can hardly bear to look her ex-partner in the eye, because she knows exactly what she is thinking of her.

'Never see her again,' Bill says, clicking the red button on the call.

THIRTY-TWO

'That's like Dad's motorbike,' Sara says to Lucy as they sit in Ajay's waiting room watching the tree ferns in the front garden shudder in the evening breeze. Lucy is all at sea and Sara is trying to keep her spirits up.

'Dad had a Japanese bike.'

'But Ajay's got a sidecar like Dad had.'

Lucy grunts.

Sara tries to think what happened to the sidecar. She thinks it got trashed in Bill's accident. Or perhaps it was before that. In any case, after Alice died, neither she nor Lucy ever rode in it again.

Too many memories surfacing everywhere.

She tries to remember why she's agreed to bring Lucy along here again to stir up even more.

Tom called after midnight on Sunday to tell her what had happened with Eve Bullock and the DNA results, and that the adult bones dated back to the 1500s. Sara was surprised by the level of relief she felt. She wants Bill to suffer for the way he

abandoned her and Lucy, but life in prison for double murder is perhaps a step too far.

Tom sounded devastated, though. 'I fucked up,' he said. 'Bill will be properly out for my blood now.'

'You were rightly acting on Lucy's witness statement,' Sara said. 'And that other set of bones on the site corroborated her story.'

'Appeared to.' Tom sounded horribly gloomy, and Sara wondered if he had found himself a nice flat after being kicked out of the home he had shared with his wife. She imagined not – a grim little bedsit fits the picture far better. She toyed with the idea of inviting him back to Carys's cosy place. They could have talked and then he could have slept on the sofa.

She decided against it. It was a disastrous idea.

'He's going to get me for not declaring my connection to him, isn't he?' Tom's voice had an unattractive hint of a whine to it.

'Would you have taken it so far had you not known him?'

'One hundred per cent I would.'

'Well then, there you go.'

She was tired. Needed to try to get some sleep before bracing herself to pass the news on to Lucy. 'Look, we'll speak soon, OK?'

Later that night – three in the morning – Carys texted and told her the same news. As well as some typical Carys crap about building bridges.

'Dream on, stepmother,' Sara said as she blearily dropped her phone back on the floor by her bed.

She waited until Lucy woke late on Monday morning to give her the news about Bill being freed. She didn't know what to expect, but it wasn't a numb 'Oh,' followed by a shrug.

'It's something else I saw, then,' Lucy went on as she stumbled towards the shower. 'Ajay'll help me.'

So that's why Sara is here, almost dragged along by Lucy to

the session Carys tried and failed to cancel. She's also here because Lucy wants her to sit in and witness whatever it is that Ajay is going to dig out of her subconscious this time.

'Relax and let go, and you go deeper. And the deeper you go, the better you feel,' Ajay says.

Lucy lies back in a fancy reclining chair, her hands on the armrests, her feet together, her eyes closed. Her hair hangs like two flame-red curtains on either side of her face, like how Sara remembers Alice's.

'And you go deeper now,' Ajay says, his voice like syrup. 'A warm, lovely feeling, through your shoes, through your feet, into your toes. That's right.'

Bill didn't kill his lover and her child. That was absurd, crazy loopyville stuff from Lucy. But something's not right, and Sara thinks this tall, thin man could hold the key.

'Now, as I count backwards from ten to one, you go a little deeper.'

Lucy's face loses all its care; every spot of tension dissolves. Right in front of Sara she becomes the sweet, happy girl from before Alice died.

Ajay talks her through the process, his voice calm and level. He takes her down in a lift, through layers of beautiful land-scapes where everything is safe, counting her down again, taking her deep into herself.

It's so intense that Sara pinches through the denim of her jeans and into her thighs to make sure she doesn't go under too. She reckons though that she probably has too many spikes to be hypnotisable.

'I want you to remember, Lucy, that you are here voluntari-ly,' Ajay says. 'You can come away from where I take you when-ever you want. Raise your fingers if you agree.'

Sara watches as, like a ghost, Lucy flutters her hand, then lets it lie back on the armrest.

He gives her some more stuff about how she is going to discover what her subconscious holds. Then he tells her to sit on a deserted beach and, with her finger, to write the number one hundred in the sand.

'Wipe it out with your hand, then write the number ninety-nine. That's good. Now wipe it out and write ninety-eight.' He carries on, taking her slowly down to ninety, then he tells her to keep going until she gets to zero.

While she's busy with that, he gets her to sit down in front of an imaginary screen and view a photograph of a time when she was really happy as a child.

Sara can't imagine what is going on in Lucy's head at this point, with numbers in the sand and imaginary TVs, but her face lights up. Under her pale blue eyelids, her eyeballs dart from side to side, like she is following a movie.

'Good, good,' Ajay says. His voice is so calm it feels like silky velvet, although when Sara surreptitiously glances at him, he seems held, like he is waiting for something to happen.

She knows from the interview training she did back on the job in Sydney that verbal and visual cues from a questioner can influence a subject. She was taught to avoid this and to use more open techniques. But what Ajay is doing is so alien to her that she just can't judge whether he's steering Lucy or letting her make her own pictures on her 'screen'.

'So now I want you to wipe that picture away,' he says, 'and replace it with a time when you were just a little bit worried.'

Lucy's smile disappears.

'Do you want to tell me what's in the picture?' Ajay says.

'It's dinner, and Mum and Dad and Sara are there.'

Lucy is talking in a baby voice. Despite the summer heat in the room, the hairs on Sara's arms prickle. This is creeping her out.

'How old are you?' he asks.

'I'm four. We're all laughing at something funny Mum said.'

'Is Mum funny?' he asks her.

Lucy giggles. 'She's always funny.'

This surprises Sara. All she sees when she tries to recall Alice is a thin, tense woman who always had a weight on her shoulders. Her patients worried her, her colleagues and the politics around the centre worried her, Sara worried her. Bill worried her.

'There's only one more slice of the cake we're having for pudding, but Dad tells me I'm too small for seconds.' In a deeper but just as unsettling voice she continues, 'He gives it to Sara.'

'Where's Mum?' Ajay asks.

'I don't know.' Lucy shakes her head and starts to look distressed.

Ajay calms her by making her check in on her sand numbers.

Was Sara such a thorn in Lucy's side? What she remembers is how Lucy inconvenienced *her*. Also how Lucy brought light back into their parents' lives after baby Danny's death just by being born, when Sara had tried so many times to make them happier: little bunches of flowers from the garden, drawings of Danny, a lopsided cake...

She brings her attention back to the room.

Ajay is now telling Lucy to put the worst picture she has on her screen. Her eyes remain shut, but her eyebrows shoot up her forehead, her hands lift from the armrests. Such is the tension that shudders through her body, she appears to levitate.

'Tell me who you see,' Ajay says. But Lucy is lost in it. Her eyes are still shut, and she is taking short, sharp breaths, sudden inhalations.

'Get off her,' she says. 'Leave her!'

'Is that Mum?' he says.

Sara looks up sharply. That's a planted thought.

'Her scarf,' Lucy says. 'The yellow one, with black squares. The tartan. He's pulling. I want to speak but I can't let him see me...'

'Who?' Ajay says. 'Is this your dad?'

Again, another plant. But Ajay seems to be as lost in the moment as Lucy is.

'It's dark,' Lucy says. 'There's a tree. Through a window.'

'What tree?'

'A hollow tree. I'm waking up but I'm very still. He's digging. And there he is, pulling her over by the tree, all wrapped up in sheets. I pretend to be asleep, but I see it all, and I want to not see it all. And he's digging again.'

She's crying. Sara wants this to stop, but Ajay is leaning forward, his sharp elbows on his bony knees, his long fingers probing towards Lucy like he wants to touch her. 'Can you look around you? What else can you see?'

Surely that's wrong, though, Sara thinks. He's getting her to look at a picture, not be part of it. Has she slipped inside it? Walked through the screen?

'I know this tree.' Lucy screws her face up tight. She's sniffing like an animal now. It looks horrible, horrifying, and Sara wants to take her by the shoulders and shake her out of it. 'Thou shall be doomed,' Lucy says.

'Doomed? Who? Him?'

'I'm supposed to be asleep.' Lucy stops sniffing. 'NO!' she screams. Her eyes fly open, and she is staring at something that neither Ajay nor Sara can see.

Sara feels like she's had a bucket of ice tipped over her.

Lucy is pulling at her hair now, batting away invisible flies from her face.

'Stop it,' she cries.

'Ajay!' Sara says. 'Make it stop!'

Briefly he acknowledges her presence, but he continues to focus on Lucy, who looks like she's having difficulty breathing.

Sara goes to him. 'You can't do this to her. Look at her!'

'Shh!' Ajay hisses, but Lucy is on her feet, gasping, like a diver surfaced too quickly.

She collapses onto her knees.

'You should have stayed quiet,' Ajay tells Sara.

'No. This is your fault.' Sara goes to her sister and kneels on the floor in front of her, trying to get her to look at her.

'I saw it all,' Lucy says, shaking like a cold dog.

'Saw all what?' Sara says.

'Mum didn't kill herself. Everyone lied. He killed her.'

'Who?'

'Him.'

'Who?' Ajay says. 'Who killed Alice, Lucy?'

Lucy looks at him, almost exploding with it. 'Dad killed her!'

'No,' Sara says. 'Remember how you thought he killed a girl and a woman and it didn't happen? You can't keep going on and on at him. He's lots of things, Luce, but he's not a murderer.'

'He is!'

Ajay stays silent, smiling, his arms folded.

Sara puts her hands on her sister's shoulders. 'Whatever this is, Luce, you need to work it out. Ajay says that what you see isn't always what actually happened, that it can be that you're working towards something else.'

'No!' Lucy says. 'This is it! He killed her!'

'You're saying Alice didn't kill herself, Lucy?' Ajay says.

Sara stands and looks at him. He's got a weird smile on his face, like he's just won a treasure hunt. And then she has a thought. 'Carys told you about Mum, didn't she?'

He smiles. 'Told me what about her?'

'About her body never being found. And you've been feeding Lucy knowing that. "Where's Mum?" I see you, Ajay.'

'Mum's body was never found?' Lucy is shaking her head wildly.

'I'm sorry,' Sara says. 'I was going to tell you.'

But Lucy carries on. 'Of course she was never found! How could she be when he buried her by the tree?' She struggles to her feet and runs out of the room.

'No, Lucy, wait!' Before Sara goes after her, she turns to Ajay. 'See what you've done?'

But he's just grinning like a devil. Like she's not there.

THIRTY-THREE

Sara hares after her sister towards the Heath. You'd never know to look at Lucy just how fast she can run. But there it is, as they sprint along the tarmac path, past pavilions, paddling pools, play parks, playing fields, dodging a couple of late-out mothers with buggies and a silver-blue whippet who tries to join in the chase.

The green hill seems to tilt towards Sara as she pumps her arms and sweats – today was one of those hot days where Capital FM warn against exercising outside, and the evening has just shored it up. Up ahead, running like she has the devil at her heels, Lucy speeds past some tennis courts and Sara gasps as she watches her run out into a road that has appeared ahead of them, narrowly missing a taxi. The driver swerves and swears some proper London at her.

Across the road, a bus stands at a stop. While she waits for a gap in the traffic, Sara watches through the window as Lucy whacks her card down on the reader. At last she gets her chance and dashes across in front of a couple of middle-aged men in Lycra breaking the speed limit on their road bikes. But by the time she gets to the bus, its doors are closed. She hammers on the glass, but the driver ignores her.

'Lucy!' she shouts as she watches her climb the stairs to the top deck.

Lucy leans across a pink-haired girl sitting by a window and opens the little fanlight at the top, grinning like she has just won a race. 'What?' she shouts out.

'Where the hell are you going?' Sara says.

Lucy laughs. 'I'm going to tell Tom that Bill murdered Alice.'

The pink-haired girl looks up at her like she is mad.

She might possibly have a point.

While Sara is on Citymapper trying to find the fastest way to get to Tottenham police station, a black cab cruises past.

She flags it down, stepping out almost in front of it.

It's a long, slow, expensive slog up through Finsbury Park and Harringay. A fug of traffic fumes hangs in the evening air like a hazy yellow photo filter. Stuck in stationary jams, drivers vent their frustration through their horns.

'Can't you find a better way?' Sara says.

'I'd take you round Stamford Hill,' the cabbie says, 'but it's even worse that way. They've dug all the bloody roads up all at once. No sense, the council. Who's in charge of planning, eh? That's what I'd like to know.'

Sara pulls out her phone, and as the driver goes off on one about loony lefties and greens, she tunes him out and tries to call Tom.

His phone goes to voicemail. She hopes it's because he's having a well-deserved few days off after the stress of arresting then releasing Bill and so won't be there when Lucy bursts into the station raving. But if that were the case, he would surely pick up if he saw it was her calling.

'Listen, Tom,' she says. 'Lucy's on her way to you to tell you the latest hypnosis so-called revelation. Bill killed Alice, apparently. Yet again, of course, she believes it all the way. Please be kind with her. I'm on my way, should be at the station in about twenty.'

'Going to be more like half an hour, love,' the cabbie says.

'Excuse me, mate.' She presses the privacy button to shut him out.

About a kilometre away from the police station, the taxi gets stuck in standstill traffic. Sara pays the driver and jogs through the fumes. Arriving at the station, she throws herself through the doors and into the reception area, where the usual crew of desperate and destitute people sit waiting to be seen.

'I'm looking for Lucy Anderton,' she says, panting so hard that her breath fogs the Plexiglas screen protecting the receptionist. 'I know you've got a ticket system, but she just came in a few minutes ago and I need to see her. It's urgent. She'll be with DS Jackson.'

'Certainly, madam,' he says, lifting his phone.

And there he is, Tom, looking ten years older than when she last saw him, standing holding the door open. 'Please come in, Ms Anderton,' he says formally and loudly so that everyone in the reception – desk staff included – can hear.

'It's Herman. I changed my name to Mum's after I left,' Sara says once the door to reception is closed behind them.

'Good move.' Tom nods as he shows her down some stairs to a grim, grey-painted interview room.

'Where's Luce?'

'With Jill – DC Peterson. She's trained in supporting people in crisis. Give her half an hour or so. She's working wonders.'

'You   probably   know   that   she's   been   seeing   a hypnotherapist.'

'I do.'

'And she's literally just run to you from a session.'

'I thought that might be the case.'

'There's something weird about this guy, like he was pleased or something, like he wants Bill to be punished.'

'She seems to be having some sort of psychotic episode. It's hard to make out, but she's going on about Bill strangling Alice with a scarf. We can take her somewhere she'll be properly looked after, if you like.'

'No, she'd hate that. Let me take her home, and I'll get her to her shrink on an emergency visit.'

Tom's smile doesn't look all that convincing. 'You'll have to sign a release. Let's go get her.' He turns to lead Sara out of the room, but with his hand on the door, he stops and turns to face her, blocking her exit.

Sara readies herself, stands tall, tries not to show the vulnerability she feels. 'What's up, Tom?'

'It's just...' He shakes his head and moves towards her.

She flinches away and he holds up his hands.

'I really screwed up, Sara. Bill has complained about wrongful arrest, and he's just called and told the boss all about how I knew him and always had it in for him. So as of tomorrow, I'm off the case, knuckles rapped. I'm putting the Bullock stuff together for my replacement. I'm a fucking idiot.'

'We all make mistakes. You were working in good faith.'

He shakes his head. 'Bill's right, though. I put my better judgement away. I hated him when I was going out with you.

'I know.'

'He did everything possible to put me down, scare me away from you. Remember how he called me the Bunny Boiler to my face? And the time when I dropped by after footie to give you some money I owed you, and he kept on asking quite pointedly where the body odour was coming from?'

'He was a jealous father,' Sara says. 'He wanted us all to stay close to him, show total devotion, and he saw you as a threat to that. Mum said it was because he loved us so much.'

Tom looks at her, an eyebrow raised. 'Really.'

'He wanted control. Like all men.'

'Thanks.'

She just manages to stop herself saying 'present company excepted', because Tom was *all* about control. He wanted to force her to love him, even when she repeatedly made it clear to him that she wanted out.

'I was a twat,' he says, as if he is reading her mind.

'Tom.' Sara takes a breath. It's time to dive in. 'If there's any question mark about Mum's death, you need to look at Carys, not Bill.'

'What?' he says. 'I mean, are there any question marks?'

'Do you know her body was never found?'

He blinks. 'But we had the cremation and everything.'

'The police agreed with Bill that all the circumstances – the car being left where it was, the note, Mum's history of depression – pointed to suicide, so he had her declared dead and didn't tell anyone that there was no body. To spare us the pain, apparently. Not everyone who jumps at Beachy Head is found.'

Tom wipes his forehead. 'Wow.'

'Yeah. Wow. So I told Carys this, and she claimed not to know, which is a bit of a stretch.'

'Why don't you like Carys? I mean, apart from the fact that for some reason she's married to Bill, she's quite nice, isn't she?'

'Nice? Carys? Oh, she puts that out, but don't you think she's too good to be true?'

'How do you mean?'

Sara tells him about Carys's sister, and how Carys blamed Alice for the disabilities that led to her death. 'She was obsessed with Mum. Obsessed. And she tracked her down through Dad, and I wouldn't put it past her to have started an affair with him to punish her.'

'Seriously?'

'Tom, I'm a great cop. I bide my time. I won't claim anything for sure unless I have proof. But I can show you everything about Carys's sister and the Alice-stalking. Anyway, if anyone pushed Mum over the edge, it would have been Carys. She's driven, that woman. Driven to be a perfect wife and step-mother, driven to avenge the death of her sister. Who knows what she did?'

'You're not suggesting...'

Sara smiles. 'I'm not another Lucy. No. I don't know. I don't have proof of anything. I'd just love to know more about Mum's car, about what was found...'

'I could look. Dig out the case files, see if anything smells.'

'Could you?'

'Unofficially. I don't want to be seen to be stirring up more Anderton trouble.'

'But this could be a chance to redeem yourself.'

Tom puts his head to one side. Somewhere in his tired eyes she sees a glimmer. Slowly he nods. His phone buzzes with a text and he pulls it from his pocket.

'Jill says Lucy is calmer. Wants to go home. You willing to take her?'

'You bet.'

If Lucy was alight when she left Ajay's clinic, she is now snuffed like a candle, all smutted and fizzled out.

'They don't believe me,' she says.

'Come on, you.' Sara puts her arms around her sister and walks her out of the station.

'I want to kill Dad,' Lucy mutters into her shoulder.

'Now—what would that solve?'

THIRTY-FOUR

'Have you seen this?' Bill holds up his phone.

He has been glued to it throughout the special Japanese breakfast Carys picked up on the way back from dropping Binnie at her new summer play scheme. It's just round the corner at the YMCA and nobody knows them there, so there's no gossip, no stonewalling, no firebombing.

They are eating at the truly horrible glass and steel table in the Airbnb. Carys had hoped a good night's sleep might be the turn of a new corner, but instead Bill has barely acknowledged her.

With yesterday's Edina childcare cancelled, the day of reconnection between Carys and Bill didn't happen. Instead, he picked up a delighted Binnie from a no doubt gobsmacked Elsa and took her to the zoo on the tickets Carys had bought for Edina to use.

Carys, meanwhile, jumped straight back into bringing the Five Oaks project back up to speed and talking over repairs to the Muswell Hill house with the insurers. Standing there looking at the wet-cinder-stinking ruins of their once-cosy nest, she couldn't see herself, Bill and Binnie ever going back to their old lives there.

The new baby could mark a new beginning.

Perhaps, once the house is repaired, they could sell up, move on, move away, perhaps to the country.

At the moment, though, all the poor baby is doing is wiping her out.

Bill seems increasingly distant and lost. Binnie says they returned from the zoo after just two hours because he was tired and his back was hurting. He stuck her in front of the TV telling her he needed to work. Carys knows this actually means needling away at starting proceedings against the police. Obsessing over the past, in other words, rather than helping her move forward and mend things.

And now he's leaning over her miso soup and pushing his phone right up to her face.

'Eh?' he says. 'What the hell is she doing now?'

Carys squints at the screen. It shows Lucy's latest Instagram post. She has taken a series of black-and-white selfies of herself holding up her scarred forearms in front of a six-hundred-year-old English oak in Brockwell Park. The photographs are beautiful, graphic, yet alarming, like a twenty-first-century Munch's take on *Grimms' Fairy Tales*. Underneath, she has written: *This mighty tree was just a sapling at the time of the War of the Roses. It has seen so much. But not as much as the poor little girl who saw her father hit her mother and strangle her with a scarf. The poor little girl who then watched him bury her in a dark, dark wood.*

'You know what she's fantasising about now, don't you?' Bill says. 'Not content with me murdering my fictional lover and love child, she's now got me doing away with my real Alice!'

He chucks the phone onto the table and runs his fingers through his hair. 'What is she thinking? Why is she doing this to me?'

Carys shakes her head. 'I have no idea, Bill. I'm so sorry. I don't even think *she* knows why.'

'It's Ajay, isn't it? I'll have that bastard's guts for garters.'

'At least if she's gone to the police they're not listening any more.'

He laughs bitterly. 'Yeah. Because if they were, that twat Tom would be knocking down the door, salivating to clap handcuffs on me again.'

She sighs, puts her head in her hands and closes her eyes.

'What?' Bill is clearly taken aback by this. It's not what Carys normally does.

'Nothing. It's just...' She looks up at him. 'I just want it all to be right again. Everything back to how it was, but with Lucy happy and the new baby here and everyone calm.'

'Me calm, you mean.'

'I hate seeing you like this.'

'It's hell, Carys. My own daughter, accusing me of God knows what.' He shakes his head. 'I suppose at least she's not making up stuff about how I touched her or anything.'

Carys shudders, thinking of creepy Mr Bullock. 'That would be horrible.'

'And totally untrue.'

'I know.'

He reaches across the awful table and holds out his hand. 'You do trust me, don't you?'

She puts her hands around his. 'Of course I do! I love you. *We* love you. Me, Binnie, the baby. Even Lucy and Sara. They'll come round.'

He shakes his head. 'That ship's sailed. It's probably my fault when you get down to it. I messed up completely when Alice died.'

'No.'

'I should have put myself aside.'

This again. It will never stop. 'You did what you could.'

'And you helped me so much.' He has tears in his eyes.

Carys pushes her barely touched bowl away. She gets up and puts her arms around him, kissing his head.

'It'll all be good.'

He continues to sob. Her mind turns and turns, trying to work out a way out of all this.

She needs to speak to Lucy about this new direction her raving has taken. It's really upsetting Bill, but it must be tearing poor Luce apart. Perhaps Carys can persuade her to take a little time out in a clinic. Spend some time away from the family. Away from her big sister.

Later, her pregnant belly queasily empty from the non-breakfast, Carys stands next to Artur by the Bullocks' back wall, watching the police cart away the last of their crime-scene paraphernalia.

'Two weeks out, then,' she says to Artur as they sip their morning tea – hers is fennel now, rather than the thick builder's she used to prefer. 'We'll add it onto the schedule, and we're just going to have to suck it up.'

Artur nods. He looks emotional. 'I can't get over that poor little girl.' He nods to the site of Martha's grave. 'They say she never saw the world outside her bedroom in all her life.'

They peer over the shoulder-height wall at the Bullocks' house, empty now, its windows covered in metal shutters, like a sleeping ghost.

The story is all over the newspapers, in various degrees of salacious detail. Apart from a brief *Falsely accused man released* story in the *Mail*, complete with a stolen snap of Bill and Carys being driven away from the custody centre in a police car, the media has turned its spotlight away from them. Thankfully they were no longer sufficiently newsworthy for the photographer to trail them, so their location is still secret.

'I know,' Carys says. 'It's too cruel, isn't it?'

DC Peterson called earlier as Carys was driving to the site to say that Tom has been taken off the case. 'Also,' she added, 'Alastair Bullock wants you to know that while he was outside your house the other night, he took a photo of a group of white boys in St George T-shirts setting the house on fire and spraying it with the racist graffiti.'

Carys's mouth dropped open. 'Does he want my gratitude?'

'It seems so, yes.'

She shuddered. 'He was camped outside my house?'

'Yeah. He apologises for that. He says he needed to keep an eye on developments.'

'What a creep.'

'We've actually been able to identify the offenders as a gang we've been wanting to nail for over a year. We're questioning them now.'

'Tell Bullock he is not absolved in any way,' Carys said. 'For anything.'

'That's an understandable position,' Peterson said.

Artur wipes his nose with the back of his callused hand. 'I want to kill this man with my own hands.'

Carys nods. She knows how he feels. If anyone did that to Binnie...

'How is she?' Artur asks. 'The little girl's mother.'

'Eve? I've got her into a private therapeutic community in Surrey. She's going to sue her parents for the abuse she and her child suffered, but the mother has already shown some remorse and has agreed to pay for her treatment. Eve may even get the house.'

Artur shudders. 'I'd sell it.'

'Me too.'

He smiles. 'She could sell it to you and Bill!'

'You never know.'

'And it's got rid of your chief objectors.'

Neither of these are new thoughts for Carys.

'Thank you for sticking with us, Artur,' she says.

'Anything for you, my dear.' It sounds so chivalrous in his perfect Polish English. He looks at her, and she notices, not for the first time, that he has quite lovely eyes – grey-blue, with long eyelashes and a small hint of fire.

'Anyway,' she says. 'Onward.'

Artur raises his mug of tea. 'To fresh beginnings.'

THIRTY-FIVE

Invigorated from spending two hours at the site, Carys cycles over to the Earthstrong office. She's got Lucy's Instagram post buzzing in the back of her mind, and knows she's going to have to do something about that.

But first she's going to focus on more positive tasks and respond to an invitation to tender for the remodelling of a school for autistic children in Hertfordshire. Good works, a strong budget and a new direction outside London. It all makes sense. Bill's in no place to discuss strategy at the moment, and she rather likes the idea of doing it all on her own, to present him with a fait accompli for a new life after Five Oaks.

She lets herself into the office – part of a converted industrial building near Alexandra Palace railway station. Tina, who has kept the ship afloat while she and Bill have had their mind on other things, is at her clean, uncluttered desk, her done-to-within-an-inch-of-their-lives nails clattering on her keyboard.

'Thanks, babe,' she says to Carys, who hands her her favourite caramel macchiato from the café next door. 'Post's here.' She nods to a thicket of mail, bound up in post office rubber bands.

'Ah, the stuff forwarded from the house,' Carys says. She gave the office address to keep things simple.

She settles down with her own herbal tea and starts to go through the post, which includes a bill for the phone line she hasn't got round to suspending yet. Yet more life admin.

It's only early afternoon, but already she feels her reserves for the day running out. She toys for a weary moment with the idea of installing a curtained-off alcove in the office with a camp bed for her to catch cat naps during her pregnancy. Then something in the post catches her eye. The envelope is addressed in a swooping script in thick black fountain pen. Like that on the note she and Lucy saw at Beachy Head, it's middle-class art handwriting – not a bit like hers, sadly. Her father drummed it into her that to get ahead in education – and therefore in life – she needed to develop a neat, functional, legible script. He even gave her writing workbooks, which she had to spend ten minutes every evening going over with him.

The difference between this art handwriting and that at Beachy Head though is that it is rather more idiosyncratic. Indeed, it looks familiar.

She wakes her computer and looks at Lucy's Instagram, scrolling back to the earlier posts she made in what Carys sees as, relatively speaking, more innocent times. She pulls up a photo of a page from Alice's book, and her mouth goes dry.

The writing on this envelope looks the same as that beside the illustrations of the trees. The unique e's that look like euro symbols, the use of the capital R rather than lower case, the classic italic s shapes...

Hands trembling, glad of the large fern that hides her from Tina in the open-plan office, she rips open the envelope. A letter falls out: three sheets of old-fashioned writing paper, covered on both sides in the same script.

If she were a Christian like her old grandma, Carys would

cross herself at this point. Instead, she breathes slowly in and out, then sits back and glances at the first page.

Dear Carys, it says. *I want you to know that I am still alive.*

'Are you OK?'

Hearing her yelp, Tina has run over to her.

Carys smiles up at her. 'I'm fine, thanks!' She waves the letter. 'Just had some good news.'

'Ah.' Tina waits for a moment, clearly keen to hear more.

Carys meets her eyes, not saying anything.

'Well!' Tina says at last. 'Better get on. I've got some stuff for you to sign.'

'Give me half an hour?'

'Sure.'

Tina moves reluctantly back to her own territory, and Carys bends her head to read the letter.

I'm writing because I have seen the gossip about what they found in our old garden and I know there will probably also be new question marks over my disappearance that will surface because of all of this. And it's possible that while tongues wag, fingers will point at Bill. Whatever anyone says, though, I want you to know that he is completely innocent. I'm sure you don't doubt him, but I must reassure you that he had nothing to do with what happened to me.

Because nothing did happen.

I had so much darkness inside me at the time I disappeared. I was worn down – I felt I was useless to my family. Sara hated me, I was sure of that, and I could see that Lucy would inevitably go the same way. Even Bill's love for me didn't help. I couldn't understand how he could love someone like me. After Hull, and then Danny dying, I felt useless. A waste of space.

And then a most unpleasant colleague became obsessed

with me, so even work ceased to be the refuge it once was. He started following me, bombarding me with messages and hassling me. When I made it completely clear that I was in no way interested, he became angry, aggressive. I was powerless to stop him. He wore down what little remaining sense of self-worth I had. I could see no way out.

So I drove to Beachy Head, with every intention of throwing myself off. I stood on the edge of the cliff, but at the last minute I was too much of a coward to do even that. I just turned round and walked away, left everything there, disappeared from everyone's life. I really believed that they would be better off without me. I live a long way away now and am pretty insignificant, just surviving. It's OK.

Bill is a great father. He has brought Lucy up far better than I could have. And I am so glad he found you – I have kept tabs on him and the girls, of course. And you from time to time, just to make sure. You are very lovely. And you and he have a daughter! I wish I could meet you, but that's not possible, is it?

I just want you to know that Bill is a good man, and if anyone tries to implicate him in my disappearance, then they are wrong, as you can see.

Don't worry about me coming back. I know I can never do that. And please don't let anyone know about this, especially Bill.

With love,

Alice Herman

Her hands trembling, Carys puts the letter down on her desk. Her initial reaction is one of rage. How could a person be so selfish? Alice says she's been keeping tabs on Bill and the girls

– and her too, for God's sake. When? Where? Her spine prickles at the thought that she has been watched – even followed. If Alice has been monitoring them so carefully, isn't she then aware of the fallout from her actions? Bill's accident, Lucy's mental health problems? This isn't the sainted, troubled Alice of family legend. This is an egotistical coward.

And then she thinks of the Alice who mutilated her little sister through her ineptitude and arrogance, and she thinks, oh yes.

That's the woman who did this.

She picks up the envelope. The stamp is one that her father would steam off and save, because the faint, illegible postmark on the envelope has not touched it. It was probably sent just before Bill was arrested, because despite being aware of all the other stuff going on, Alice makes no mention of that.

Carys shivers. Alice has handed her this bomb, and it has blasted her into a new dimension, one she alone occupies. She knows she can't tell anyone about it, because it would smash the foundations of her life. But also here is unequivocal proof that Lucy's new accusations are wrong.

So one thing is very clear, and very urgent: she has to stop Lucy before she does any more damage.

She texts her, telling that she has to see her right now.

The reply comes back instantly.

Good. Meet me at the Hardy Tree, four sharp.

Carys looks up the photographs of Alice's book on Lucy's Instagram. The Hardy Tree is in St Pancras churchyard, an ash tree planted among a pile of tombstones discarded when the graveyard was dug up to make way for the new railway. Thomas Hardy, who was an architect before he was a novelist, oversaw the project. Because of this, Alice has named it, in that distinctive handwriting, *Bill's tree.*

Carys notes it on her Google Maps, then deletes the messages between her and Lucy.

Bill can't know about this.

Like he can't know about Alice.

Or Emily.

THIRTY-SIX

Carys is at St Pancras graveyard early, because after Alice's letter, there was no way she could concentrate on putting together a tender. It's with her now, burning through the corduroy of her bag and the linen of her dress, branding her leg with the heat of its revelation.

Everything is changed.

All the pain everyone went through didn't need to happen. Bill wouldn't have had his accident. Sara would have stayed. Lucy would have been happy.

But then Bill and Carys wouldn't have married. Binnie wouldn't have been born; this baby wouldn't exist inside her.

Should she be *grateful* to Alice for being such a cowardly deserter?

She walks round the Hardy Tree, which looks like an agave flower rising from a plant of gravestones. Alice must have envied it for its resilience.

She feels very different now about trying to see things through her predecessor's eyes. The eyes of a bolter, a runaway, a weakling: they have lost all authority.

She sits on a nearby park bench, closes her eyes and lets the sunlight, filtered through the leaves in this little oasis, play on her face. Behind her, an enormously tall yellow brick wall shields this ancient place from the modern intrusion of St Pancras station. The sound of the trains is hidden too by the racket of the traffic thundering down Pancras Road.

If she could just sleep for a little while, perhaps she could let this news, which sits in her like scum on pond water, settle a little...

'Hey.'

She starts and opens her eyes. Perhaps she drifted off. Lucy stands in front of her. She has cut off all her hair and it stands on her head in little uneven red tufts. Her drug-plumped features look drawn and marshmallowy, she has dark rings under her eyes, and her skin has gone beyond pale and into the light greys. Her little doodled-over canvas rucksack, which dangles from her right hand, skims the ground, all forlorn.

'Oh, Lucy.' Carys takes her hands. Amazingly, Lucy lets herself be drawn down onto the bench and held. All of Carys's compassion flows into this broken, mistaken girl sobbing into her shoulder.

'No one believes me,' Lucy says, finally pulling herself away. She looks feral, the whites of her eyes red. 'Not even Sara. Not Tom.'

'You did go to the police, then.'

She looks at Carys aghast. 'Of course I went to the police. I saw Bill murder Alice.'

'But did you?'

'Yes.'

'But you were certain that he murdered a lover and a child, and that didn't actually happen.'

'That was on the way to remembering the truth. Ajay says—'

Carys holds up her hands. 'I don't want to hear what Ajay says.'

'What? Why? You found him. You said he was the best. And you were right. He is! He's helped me see the truth!'

'He's dangerous, Lucy.' Carys takes a breath. 'Do you know he worked with your mum?'

Lucy shakes her head and laughs. 'No, he didn't. He would have said.'

'He worked with her and he made her life hell.'

'No.'

'He was obsessed with her. He's used me and he's used you to get back at Bill because he is jealous at him for having had Alice's love.'

'No. You're lying,' Lucy says. 'And I know why. Bill has brainwashed you. He's the one who's dangerous. Really danger-ous. He may be all pretend perfect, but he's far from it. He's dangerous, dangerous, dangerous.'

'No. He's not. He's having a hard time at the moment—'

'He's always having a hard time. Don't you see? You're always excusing him for something. And do you know what that is, right in his rotten heart? It's that he murdered his wife.' Lucy nods and points at Carys, touching her chest with her finger. 'You need to be careful. One wrong step and he might do it to you too. You think you're in control, but you're not. My mum was perfect. She loved us all so much, and he took her away.'

This is too much. 'That's not how it was,' Carys says. 'Your mum wasn't perfect. She was a human being like all of us. She was weak, and she was a coward and she left you—'

'No! Even if she had killed herself – which she didn't, because she was murdered – it would have been because of an illness. You said that. You've always said that.'

'No, Lucy.'

'It was like cancer, or heart disease, you said. She had a poorly soul.' Lucy glows, like a saint possessed by love.

Carys can't bear it. This has to stop. Lucy has to stop

blaming Bill, and most importantly, she needs to know the truth. Sometimes you have to be cruel to be kind.

'Lucy. Your mother is still alive. You have to hear this. She walked out on you all.'

Lucy stares at her open-mouthed, looking like she's torn between laughing and howling. 'No. No. Bullshit! Why are you saying that? Of course she wouldn't do that. She loved us too much to do that.'

'I'm afraid she did do that.'

'She didn't. She was murdered. By my father. By your husband.'

And suddenly Carys realises what all this is. It's a story Lucy has made up to protect herself from the fact that her mother left her voluntarily – either by suicide or, as what actually happened, choice.

Feeling so sorry for her, but desperate for the truth to put a stop to her wild accusations, she reaches into her bag.

'She's still alive, Lucy. She sent me this.' She hands Lucy the letter and braces herself for whatever the fallout will be.

Is this the wisest or the stupidest thing she could do?

All she knows is that she agrees with Sara that there is messed-up shit going on in the family and it needs to stop.

As Lucy reads the letter, sitting as still as the angel statue guarding the grave behind her, Carys counts in her head, like a soldier who has just thrown a grenade. She's reached eighty-two when, in a move so sudden it makes her gasp, Lucy screws the paper into a ball, flings it on the ground and shakes her head so wildly the flesh on her face can't keep up.

'No, no, no!' she says. 'No. This isn't true.' She's on her feet now. 'I *know* what happened, Carys. This is a fake. Why are you doing this? I thought I could trust Sara, but no. I thought at least I could trust you, but you do this? *You do this?*'

Howling, she grabs her rucksack and takes off, tearing down

the gravel path that leads through the crumbling graves and
onto Pancras Road.

'Lucy!' Carys calls out. But Lucy is running like she has the
devil at her heels.

Carys picks up the letter and stuffs it in her bag, which she
slings over her shoulder. Then she sets off after her.

Fit from all her cycling, she thinks she will easily catch up
with her. But Lucy is fast. And Carys's bladder is full, her tits
hurt, and something in her body is telling her not to give the
running her all for the sake of her baby.

Put your real child first, it says, over the one you've inherited from a selfish witch.

So Lucy gets away. But Carys keeps her in her sights as she
pelts along the road, down the side of the back of the station, the
functional part of the building, so far removed from its grand
front end on Euston Road.

Lucy turns left into the station, which is a problem, as it will
be easy to lose her in there. As Carys follows her, she spies her
taking a sharp left to throw herself under a ticket barrier,
heading towards the Thameslink platforms.

As a station guard joins the chase to catch the fare-dodger,
Carys slows and fumbles for her phone, whacking it down on
the card reader to open the gate. She takes the stairs down
rather than the escalator, which is crowded now with rush-hour
commuters. In doing so, she gains some advantage on Lucy and
the guard, who get clogged up with a group of those infuriating
people who stand on the left-hand side.

By the time they reach the first landing, Carys is hot on
Lucy's heels. But Lucy launches herself at the second escalator,
almost tumbling down it. Again Carys takes the stairs, but this
time she loses ground.

Lucy turns left and runs along the crowded platform,
barging past the thick knot of people waiting for the Brighton
train, which is just arriving at the other end of the platform.

Carys tries to catch up. The train comes up behind her, its brakes squealing as it slows, ready to stop.

Lucy looks back over her shoulder, still running ahead of the slowing train. For one second her eyes meet Carys's, and Carys sees her fear, her horror, her I-don't-want-this-any-more.

And then she is gone. Down onto the rails and under the front wheels of the train just before it hisses to a stop.

'LUCY!' Carys yells.

Somewhere by the front of the train, a woman screams.

A man shouts.

Another woman cries out, 'Jesus Christ. No.'

Carys realises the voice is her own.

THIRTY-SEVEN

It's 4 a.m. That part of the morning that feels cold even in midsummer. Carys helps Bill into the side bay where they've put Lucy. He is so broken by this she wonders if he will ever recover.

And it's all her fault.

She tries to think back to standing with Artur yesterday morning, chatting at the Five Oaks site, feeling that something newer and better was happening, a new start.

It feels like several thousand years ago.

And now here is Lucy, lying on her back, her mouth slightly open, her recently hacked hair hidden underneath a turban of bandages. A tube snakes in through her cyan lips and, Carys imagines, goes some way deep into her lungs. It's attached to a section of semi-transparent blue tubing that rests on her shoulder, filtering oxygen into her.

Her eyes – both with perfect, heartbreaking comic-book shiners – are taped shut. Her chest, left accessibly bare above a sheet positioned to cover her breasts, is almost invisible under a thicket of needles and wires going in and out of her. Her arms lie cushioned by waffle blankets, her hands bristling with yet more cannulas and tubing. Bags of various in and out liquids – each a different colour and opacity – are slung around her bed, and a rolled-up towel stops her head from lolling.

Around her, noises – beeps, pumps, squirts – provide a low-level percussive background, and the clean tang of sanitiser is tinged with a waft of bad breath and a slight undercurrent of faeces.

Some stroke of luck made Lucy glance off the front end of the slowing train and pitch down into the gulley between the wheels. Both of her legs are broken, and she has flail chest, which is as bad as it sounds. Her ruptured spleen has been removed. But worst of all, she received a blow to the head that not only fractured her skull but also gave her brain 'a proper pummelling', as the kind but rather gung-ho surgeon told Bill, Carys and Sara after he came out of an eight-hour session in the operating theatre.

Poor Lucy's body is now as broken as her spirit, and Carys wants to slam her own head against the wall over and over again, because yes, it's all her fault.

She is as responsible for this damage to Lucy as Alice was for what happened to poor Emily. It doesn't even have the tiniest whiff of revenge to it.

They're keeping Lucy in the netherworld of an induced coma. Without this slowing-down, the surgeon explained, her body would perform radical triage and shut off blood flow to the damaged sections of her brain, thus killing them. 'This way gives the brain time to heal,' he said.

Carys hates all this talk, which reduces Lucy to a collection of damaged parts.

Parts damaged by her.

As she takes all this in, she wonders if she should tell Alice what has happened to her daughter. But she almost instantly wipes this alarming thought from her head. She doesn't have any contact details, and more importantly, Alice doesn't have any right to know.

'Oh, Luce.' Bill pulls up one of the two plastic chairs beside the bed and sits, pressing his cheek onto the bare flesh of his daughter's arm. He closes his eyes. 'Why did you do this?'

Carys stands a little way back. She knows exactly what the answer to that is, but there is absolutely no way she can tell him. A part of her that she knows is despicable is worrying about what happens when – if – Lucy wakes up and tells him. She stamps the thought right down.

'My love,' Bill says, 'when you come back to us, I'm going to move heaven and earth for you. We'll put all this behind us. We've got a little baby on the way, and he or she is going to love you so much, and you are going to be such a great big sister.'

Carys sits on the chair on the other side of Lucy and rests her hand on her shoulder. 'Binnie sends her love. She's going to make a card for you and the nurse says she'll pin it on the board behind your bed.'

Carys tries to forget how upset Binnie was at the news about Lucy by thinking about the new home she'll find for everyone. It'll have to be accessible, so if Lucy doesn't entirely recover from this she will be able to live as full a life as possible. A modernist single-storey building, perhaps, in a leafy part of Cambridgeshire. Or even Suffolk. Somewhere with fresh air so they can breathe in a new life and leave all of this behind them. Big windows, lots of wood.

She pulls herself up. This is not what she should be thinking about right now. She does a quick stock-take. Binnie is, finally, with Edina. Bill was in no place to even think about objecting. Edina also agreed to have Nonna and drove to the hospital to pick up both girl and dog after Bill, in a panic and not really thinking, brought them with him in a taxi.

Sara is in the relatives' room, waiting her turn to see Lucy, because only two visitors are allowed at a time. The nurses and doctors are busy on the other side of the glass wall of the cubicle, attending to patients spaced around the room like ghost ships anchored to life support. From time to time the nurse Lucy shares with one other suspended soul comes in and checks her monitors and types something into the computer terminal at the end of her bed.

Carys and Bill fill the spaces with talk they imagine will cheer Lucy if she can hear it. They tell her about the Airbnb, how lovely it is to actually live in central London, like being on holiday. Carys talks about the trees they have yet to see from Alice's book, Bill recalls holidays they went on back when Alice was around.

Why the Alice holidays? Carys thinks with a sharp, vicious pang. But she deserves all the punishment she gets tonight. And Bill is almost smiling as he conjures that time in Crete when Alice bought Lucy two ice creams, one for each hand, and Lucy cried at the sheer joy of it.

'Fuck.'

Carys wheels round. Sara has snuck in and is standing behind her, her hand over her mouth, looking at her sister. 'What the hell?'

Bill looks sharply up at her. 'We're only supposed to be two at a time.'

Sara looks at Carys. 'What have you done to her?'

'Sara!' Bill says, like she is still his toddler daughter.

'She's upset.' Carys stands and puts her arm around Sara's tense shoulders and guides her into the chair she has vacated. 'The nurse says Lucy can probably hear us. Tell her nice things.'

And Sara starts reaching into the same memories that Bill has been playing, and as the two of them bow their heads close to Lucy, whispering a litany of good times past, the years of division and hostility seem to melt around them.

The nurse comes in again to check on Lucy, and stops, looking disapprovingly at the surfeit of people at the bedside. Carys apologises, puts up her hands and bows out.

Leave the blood ties to get on with it.

She glances around for her bag, then remembers that she doesn't have it with her, that at some point she lost it. Perhaps she dropped it on the platform, perhaps she left it in the ambulance as she sat beside Lucy, so numb with shock that the paramedic briefly turned her attention her way.

She'll have to cancel her bank and credit cards, notify the police. Oh God, her wallet, containing not only two hundred quid but also Binnie's little note, scrawled when she was three: *I lov yo mummy*, neatly folded and tucked inside a small St Christopher locket that also contains a tiny picture of Carys's mum and dad at her own christening. All irreplaceable.

But all just things, stuff, while not twenty metres away from her, Lucy lies lost between dead and alive.

She retires to the relatives' room, kicks off her Birkenstocks and lies flat out on a sofa probably chosen because of its suitability for people to do exactly this.

She feels like the last string of a pulled-out piece of toffee, the moment before it breaks. Her ears still ring with the awful silence that fell after she called out and everyone on the platform realised what had happened. The horror of not knowing what was left of Lucy until the train was backed up and the rescue workers reached her still sits in her stomach.

It is her fault. All this.

She came into this family like an avenging angel and has pulled them apart. Without even trying – without even wanting to – she has balanced the scales of justice for Emily. A damaged brain for a damaged brain. An atomised family.

And although this was largely her aim when she was a

teenager, from where she stands right now it is the worst possible thing that could have happened.

She has to put things right.

With that thought, somehow, somehow – perhaps her body's response to some whispered message from her baby – she sleeps.

THIRTY-EIGHT

Someone lifts her legs and puts their arms around her ankles, and like a pearl diver she surfaces, clutching her dreams. Bill is sitting at the other end of the sofa, gazing at her.

'You looked so beautiful there,' he says, stroking her bare feet.

Carys rubs her eyes and props her head up on the sofa arm. 'How is she?'

'They're doing something to her.'

Alarmed, she tries to extricate her feet from his hands so she can get up.

'It's routine, not an emergency,' he says, keeping hold of her.

'Tea.' Sara backs through the door with three mugs. She hands one to Bill, places another on the lino by Carys, then sits in the armchair opposite them.

Carys swings her legs round and takes the tea. They sip in silence.

'I want all this to stop,' Sara says at last.

'Yes.' Carys nods.

'Put me at the top of that list,' Bill says.

But Sara is looking right at Carys. 'You haven't told him, have you?' she says.

Carys swallows. 'Told him what?' Because she isn't sure which of her many secrets Sara is referring to.

Sara turns to Bill. 'If there's any question about how Mum died, you need to look at your wife.'

Bill closes his eyes. 'What the hell are you talking about now?'

'Tell him, Carys.'

Carys shakes her head. 'We don't need to do this now.'

'Wait. What?' Bill says, looking at her. 'Do what?'

Sara sits back and folds her arms. 'Carys hounded Lucy to this.'

Carys puts her hands over her eyes. She can't believe Sara has chosen this moment to do it.

It's what she deserves, though.

'Lucy was – is – in the middle of an episode triggered by that hypnotherapist Carys put her onto. Carys asked to meet her – Luce showed me the text – but instead of offering her comfort, she says things to her, no idea what, that so freak her out she ends up throwing herself under a train.'

Sara smiles grimly, like she has finally put Carys in her place, which, of course, she has.

Bill looks at Carys. 'What? Is that true?'

Carys nods.

In all the upheaval and difficulty of the past twelve hours, she blurted the totally unconvincing and impromptu explanation that on her way to get a train up to St Albans to view the site for the school project she has yet to tell him about, she saw Lucy running through the ticket gates in a distressed state, so she followed her.

In shock, Bill bought it entirely. But now he's looking at his wife with the face of a man betrayed.

'You promised you weren't going to contact her,' he says.

Carys just looks at her feet. Her nice little pedicure is beginning to go at the edges.

'And while I'm shovelling Carys's shit, can she tell you something else?' Sara says.

'No,' Carys says. 'Please, no.'

'What?' Bill says.

'I can't.'

'Best leave it to me, then,' Sara says. 'So, Bill. You know the baby Mum made the mistake with in Hull? After she'd worked two full shifts in a row and the mother said she wanted a natural birth and she went along with it too long and the baby suffered brain injuries?'

Carys breathes in sharply. That's not the story she heard from her parents. She wants to beat a path to the door, to the street, to the motorway, to the ocean. Anywhere other than here.

'What is this?' Bill says.

'That was Carys's mum wanting the natural birth. That baby was Carys's sister.'

'No,' Bill says. 'That's not true. Is it?'

Carys can't meet his eye.

'Carys didn't just arrive in your office twelve years later because she liked your groundbreaking eco approach to architecture. No. She tracked you down because she wanted to get back at Alice.'

Bill is looking at Carys in the same way he might regard a wall built badly by a drunken brickie.

'Is this true?' he says.

She can't move her head or open her mouth.

'Like I said,' Sara says, 'if there are any question marks over how Mum died, this is the person you need to ask.'

Bill looks at Carys like he might cry. 'You sought us out?'

Carys finds herself nodding.

'And that was your little sister?'

'Yes.' Her voice feels like it's coming from a metre behind her.

He frowns. 'Did you ever meet Alice, then?'

Carys closes her eyes and nods again.

'I never knew you met her,' he says, astonished.

'She did.' Sara's voice is low, like it's rumbling from the bottom of a deep, nightmarish ocean. 'She probably met Mum time and time again. Sweet Carys, reminding poor Alice of her terrible mistake, the mistake she needed no reminding about. The mistake that caused a breakdown and a life of regret and self-flagellation. Sweet Carys. Sticking the knife in and twisting it again and again.'

Carys looks at her through stinging eyes. 'I saw her once.'

Once was all it took to forgive her for what she'd done to Emily. Alice convinced her in that one meeting that she was at heart a good woman, who had done the time psychologically for a terrible error.

How wrong Carys had been, given what she now knows.

'I met her once, when she was dropping Lucy off at school. I was upset at first and confronted her. Lucy saw. I don't know how much she heard. I'm sorry.'

'The question is, Dad,' Sara goes on, 'and I'm speaking as a recently divorced woman whose husband was screwing someone else behind her back: Were you just another way for Carys to get back at Alice? What exactly was the sequence of events?'

Bill is on his feet now. 'No!' he roars. 'I did not cheat on your mother!'

'There's no need to shout.'

He gathers himself, sits down with his back to Carys so that he can just speak to Sara. 'I would never have done that.' He takes her hands. 'Look. Life was too much for your mother. She killed herself because of the grief of losing Danny, the pressure of work, the guilt from Hull, which I now know she was not being allowed to forget.' He throws a look over his shoulder at Carys as he says this.

If only she had her bag, she could uncrumple the letter, hold it up and wave it like a victory flag, show Sara and Bill that, along with them, she too is an innocent victim of Alice's cowardice and deception.

But her bag is missing, and to tell them about the letter without proof at this moment would look like the act of a desperate woman.

Which would be pretty accurate.

'And then,' Bill goes on to Sara, 'your Tom going on at her, and on top of that, Carys's precious Ajay...'

'I'm sorry. I'm sorry.' Carys is crying now.

'...stalking her and making her life a misery.'

'Wait. What?' Sara says. 'Ajay stalked Mum?'

'He worked at her centre back then,' Bill says. 'He was obsessed.'

'I knew there was something off about him,' Sara says.

'She was afraid for her life,' Bill goes on. 'He even threatened to kill you and Lucy to make her suffer.'

'What?' Carys is horrified. Alice didn't mention that in the letter. 'You never told me that. Did Alice know?'

Bill looks round at her and it's as though he can see right through her. 'Why do you ask?'

'I... I...' Carys feels the weight of what she is keeping from him, but she can't let it out. She can't.

'He stalked Carys too.' Bill turns back to Sara. 'And she stupidly fell for his patter, which is why Lucy is there.' He points towards the wall, on the other side of which Lucy lies in her coma. 'Ajay Gupta hates me. He wants everything I've got. And he drove Alice to her death. She killed herself to save you.'

'Oh, Mum.' Sara is as near tears as Carys has ever seen her.

Bill turns to Carys. 'And now I find out about you, about

how you only showed any interest in me because you wanted to get your hands on my wife.'

Carys is on her feet, reaching out for him. 'It's not what it looks like. Yes, I wanted to meet Alice, try to understand what happened—'

'Get your revenge, you mean,' Sara says.

'—but I fell in love with you, Bill.'

'And Alice dying was pretty handy for you, wasn't it?' Sara says. 'Cleared the field, ready for you to step right in with the Florence Nightingale act.'

This is too much for Carys. 'Please. Just shut up!' Her voice comes out as a screech. Like that of a demented harpy.

Sara raises a triumphant eyebrow. 'Ah. Now she's showing her true colours. Haven't seen this side of her before, have you, Bill – sorry, Dad?'

Carys looks at Bill, who is staring at her like she's a stranger.

'So Alice's body was never found,' Sara goes on. 'And who knows how much Carys is to blame for her death. Who knows what she knows about it, what she hasn't told us.'

Bill keeps his eyes locked on her. 'Is there anything you want to tell us, Carys?'

Despite the fact that she is burning to tell them Alice is still alive, Carys says nothing. They wouldn't believe her. It would be an utterly disastrous step for her to take.

'I'm sorry. Really sorry. But I had nothing to do with Alice's death,' is all she can say. 'I spoke to her once. I was satisfied that she had accounted for what she had done in the way she'd led her life since she left Hull.'

'Like you're some moral arbiter,' Sara spits at her.

'Enough now, Sara!' Bill swipes his hand through the air. 'I... I...'

He can't find the words. Instead, he grabs his cane and heads for the door. He goes fast, but his gait is uneven, lumbering.

Like that, Carys suddenly sees, of an old man.

She makes to go after him, but Sara puts her hand on her chest and pushes her backwards.

'You've done enough damage chasing after people. You stay here with all the messes you've created and let me go after my father. Don't you think you've put him through enough?'

Angry as she is with Sara, Carys does as she's told.

Alone in the room, she sits on the sofa, and tries her very best to breathe. In her pocket, her phone vibrates. It's Edina, asking how things are going. Carys texts her reply:

Grim. Are Bins and Nonna OK?

Edina replies that everything is grand, and she and her wife are happy to play mummies and mummies as long as they need to. She adds a photo of Binnie, Nonna and a beautiful blonde woman who looks about twenty, and signs off with a kiss. For one second Carys wonders if she's messing up here too, allowing Binnie to stay with a stranger. But unlike Carys, Edina is a good judge of character. That child bride will be a lovely person.

The only worry Carys has about that part of the situation is that Binnie won't want to come back to her flawed, lying weasel of a mother.

'Mum?'

Carys looks up. It's Lucy's nurse Dorothy, a kindly older woman who reminds her of her grandma.

'You can go back to Lucy now, my dear.'

As they walk back to the ICU, Dorothy turns to her. 'Did Dad and sister go get some rest?'

Carys nods. In a way, she supposes that's right. Rest from her.

She sits beside Lucy, and for the first time in her life, she prays.

'Carys?'

Recognising the voice, but not quite believing it, she looks up.

THIRTY-NINE

'I can't believe it.' Ajay is looking at Lucy with so much horror, guilt and shame that for a brief moment, Carys almost feels sorry for him.

'Who let you in here?' she says. 'Go away.'

He is a deathly yellowish pale. He pulls a chair up next to hers and sits facing her, like a sinner seeking absolution from a priest. 'How is she?'

'How do you think?'

He grabs her arms. 'This wasn't meant to happen.'

She tries to shrug him off, but his grip is strong. 'Oh, wasn't it?'

'Is she going to die?'

'Quiet, Ajay. She can hear everything that's going on.' She wrenches herself out of his grip. 'What do you want? Why have you come here?'

'I'm so sorry.'

'Couldn't you see that messing around with her brain was going to cause trouble? That a self-harming girl was only going to do more damage to herself if you led her down the path to crazy?'

Ajay's face hardens. 'I didn't do that.'

'You did! You filled her head with the most outrageous bullshit.'

'No. She did it herself. It was a process, a path to unlocking the truth.'

'"A path to unlocking the truth"?' she says, mocking his reedy voice. 'This crap now about Bill killing Alice?'

'It's not crap.'

'It is. I know for a fact that Alice isn't dead.'

He blinks, horror on his face. 'You what?'

'If I had it, I'd show you—' She tells him about the letter.

He looks at her, open-mouthed. 'No,' he says. 'Someone's playing a trick on you.'

'Playing a trick?'

His pallor has gone. 'She's dead. I know she's dead.'

Carys looks at him, her eyes steel. 'I thought you might have killed her, in fact—'

'What?'

'—and you nearly did: stalking her, making her life unbearable, threatening her...'

'I didn't do any of that!' He grasps her knees, his fingers digging into her flesh.

She readies herself to shout for help, but she has to go on. She has to tell him what she thinks of him, and what she now knows. 'You did, Ajay. She told Bill about it. And you threatened her children! How could you do that? If she *had* killed herself, *you* would have been responsible for it. She says so in the letter. As it is, you are the main reason she walked away from her family.'

Ajay gasps in disbelief. 'What?'

'She tried to kill herself, but she couldn't do it, so she disappeared.'

'You believe that?'

'You hounded her until she was unable to bear it any more.'

He takes his hands from her knees and grabs her arms and shakes her. 'I *loved* her and she loved me.'

'You're deluded. She didn't love you. She loved Bill. But she didn't love herself, and because of you, she was frightened for her family.'

'She was frightened of Bill!'

'*You're* frightening *me*. Let me go.' He loosens his grip and Carys shakes herself free again. 'I'm not listening to your bull-shit any more. I can't believe I didn't see through you right from the start.'

He falls to his knees and looks up at her in a way that so shows the level of his delusion it makes her want to vomit. 'She told him about us and he wouldn't have it. The day she died—'

'You stalked me too, tracked me down to Coldfall Woods.'

'—she came to see me in my room. She said Bill had told her that if she left him, he would kill her.'

Carys stands and moves away, backwards against Lucy's monitors. 'That's just your fantasy. That's not Bill!'

Ajay follows her on his knees. 'You have to be careful with him. He's dangerous.'

'Is that what you told Alice to try to get her away from him? Listen: you can't have Alice and you can't have me, and even though you nearly got hold of Lucy's soul, you can't have her either.' She dodges around him and dashes to Lucy's bed, standing guard in front of her.

Ajay looks more like a spider than ever as he struggles to his feet and stands to face her. He keeps his distance, but he is so much taller than her she feels like she is under a crane swinging a dangerous load. Every part of her is telling her to run, but she can't leave Lucy alone with him.

'Look.' He holds out his hands, trying to show that he is speaking sense. It doesn't work. 'What Lucy saw in the last session—'

'That Bill killed Alice? Alice who's still alive?'

'—is the truth. We're nearly there. We'll find her poor body soon enough.'

'Ajay. There's no "we" about it. There never has been. There's no body, either. You're out of this.' Carys has had enough. She steps out of Lucy's side room and summons Dorothy. 'Can you get security, please? I want this man kept away from Lucy.'

Dorothy nods and hurries off.

'I'm going to keep an eye on you both,' Ajay tells her. 'And if I can save you from him, I certainly will.'

'You're not coming near any of us ever again. I'll involve the police if I have to.'

Two uniformed security guards appear and position themselves either side of him.

'Come on, mate,' one of them says. 'Let's leave the poor girls alone.'

When they try to take his arms, Ajay holds them up in the air. 'Don't touch me. I'm coming.' As he is hustled out, he turns to look at Carys. 'He's dangerous, remember, Carys. And I'm always here if you need me.'

She turns her back on him.

'We can get a picture from the CCTV, and I'll put a card up by the buzzer at the nurses' station,' Dorothy says, once Ajay is safely the other side of the ICU doors. 'Even if he gets in downstairs, there's no way he'll be allowed onto the ward.'

Carys takes her hands. 'Thank you,' she says.

Alone with Lucy, she lays her forehead on the blanket on her bed and prays for forgiveness for ever putting this poor girl into Ajay's clutches.

FORTY

'It really does look like it's growing strawberries,' Tom says as, rucksack slung over his shoulder, he walks up the box-lined path towards Sara, who is taking photographs of the fruiting tree.

She turns, and despite the fact that her soul feels like it's on the bottom of her shoes, the sight of him makes her smile. 'It's just like Mum's drawing, isn't it?' She points to Alice's book, which she has brought from the hospital and which lies open on the bench behind her, only a little damaged from its encounter with the train.

While she was sitting with Lucy this afternoon, she arranged to meet Tom here in Waterlow Park, the 'garden for the gardenless' in north London. All around her, other people are having their summer-evening fun. A gang of children chase each other over the lawns while their parents loll by the remains of a picnic; a Lycra-clad fitness group run round football markers; a group of lads giggle in a skunk haze. Other lives, going on, while hers festers like bacteria in a Petri dish.

The strawberry tree was next on Lucy's schedule. As she sat beside her hospital bed, Sara decided to keep the visits going. She's photographing the tree for Lucy's Instagram page and feeling sorry that she hasn't got her little sister's eye for a striking image.

'Shall we?' Tom points to the bench.

Sara closes the book and puts it back in her bag, and they sit.

'Well then, here we go.' He unzips his rucksack and takes out two paninis and a couple of bottles of Heineken. 'You must eat.' He hands one of the paninis to Sara and uses an opener on his key ring to pop the tops off the beers.

'You shouldn't have,' she says as she unwraps the sandwich. She is, she realises, starving.

'But I did. Napkin?'

Sara could weep. Since she arrived in the UK – most of her life, in fact – she has been the one doing the looking-after. To be cared for like this feels strange and wonderful. And then she remembers how Tom's almost pathological looking-after of her after Alice's death suffocated her.

'I'm all right, thanks,' she says, pulling a tissue from her pocket.

'How is she?' he asks as they eat.

'They plan to keep her in the coma for at least a week.'

'Who's with her?'

'Now she's settled, we have to stick to normal visiting hours, which are over. I've arranged with Carys that she does the mornings and I do afternoons so we don't have to see each other.'

'Why so?'

'This morning – which seems like a year ago – I told Bill about how Carys used him to track Mum down.'

'You did? Whoa.'

'I know. Timing was a bit shit, but he has to know.'

'So who'll he be visiting Lucy with?'

Sara shrugs. 'Up to him. I'd rather be on my own, though.'

'What did he say when you told him?'

'He was devastated, of course. But it's important he knows the truth about just how twisted little Ms Perfect actually is.'

Tom frowns. 'But she's stayed with him, hasn't she? And she stepped in and looked after him after your mum died. And she took Lucy on.'

'Hey! Whose side are you on?'

He holds up his hands and smiles. 'The side of fairness, integrity, diligence and impartiality.'

'Yeah, yeah, Mr Policeman. But Carys is a pathological carer, plus all that was probably fired by guilt at driving Mum to her death – or worse.'

'You're not suggesting...'

'She's always been a social climber. Marrying Bill bought her a place in society, a lovely house, a fast track to a partnership in the firm. Oh, and she got her hands fully on that, by the way: changed the name, made it just him and her and an admin person, set them off on doing this affordable housing, blah blah.'

Tom frowns. 'You're very bitter.'

'Of course I'm fucking bitter.'

He eats the last piece of his panini, wipes his fingers with his napkin and turns to face her. 'OK. I've been doing that research you wanted me to do. Looking through the evidence from Alice's death.'

'They've still got it?'

He nods. 'It appears that despite the suicide verdict, a DC Amandeep Kaur in Sussex smelled a fish and applied for all the materials to be archived.'

'Wow. Did you speak to her?'

'She's no longer with us, sadly. Leukaemia.'

'Damn.'

'But she did a great job. Itemised everything from the car Alice left at Beachy Head, pointing out the elements that caused her concern and why. She was new, a trainee detective, and no one took her seriously, so she must have had a battle to get the exhibits archived. And then she went off sick soon after and never came back.'

'What a waste.'

'Yeah. But this is such a fine legacy.' He draws an iPad from the padded pocket of his rucksack and pulls up some photographs. 'The interior of Alice's car. What do you notice?'

'Are you giving me a detective test?'

He smiles. 'No! I want to see what you think, coming at it fresh.'

She takes the iPad and zooms in on the photograph, holding the screen close to her face. 'It's a mess – Dad always said she drove a dustbin, not a car. Look – coffee cups, a notebook lying in the passenger footwell. A half-eaten pasty in the bit between the driver and passenger seats. There's the little cat I made her when I was a kid, to hang from the mirror.' The sight of the hand-painted pink model, made from some kit she got one Christmas, hurts her chest. It disappeared from her life along with the car and her mother.

'OK. What else?'

She scrolls through the photographs. 'The back seats are folded down. That's unusual. They were usually up because she drove us to school and clubs and stuff. There's a dirty spade in the boot. Weird. Oh, hang on: she and a couple of the other people at the health centre were working on the garden there when she disappeared – they called it the calm garden. She'd been going on at me, trying to rope me in...'

For a second, the anger at how her busy, connected, brilliant mother was snuffed out means that Sara can't go on. She takes a deep breath then dives in again, scrutinising the photo on the screen. 'And there's a blanket by the spade, with dark patches on it.'

'Good. Forensics say that's oil, not blood. Go back to the pictures of the front seats.'

'There's a pillow on the passenger seat, which is reclined a bit. Mum always kept a pillow in the boot in case either of us needed a nap.'

'Good detail. And?'

She frowns, looking at the photograph. Then, with a jolt, she spots it. 'Fuck sake.'

'Are you seeing it?'

She nods. 'The driver seat is pushed way back.'

'Yes.'

'Mum was barely five foot one, and she always drove close up, like she was hugging the wheel.'

'That's what I remember. We laughed about it, didn't we?'

She looks at him. 'We did.'

She zooms in and sees the acres of space between the seat and the muddy pedals. Too far for Alice to reach. 'Perhaps she pushed the seat back before she got out?'

'Possibly. I'm sure that's what Amandeep was told when she flagged it up. Everyone wanted a neat suicide verdict.' Tom takes the iPad and brings up another photograph. 'Here's the note.'

Sara knows about the note, about what it said, but she's never actually seen it. It's a sheet torn from a prescription pad with *I'm sorry* written on it in what looks like Alice's handwriting – the thick pen, the small capital Rs, the italic flourish.

'She was really strict about prescription pads. When I was about eight, I got hold of one from her bag and wrote pretend scripts on it for my dolls. She went ballistic.'

'If she was suicidal, she was probably beyond caring.'

'True. It just seems odd, though. Why use that when that notebook is there? Hold on.' She zooms in on the pasty. 'That's meat, isn't it?'

Tom takes the iPad and scrutinises the grey mulch in the chewed pastry. 'Looks like a Ginsters classic.'

'Mum was a staunch vegetarian, and she was a proper clean

eater, too. It had to be organic and home-made for her. She'd never touch anything like that.'

'So what are we saying? She could have pushed the driver's seat back, she could have had a sneaky meat pasty habit, she could have had a snooze in the passenger seat before walking to the cliff edge, she could have seen the poetic virtues of writing a suicide note on a prescription pad and she could have wrapped an old engine or something in a blanket and driven it to the tip en route to killing herself?'

'Please, Tom.'

'Sorry. Or...'

'A tall meat-eater drove her there while she was sleeping and pushed her off?'

'Could be.'

'So not Carys, then.'

'Do you really think Carys is capable of murder?'

Sara thinks for a few moments. 'No. I think she's a coward, a liar, a user...'

Tom looks at her. 'Not a sister and daughter trying to find justice?'

She pointedly ignores the parallel he is clearly drawing, and goes on. 'A gold-digger...'

'Who genuinely fell in love with a man and took him on, shattered family and all.'

Sara sighs. 'You always were a romantic.'

'Still am. And that's how it looks to me. Once she was in, she couldn't tell the truth. Perhaps kept putting it off and off until it was too late.'

'Can we go back to the evidence, please?'

Shaking his head, he holds up the screen. 'OK. So this person then faked the suicide note – not hard to do with such characteristic handwriting.'

'Had to be someone who knew what it was like, though.'

'I want to show you what was found caught in some

hawthorns on the edge of the cliff.' He brings up another image and hands her the iPad.

She suddenly feels horribly weary. 'Mum's yellow tartan scarf.'

'Yup. That's where they found it. This' – he swipes to another picture – 'is when I guess Amandeep laid it out to be photographed. See here?'

He points to where the scarf becomes narrower in the middle of its length. The tartan is elongated, and the fabric looks like it is at the very end of its stretch before breaking.

Sara looks at him, horror in her eyes. 'Like it's been used to strangle someone. Like Lucy said, and we all thought she was talking rubbish.'

'The girl who cried wolf?'

The ham and cheese sit heavily in Sara's stomach. 'Don't.'

'And finally there's this.' Tom shows her a photograph of a motorbike trailer. 'Abandoned in the next car park. The official view was that it had no connection to the inquiry. But look at it. Who dumps a brand-new motorbike trailer?'

'Perhaps someone was going to pick it up later?'

'Amandeep clearly took a trip down there later off her own bat, because she notes it was still there six weeks after the "alleged suicide of Ms Herman".'

'But if someone wanted to hide it, why didn't they push it off the cliff?'

'That would have looked way more suspicious.'

'So if we're going along with our meat-eating tall person, we're looking at a motorbike getaway from the abandoned vehicle.'

Tom nods.

'You know this all points to Dad?' Sara says.

'Yes.'

'But it can't have been him. Despite everything, he loved Mum with all his heart.'

'They argued.'

'Doesn't everyone? She was difficult. And she had her own challenges. But I sometimes felt left out because they were so tight together.'

'Children don't see everything.'

'Even so.'

'So who else could it be?'

'Ajay's tall and he has a motorbike. And Dad said this morning that he stalked and threatened Mum.'

'He said that when we had him in custody and I didn't believe it.'

'I wouldn't have believed it before I saw him in action with Lucy.'

'I thought Bill was just trying to deflect his own guilt at what he had done in The Wilderness. I'm so stupid.' Tom slaps his forehead. 'He said that Ajay was manipulating Lucy to get back at him yet again. To make his life hell.'

'My God. Poor Lucy.'

Tom shakes his head. 'I should have listened to him.'

'I actually witnessed Ajay planting Bill's name during that last session. When Lucy said she saw someone pull the tartan scarf around Mum's neck, he asked specifically if it was Bill.'

'Don't ask leading questions. Interview Technique 101,' Tom says.

'I know! I thought it was odd, but you know, hypnotism. It's different.'

'It isn't.'

'So we think that at the very least, Ajay used Lucy in some sick game to get at Bill?'

'At the very least.' Tom grabs her hand. 'And I hope this proves to you that however much of a stupid idiot I was when I went to Alice and tried to get her to make you stay with me, the fact that I was one of the last people to see her had nothing to do with her death.'

She pulls her hand away and stands, looking at him open-mouthed. 'Is that what all this is about? To prove your own innocence?'

'I've felt so guilty about it.'

She looks at him, disgusted. 'You want me to forgive you?'

'No! No. I want justice for Alice. Whatever it takes.'

But Sara doesn't hear this, because she is walking away, leaving the beers, the evidence, Tom, behind.

He knows better this time.

He lets her go.

FORTY-ONE

'What the hell are you doing?' Carys asks.

'I'm looking through your things,' Bill says, although it comes out more like 'I shlooking shroo tor fins.'

He is drunk.

She hadn't wanted to face him after the showdown this morning. So when Sara texted to dismiss her from Lucy's bedside for the afternoon, despite having slept perhaps two hours tops, she got a bus to the Five Oaks site office. She had phoned Tina earlier to give her the news and to pass on her apologies to Artur for not being on site first thing as planned. So, when she turned up, every single builder looked at her with toe-curling pity, as if she had been bereaved.

Not feeling worthy of their sympathy, she spent the afternoon cracking the whip on the building site, so by the end of the day most of the men probably hated her as much as she reckons she deserves.

She then had to rush to pick Binnie and Nonna up from Edina's.

'You've not been at work?' Edina said.

Carys nodded, trying to keep back the tears so as not to upset Binnie any further.

'Call me,' Edina whispered to her as she handed over the bag containing dog and child essentials. 'We had fun, didn't we, Binnie?'

Binnie nodded.

So much fun, in fact, that as they walked the three miles or so back to the Airbnb – Carys was spinning the hours out as much as possible before having to face Bill – Binnie said she wanted to visit Edina and Juliet every day.

'But what about your new play scheme?' Carys asked.

'I hate it. I don't know anyone. I want to go back to my old play scheme with all my friends.'

'You'll make new friends soon enough.' Going back would be impossible for Carys because bloody Fiona is still muck-raking on her bloody blog.

'No smoke without fire' is the grotesque slogan this week, underscored by 'watch your kids around certain individuals' and supported by accounts about communities in other parts of the world that may or may not have 'unknowingly had paedophiles and child murderers in their midst'.

There is no apology on the blog for all the shit Fiona flung their way. And that omission means that the nasty hints and insinuations not only cover the Bullocks, but also continue to stain Bill and Carys.

What, Carys wants to know, did she and Bill do to make Fiona so mad?

Even though she's on holiday, Elsa has been in touch, having taken the temperature via the alpha mums' WhatsApp group that has never admitted Carys. She advised Carys that it would be better for Binnie if she continued to stay away, 'until they find something else to get their French manicures into'.

She also said she had heard about poor Lucy – how on earth? Carys thinks – and hoped she made a speedy recovery.

Carys had forgotten to bring Binnie an afternoon snack, so halfway back, the prospect of a whole summer without friends prompted an outburst of such epic proportions that an older white woman stopped and, in clipped tones that made her meaning absolutely clear, accused Carys of being a terrible mother.

So here she stands in the doorway to the living room, strung out, a post-meltdown Binnie trailing behind her. And there is Bill, sitting drunk on the sofa with her belongings all around him – the box file she keeps with the household admin in it open and spewing its contents, her many work and personal notebooks, the laundry basket, which is at his feet, her unwashed underwear all around.

For once she is grateful for the fire: her journal, which has *everything* in it, no holds barred, is still tucked under her T-shirts in her chest of drawers back at the house. The shoebox that Sara handed her, with the evidence of her shameful obsession with Alice and then Bill, is in the house too, hidden at the back of the winter-coats cupboard.

Bill shows no shame at being caught snooping. And he is not just drunk. He is slurringly, stonkingly legless.

'Just looking to see if I can find any more of your stinking lies,' he hisses at her.

He can barely focus. She notices that her bag is on the kitchen worktop, the one that she lost when Lucy had her accident. She lunges forward and grabs it. A label is attached to it.

You left this in my ambulance, it says. *I got your address when I checked in on Lucy. I hope she improves soon xxx*

The kindness of strangers is not lost on her, but she is too busy making sure Alice's letter is still inside to dwell on it.

It's there.

It appears then that Bill hasn't found out about her other deception. But never mind: he's busy enough going on at her about all the rest of her failings.

'You lied to me about Ajay, how we met, your connection to Alice. What else are you lying to me about?' He stands, swaying, spilling papers and knickers and notebooks on the floor, and points at her belly. 'Whose fucking baby is that anyway?'

He stumbles towards her, and she angles herself to protect Binnie. But he doesn't make the distance. Instead, he falls flat on his face.

Carys has had enough. 'Come on, Bins.' She takes her daughter's hand and leads her out of the room.

Binnie is so shocked by the sight of her paralytic, raving father that she has forgotten all about her own troubles.

After packing two small overnight bags, Carys takes Binnie and Nonna out onto the street. They walk through the sweaty, fun-drunk summer-evening crowds towards the river.

'Where are we going, Mum?' Binnie says.

'You'll see.'

Carys boldly leads her through the covered market and beyond, down a colonnaded driveway past a topiary cat and a fountain made of glass fish. They pass a couple of snooty-looking top-hatted doormen and swing through a revolving door into the grand foyer of the Savoy. Using the company card, she books them into a dog-friendly luxury king river-view suite for four nights.

'Mum!' Binnie says when she overhears the desk clerk tell her how much it is going to cost.

'We're worth it, Bins,' Carys says. And to prove she means it, she takes her six-year-old daughter to dinner at the Savoy Grill, and afterwards they watch *Frozen* from the comfort of their thousand-thread-count duvet, the Thames twinkling darkly outside their window, Nonna snoozing at their feet.

Binnie falls asleep, curled up against her.

Bill is just having a terrible time, Carys tells herself. He is a good man. He will come round. It will all be fine. It just needs patience. She whispers it over and over, willing herself to believe it.

Finally she closes her eyes, and as she falls asleep, she wonders what her parents would say if they knew where she was.

Then she realises.

They'd tell her to come home.

FORTY-TWO

Tick tick boom. Tick tick boom. The rhythm of the machines keeping Lucy alive thumps in Sara's head. Pleased with her progress, they have taken her off ventilation after just forty hours and are weaning her out of the coma.

'It's like being born,' Dorothy, the lovely older nurse, told Sara as she ushered her out of the room so they could remove Lucy's ventilation tube. 'They need time to come back into the world.'

Dorothy has said that Lucy could come round any time in the next eight or so hours. Sara has permission to stay beyond visiting hours, and she has reassured the overworked nursing staff that she will deal with notifying Bill and Carys of any developments.

She won't, of course.

Carys doesn't deserve to know.

Neither does Bill, thanks to what Sara assumes to be – given his lack of contact – his continuing association with her. Even knowing what he now knows! Carys must have wangled herself back into the right, painted Sara in the wrong. No change there.

Bill is a sap.

She's minded to tell them that she's had it with the lot of them and it will just be her and Lucy after all this, facing the world unparented but with each other. However cold and lonely that feels right now.

She hunkers down into the darkened cubicle. It's 10 p.m. and all she has done since she saw Tom yesterday evening is sleep, eat and walk and walk, filling in the time before she can be back here. Because this is where she needs to be: alone with Lucy, making plans for the better life she will build for her as penance for sleepwalking through their mother's death and all the suspicious circumstances around it.

As part of this, she will make sure that Ajay is brought to justice for everything he has done to her family.

She's sure now that he killed Alice. Having spent the past day thinking it over, she can see no alternative. With the hindsight of knowing how he stalked and threatened her, she can see exactly how he manipulated Lucy in the hypnosis session to picture her father murdering her.

Bill: a murderer!

He really loved Alice, and however much Sara despises his weakness, there's no way he's capable of doing anything so awful. The whole sorry Five Oaks business was a dry run at seeing him as a killer, and it just didn't fit.

She reminds herself that it is the sorry Martha Bullock business now. She spends a couple of minutes thinking about that poor lost little girl. But still her mind returns to Bill.

He was such a great father when she was little. Even though he was busy, he gave her – and Lucy in her turn – all of his spare time, taking her to the park, the zoo, the museums. His big fault is that he loved his girls and his wife too much, and found it almost impossible to let them go. Hence his rudeness to Tom, whom he saw as a threat, and his collapse when Alice died.

No. It has to be Ajay. And Sara is furious at Carys for

having been so gullible as to allow him near Lucy in the first place.

'But before we sort all that out,' she says to Lucy, who so far is showing no sign of waking up, 'let's get you out of here.'

Tom has tried to call her a dozen times since their meeting in Waterlow Park, but she can't bring herself to speak to him. She has texted him just once, telling him to leave her alone and to do his damn job, honour Amandeep Kaur's work and put the evidence together to make a case against Ajay.

Her brain is too full for whatever personal games he is playing.

Lucy smacks her mouth drily.

Dorothy has given Sara a little sponge on a pink plastic stick to wet her lips. She holds it up for her now, and, amazingly, she takes it between her teeth and sucks at it.

'Wake up, Luce,' Sara whispers, her heart thumping fast enough for both of them.

Lucy stops sucking and her jaw slackens again. Sara replaces the sponge in its water glass. The flutter of hope settles back in her chest and she goes back to turning over the circumstances around her poor mother's death.

Everything she and Lucy have gone through as a result of believing that Alice chose death over them was because a rookie detective's great work was disregarded. To add to the pain, Amandeep Kaur's investigation was probably ignored because she was young, Sikh and a woman.

Sara carries on watching, hoping and praying.

A while full of nothing but *tick tick boom* later, she hears a quiet male cough behind her. Thinking it's Lucy's other carer, a handsome tattooed nurse called Mark, she gets up.

'I'll get out your way,' she says. But as she turns, it's not

Mark she sees, but Tom. He's standing in the entrance to Lucy's cubicle in his linen work suit.

'How did you get in?' she asks.

He flashes his warrant card.

'That's misuse.'

'Sorry, but I didn't know how else to talk to you. You weren't exactly returning my calls. How is she?'

'They're bringing her out of it, slowly. What do you want?'

'May I?' He indicates the second chair.

Nodding so slightly it is barely a yes, she returns to her own seat. He hangs his jacket on the back of the chair and sits.

'So?' she says, as they watch Lucy like she's a flat-screen TV.

'I've been doing some digging on Ajay.'

'Yes?'

'You know Bill said he worked in Alice's health centre?'

'Yup. So?'

'I went back there and asked if anyone remembered him.'

'And?'

'I spoke to the receptionist, a sixty-year-old woman called Sandra Noakes—'

'Oh, bloody Sandra. Nose into absolutely everything.'

'Interesting. Well, she looked at me and I could tell she knew something. She asked to speak to me in a café round the corner. I sat there and waited – it was nearly her lunch break – and she came in looking over her shoulder.'

'Such a drama queen. What did she say?'

'She told me she thought there might have been something going on between Alice and Ajay.'

'So she clearly misread the stalking.'

'Probably. He's pretty convincing, isn't he? Had us all fooled. I didn't want to prejudice her by telling her about that, in case we need more from her. Even now, all these years later, she wells up when she's talking about Alice.'

'Everyone loved Mum.'

Tom nods. 'She was so alive, wasn't she, so interesting, so beautiful.'

'She was.'

'You know, thinking about it, I never really understood how she ended up with Bill.' Tom is trying to get Sara to look at him, but she won't. 'He wasn't bad-looking for an old guy, but he just seemed, I don't know, dull and borderline hostile.'

'He didn't exactly save his best bits for you,' Sara says.

'Sandra said much the same thing about him, though.'

'A bit unprofessional of her to have an opinion.'

'She said they were all so shocked about Alice killing herself. No one at the clinic saw it coming. In the days leading up to her death, she had seemed so happy.'

'That's not what I remember.'

'A brave front, perhaps? After Alice died, Ajay handed in his resignation.'

'Fishy.'

'Yup. He kept dropping by, though, asking about the family. Sandra said she never went into detail – she respects patient confidentiality too much...'

'Ha! As far as I remember, she's the biggest gossip around.'

'... but she did tell him about a month ago about Lucy going into hospital after she cut herself.'

'Oh, *come on*, Sandra.'

'So we now know how Ajay found out about Lucy, and—'

'The Doom Tree.'

They both look up.

Lucy is lying with her eyes wide open, staring at the ceiling. She speaks in her little-girl voice, but it is dry and hoarse and barely audible.

Sara gasps. 'Luce?'

'I'm in the car, right by the Doom Tree, looking at the bit where the roots make a little arch, and I've woken all sleepy, like

Daddy is when he's had too much wine. My sleeping bag is damp. It stinks of wee. I pretend to still be asleep, but he's in front of the tree digging and the smell of the earth and the sound of the spade make me feel sick.'

Her hands claw the air; her eyes close, but she still speaks. 'He's got her wrapped up in a white sheet. He drags her into the hole. He's got the spade and he's filling the hole back in.'

Her body is shaking, her voice rising. Sara grabs her hands.

'You don't need to worry, Lucy. It's me, Sara, and Tom's here too.'

She knows she should tell the nurse that Lucy is awake, but she wants – needs – to hear this.

'I close my eyes, pretend to sleep, or he'll get me too and put me in there with Mummy.'

Tom and Sara look at each other. 'The mud in the driver's footwell,' Sara says.

'The spade,' Tom says. 'What was she saying? The Doom Tree?'

'The map,' Lucy says. 'The book.'

'It's not here.' Sara wants to kick herself. She knows exactly where it is, and that's back on the coffee table in the Stoke Newington flat.

'Phone,' Lucy says. 'My phone.'

Her hands not moving as fast as she needs them to, Sara unlocks Lucy's bedside cabinet. Inside are a number of items that will help her 'land', as the consultant called it, when she wakes up – photographs, her sketchbook and her phone, which Sara holds up to Lucy's face.

Because of the bruises and cuts, the bandage covering her hair, the face recognition fails to work.

Sara puts her mouth close to Lucy's ear. 'What's the passcode, Lucy? How do I get into your phone?'

Lucy's eyes are closed. 'Mum died,' she says, through cracked lips.

'I know, Luce. Can you do the sponge thing?' she says to Tom, nodding at the pink swab in its water glass.

The phone needs four digits. She tries Lucy's birth date, but it doesn't work.

'Mum died,' Lucy says again.

'Try the date of Alice's death,' Tom says, dabbing at Lucy's lips.

'Oh! Oh, my love.' Tears in her eyes, Sara types in 3006 – the thirtieth of June, a date tattooed on her brain. The phone springs to life. She scrolls through Lucy's photos – a series of grim selfies as she cut her hair, videos of her talking at the camera. Deciding she needs to have a look at that lot later, she keeps going, back through photographs of trees and close-ups on the relevant pages of Alice's book, until she comes to a series of pictures of every page. It doesn't take long before she finds the page for the Doom Tree, which is in Epping Forest.

'Of course,' she tells Tom. 'Mum used to take us there. We hid in its trunk when we were small enough. You can climb up inside it, and there's some writing there.'

'Google Map. Pin,' Lucy says.

Sara opens Lucy's Google Maps and zooms in on Epping Forest, and sure enough, there it is, exactly.

'We're going to find our mum,' she says to Lucy. 'We're going to find out where Ajay put her.'

'Not Ajay.' Lucy shakes her head. 'Dad.'

'Bill?'

Sara and Tom eye each other, horrified.

'Tell Carys,' Lucy says. 'Dangerous. Now.'

Confused, her hands shaking, Sara tries to call Carys. But of course she doesn't pick up. Tom grabs her and pulls her away from Lucy's bed.

'But do we believe this?' he whispers. 'It's not just stuff Ajay planted?'

Sara frowns. For a second she was so certain. But Tom has a point.

'Can you get a team up to Epping?' she asks him.

'Look,' he says, pulling on his jacket, 'I'll run it past the boss. And if she doesn't buy it, then I'll go up there on my own. We need to know if there *is* something there. Then we might uncover other evidence.'

'Keep in touch,' Sara says.

On his way out, he brushes past Nurse Mark, who is hurrying towards the bed.

'Are we awake, then?' he says, looking at Lucy, who is smiling up at him.

'Yes!' Sara says, taking Lucy's hand. 'Yes, we are!'

'Go, go with him,' Lucy says, her voice a harsh rasp. 'Take my phone. Go!'

'You sure?'

'Yes.'

Sara kisses her sister, then rushes past a confused Nurse Mark, out of the ward and after Tom.

FORTY-THREE

Seven thirty in the morning and Carys's phone is showing yet another call from Sara. All through the night they've been coming.

She stops at the pedestrian crossing on the Strand, gives Nonna's lead to Binnie and rejects the call.

If it's about Lucy, the hospital will call. Otherwise she has no business at the moment with Sara.

Once more Sara leaves a voicemail. This infuriates Carys. Does she really think she's going to waste her time listening to it?

She throws her red cotton stole over her shoulder and she and Binnie continue on their way to the new play scheme. Carys had a word with them yesterday about Lucy's accident, and the super-responsive play workers helped Binnie find a friend, another new girl. She's far happier now.

Carys and Binnie have also been soothed by the two nights they've spent at the Savoy, away from Bill. The best part for Carys was curling up on the bed with Binnie, her baby in her belly, imagining that this was it. That this was all she had to worry about in the world: bringing up her two children and making sure they had enough to live on. She edited out their present luxury and scaled it back to a cosy, comfortable flat, clothes to wear, food on the table. After all, that was the best she ever imagined for herself back when she was growing up.

How did she ever allow herself to end up here, in this wealthy, messed-up family with its Netflix-level traumas and terrible secrets?

Oh yes, she reminded herself as she and Binnie gazed out at the twinkling lights of the London Eye slowly revolving in the distance.

Love.

She fell in love with Bill.

She has to remember that.

And that's what she has in mind as, after dropping Binnie off, she and Nonna head back down Charing Cross Road to the Airbnb to try to broker some sort of peace with the man who has been her rock for so long.

The cracks are so bad right now that Bill didn't join her at Lucy's bedside yesterday morning. She hopes he went in when Sara was there, but there's no way of telling. She can't ask the nurses, because it would look odd, her not knowing if her husband has visited their daughter.

She's hoping she will be able to persuade him to come to the hospital with her today.

Using her key card, she lets herself into the Airbnb lobby, smiling at the concierge, who barely looks up from her phone. So much for twenty-four-hour security.

As she rides up in the lift, she looks at herself in the multiple mirrors. Weirdly, unusually, she likes what she sees. She and Binnie have made ample use of the Savoy swimming pool and the luxury toiletries that come with their room. She even felt safe enough to leave Binnie and Nonna while she had a pregnancy massage. She is positively glowing.

Her hormonally acute nostrils flare the moment she opens the front door of the flat. The hot, stuffy air brings with it the stench of rotting food and stale alcohol. Pressing her stole to her mouth, she rushes to the bathroom to vomit.

As she enters the living room with freshly washed face and sucking a peppermint, she finds Bill passed out on the sofa. Nonna trots over to him, takes one sniff, then removes herself to the other side of the room and settles by the door.

A half-eaten burger sits on the coffee table; six beer cans, two wine bottles and two Talisker bottles lie on the carpet – all empty. The TV screen is broken, and all the belongings Carys left behind when she and Binnie walked out are strewn about the flat. She follows the trail to the bedroom, which clearly hasn't seen much sleeping, as the duvet is piled in a corner, its cover ripped and wine-stained.

One of the first thoughts she has is that this is going to totally screw her Airbnb profile. But worry for Bill quickly takes over. He has clearly relapsed big-time.

It's all her fault.

She rushes back to where he is lying flat on his back and checks his pulse. As he grunts and stirs, her compassion for him is replaced by anger once more. Rather than addressing a stressful situation by wallowing in alcohol, he should be with his daughter, who is lying half-dead in a coma not more than twenty minutes' walk away.

She slaps him around the face. 'Wake up, Bill. Wake up.'

'Wha...' His eyes roll back so they show only the whites; a line of drool connects him to the sofa.

She wants her man back. Not this wrecked shell.

Then, suddenly, he comes back to consciousness. He sits up with such force when he sees her that it is as if he has had an electric shock.

'You,' he says, his upper lip curling.

He is there in body, but when she looks into his eyes, Bill has left the house.

'Have you enjoyed staying at the Savoy at my expense? Eh? Miss "Council House from 'Ull".' He imitates and intensifies her accent. 'Bet "Mam-Gu and Grampa" never guessed their little girl would ever stay anywhere so posh.'

'How did you know?'

He holds up his phone, smiling. Carys's mobile shows up on his Find My iPhone.

Her mouth falls open. 'What?'

'I know exactly where you are. Well, you know all about that, don't you? Keeping tabs on people.'

If she hadn't already emptied her stomach, Carys would have vomited with the disgust that itches up her insides. She moves around the room collecting up her stuff, then gets a suit-case from the bedroom and crams it all in. She takes another and fills it with Binnie's remaining things.

'You can't get away from me,' Bill says. He's on his feet, stag-gering after her. 'I'm going to make you pay for what you've done.'

'I'm not doing this. Nonna!' Carys calls the dog, who comes to her obediently, making a wide circle to avoid Bill. She clips on her lead, then wheels the two suitcases out of the flat. Behind her, Bill shouts, in a proper rage now, for her to come right back this instant.

She gets dog and luggage into the lift and the doors close behind them.

Out on the street, she sits on the nearest bench and, with Nonna beside her, turns off location-sharing on her Find My iPhone. As she's doing that, a message arrives from Ajay's number. If it weren't for the photo preview that appears on her screen, snatching her full attention, she would have binned it unread.

The photograph is of Alice and Ajay kissing. It's a properly lustful and longing kiss that reminds her of her early days with Bill. She opens the message and sees the other two photographs, which are clearly leading up to the first. In them, Alice looks up at Ajay, her face alight, her hands on his shoulders, as he reaches out his arm to take the photo.

Finally she reads the message accompanying the images.

Please. I need to talk to you. I believe you are in danger. Can you make it here today?

She tries to put these images, this message together with what she knows from Alice's letter. She was having an affair with Ajay, but still she ran away?

It just doesn't seem likely. The tiny, neat, contrite woman she met outside Lucy's school surely didn't lead such a messy life.

But here is evidence that clearly she did.

Perhaps these photographs pre-date it all. Perhaps Alice had an affair with Ajay, tried to finish it, and he couldn't accept it so started following her. She knows this is a common stalker scenario.

Nonna whines as Carys folds her arms over her knees and rests her head on them. She stays there for a while, breathing, trying to put it all together. Part of her wants to just get back to the hotel, burrow under the duvet and hide until it's all over.

But she knows it won't be all over.

'Are you OK, love?'

She looks up. A young man – boy, actually – is standing over her. He has a kitbag on his shoulder, track marks on his bare arm, a dog who hangs beside him despite the lack of a lead. His face radiates kindness.

He sits beside her. 'It's just you look like you're in a bit of trouble.'

He must have thought she was one of his own, all dishevelled with the two suitcases and her own mutt. She smiles up at him, her Good Samaritan, her reminder that all is not awful in the world.

'You're right,' she says. 'I'm in a lot of trouble, and I don't know how I'm going to sort it.'

'Here.' He reaches into his kitbag and offers her a can of strong lager.

He has the cracked voice of an addict, which reminds her of poor Eve Bullock and, despite her own current situation, how much worse so many people have it.

She smiles and declines his offer. 'I need to keep a clear head, thanks.' She starts to get herself together, ready to head off to the hotel.

'I'm Devon,' he says. 'Devon Stephens.' He touches his dog's head. 'And this is Scout.'

'Carys.' She holds out her hand for him to shake. 'And this is Nonna.'

'You know what I've found helps?' he says. 'In every instance?'

'Go on,' she says.

'Kindness, babe. That's what works.'

She looks at him, his lovely face under its layer of street grime.

'Where are your family?' she asks him.

He smiles. 'Scout's my family. My mum died, my dad didn't want to know.'

'I'm sorry.'

'Scout does me fine.'

'Here. Would you just mind my bags and my dog for a moment?'

'You trust me with your stuff?'

She looks at him and nods. 'Yes. Yes, I do.'

He smiles. 'Sure, then.'

She heads to the bank a short distance away, sticks her cash card into the hole in the wall and draws out the maximum £350. Then, using her phone, she buys a Travelodge gift card in Devon's name that should do him for a week in central London.

He's still there when she gets back. Nonna and Scout have made great friends, and Devon has his nose stuck into a paperback. She hands him the cash and gets his number off him to send him the gift card.

'You don't have to do this,' he says.

'Believe me,' she says, 'I do.'

She needs to sort things out with Ajay. Tell him the truth. Whatever he's done, however manipulative he has been, he needs to know that Alice is still alive and, most importantly, that Bill is innocent and although he's being a complete arsehole at the moment, she is definitely not in danger from him.

With another hour to go before she is allowed in to see Lucy, she heads off to get a bus up to Ajay's. A loud Extinction Rebellion demo is going on in Trafalgar Square. She pushes through the chanting crowd and sits at the bus stop down the side of the National Gallery. She runs her fingers through Nonna's curly topknot. Although she doesn't know what she's going to do with her when she goes on to the hospital, she's glad she has her with her, as a sort of emissary from Alice's past for her visit to Ajay.

Or possibly, should she yet again be wrong about him, as something approaching a guard dog.

She sits and waits, and yet again Sara tries to call her.

Still furious with her stepdaughter for making a terrible situation a million times worse, but trying to be more Devon Stephens, she picks up.

FORTY-FOUR

It took Tom a while, but in the end his detective work was taken more seriously than DC Kaur's had been. His boss gave him twenty-four hours from six this morning and a search team including ground-penetrating radar and a cadaver dog. He also got clearance for Sara to be present, based on the fact that she is a police officer in Australia.

'Ma'am's a bit sweet on me,' he said. 'Can't ever say no.'

More fool her, Sara thought, but she was grateful that she could be present, even though she had strict instructions to stay firmly out of the way.

They were up at the site early doors, everyone in forensic suits. A track made it possible to get the vehicles right up close, so they set up pretty quickly. Sara helped by talking through what Lucy had said about where she was in the car, and where the digging must have been in relation to the hollow of the tree.

While the team worked, she sat in Tom's car and watched, trying to imagine what it had been like for Lucy on her own that night, watching her mother being buried.

The night Alice died, Sara had stayed out. She was at peak teenage rebellion, and had been to a party with some student boys she and a friend met in a pub. She'd taken a couple of pills, drunk too much and ended up going back to one of the boys' bedroom in a hall of residence down near Russell Square, doing the walk of shame back up to Muswell Hill at about eleven the next morning. She had failed to let her parents know that she was going out or that she was staying out, and she was expecting to have music to face on her return.

What she hadn't foreseen, however, was the police car parked outside the house. Nor had she imagined she would find a weeping Bill being consoled by two uniformed officers in the living room.

'Thank Christ you're safe,' he said, running to her and enveloping her in his arms. 'I thought she might have taken you with her.'

Lucy was upstairs, sleeping, he said. She was ill – flu or something. She'd been delirious in the night and he'd had to deal with it on his own, while worrying about Alice, who hadn't come home. Sara remembered the note of accusation in his voice, implying that in some way she had deserted him in his time of need. But with all the more important things that happened that night, she never did get into proper trouble. The student boy was forgotten, too, and she found she had nowhere to turn but back into Tom's all-too-willing arms.

And now there he was, overseeing the search for Alice; faithful old Tom, still supporting her.

Remembering the writing she'd seen inside the tree as a child, Sara slipped out of the car and slid into the hollow trunk, hunkering down into the earth, the police team too busy to notice her. She shone her phone torch around the innards of the tree until it hit its mark. Some time, possibly centuries ago, someone had carved:

Thou who treadeth on this tree, thou shall be doomed.

She shuddered.

Then her torch picked up some other lettering just beneath

it, which must have been added since she was last here as a
child:

Bollox.

It almost made her laugh.

And then she realised. If Lucy had been here and had seen
the burial, then Bill lied about her being ill in the night while
Sara was with her student boy. If Alice was here, then Lucy was
here, so then surely it has to be Bill, not Ajay, who killed her.

Unless Ajay planted the whole thing in Lucy in the earlier
sessions, and it all came out after the accident.

That was what Sara wanted to believe. Ajay was, after all,
her mother's stalker. And her dad used to plait her hair and
make her Little Mermaid and SpongeBob SquarePants birthday
cakes.

Sick with confusion, she slipped out of the tree and back
into the car.

And now Tom is working with the ground-penetrating-
radar guy, who is passing a machine that looks like a giant lawn-
mower over the marked-out ground, working backwards and
forwards away from the tree.

Sara is on her phone, trying once more to call Carys, not
quite knowing what she's going to say. She wants to tell her to
be careful, just in case Tom finds Alice. Just in case she and
Binnie are in danger.

This time, amazingly, Carys picks up.

The first thing Sara hears is people chanting – some kind of
demo going on in the background.

'Will you please stop calling me,' Carys says. 'I'm not ready
to talk to you yet.'

'Carys? Carys? Stay with me!' Sara shouts down the phone,
fearful that she won't be heard with all that racket.

'You really chose your moment, didn't you?' Carys is
saying. 'Bill's collapsed completely. He hates me. Why did you
have to tell him then? At his most vulnerable moment. *Quiet*,

Nonna!' The dog is barking along with the chanting protesters.

'You have to stay away from him,' Sara yells.

'Shh,' Tom calls to her. He and the guy have stopped and are looking at something on a monitor on top of the machine.

'Listen to me, Carys,' Sara says, her voice an urgent whisper. 'We're in Epping Forest and we're pretty sure this is where Mum's buried. Near the Doom Tree in her book. You have to keep away from Bill: he could be dangerous. You have to go to the flat and lock yourself in.'

'I can't. I don't have a key, remember? And anyway, I don't know why you're in Epping, or who "we" is, but I have proof that Alice isn't dead,' Carys says.

Sara almost drops her phone.

'I have a handwritten letter from her saying that she's very much alive.'

'What?'

'Look, I haven't got time to go into it now. But you're wasting your time up there. I've got some things I need to do before I get to Lucy. How was she yesterday?'

'Carys. She woke up.'

'She what? Why didn't they tell me?'

'I said I would.'

Carys sounds outraged. 'Why would you do that?'

'I've been calling and calling you. Why didn't you pick up?'

'Is that why you're up in Epping? Lucy's had another "vision"? Haven't we had enough of that? Did Ajay blag his way back into the room?'

'It's not like that.'

'Look. You just need to know, Sara, that your mum wasn't the saint you all think she was. She chose to run away from you. I didn't want to tell you this, but there it is. The truth.'

'No,' Sara says. 'I don't believe it.'

'I'm sorry, but it's true. And look at all the fallout that's still going on. I'm sending you a photo of the letter so you can see I'm not lying.'

'Where are you now? What are you doing?'

'I'm sorting shit out, Sara. Sending you the letter now.'

Behind Sara, the cadaver dog starts barking. She swings around to see a flurry of activity as the team move over to where the Alsatian is pawing at the ground.

'Carys, listen, they—'

But there is silence at the other end. Carys has hung up.

Sara's phone pings. It's a photo of the letter. It looks right, but she just can't believe it. And there's something about it, something just a bit off. Unable to put her finger on it, she holds her phone right up to her face and zooms in on the handwriting.

She gets out Lucy's phone and finds one of the photographs of Alice's book.

And there it is. In the letter, every single r is written like a small capital R. But that's not what Alice did. Her r's on the end of words were normal lower case.

The letter is a fake.

Tom calls out, 'We have a find!'

In a stupor, Sara walks towards where the dog is sniffing and scratching. Carefully the team starts to dig.

'You may want to go back to the car,' Tom says.

'I'll stay here if that's OK. I promise I won't get in the way.'

He looks at her and nods.

It's not a deep grave. In twenty minutes Sara sees a tatter of white material. One of the team lifts the fabric and there's the friendship bracelet she made for her mother when she was ten. The one Alice said she would never take off.

And she was true to her word.

Sara closes her eyes. Here is her mother. At last. It's a strange sort of relief to have found her. But it doesn't last long, because the important question now is who did this to her. Was it Bill?

Or is Ajay cleverer and more evil than it's possible to imagine?

She knows what she wants to believe.

Sara tries calling Carys again. Of course this time she doesn't pick up.

She has to find her, get her to safety, away from both those men. She looks on Lucy's Find My iPhone, but Carys isn't there. She stares at the screen, trying to think. Then she sees it. Nestling between HappyCow and Depop on Lucy's home screen she spots an app called Where's My Doggy?

Lucy said she had a dog tracker to follow Nonna. Praying to all the gods she can think of, Sara fires it up.

Almost instantly she finds her. She's moving swiftly up Fleet Road, nearly up to Hampstead Heath. She and Carys must be on a bus. And Sara knows exactly where they're heading.

She feels sick.

'Tom,' she says. 'Can I have a car and a driver, please? Carys is on her way to Ajay's.'

'You can have me,' Tom says. 'I'll leave this with the CSI.'

In ten minutes, they are blue-lighting down through Loughton, heading south and west in heavy traffic towards Hampstead.

Sara turns to Tom. 'Can you go any faster?'

But they come up against a massive knot of stationary vehicles. A lorry has jackknifed across the road. Even if anyone felt minded to move aside to let them through, there's no space for it.

'I don't believe it,' Sara says.

Tom looks over his shoulder at the jam that has already built up behind them. 'We're never going to get out of this.'

'We have to. Carys's life could depend on it.' Sara jumps out and starts directing the drivers behind them to make a space for Tom to turn the car around.

FORTY-FIVE

The front door to Ajay's clinic is closed. The building looks empty, uninhabited even. The foliage in the front garden that Carys so admired now seems thick and oppressive. It blocks out the sunlight, making her feel like she is in a cave. Bindweed creeps over his motorbike and sidecar, which look like they haven't been touched for weeks.

She hammers on the door and then peers through the letter box. At the end of the hallway, the door to the rest of the house opens and Ajay skitters down the tiled passage.

'Hey,' he says as he opens the front door. He looks drawn and tired. 'Thank you for coming. Come in.'

Nonna growls.

'What is it?' he says, bending to stroke her nose. She snaps at him. He straightens up and smiles at Carys. 'She's probably wondering where Fig is. He's out with the dog walker.'

He looks thinner than ever, and instead of his usual loose shirt and trousers, he's in a tracksuit that hangs off him, looking suspiciously like it has been slept in. He appears unwashed – although not as badly as Bill – and the several days' beard growth looks oddly out of place on his feminine face.

'Where are your patients?' she says, still on the doorstep.

'I've cancelled them. Haven't got the heart at the moment. I'm giving myself some headspace.' He taps his temple with a long finger. His eyes are bloodshot. 'We can't speak out here. Come in, Carys.'

In the shady front garden, Carys's spine prickles. Every part of her is telling her not to go into this house. What if he hypnotises her without her knowing? What if he makes her throw accusations at Bill too?

But she needs to know more about the photo, which seems so thoroughly to contradict what Bill told her about Ajay. And in any case, what does she have to lose?

She steps into the hallway. But Nonna won't come. She sits on the step outside.

'It'll be the chilli powder,' Ajay says. 'I put it around the doors this morning to stop the ants. Fig hates it too.'

Carys is dubious about this to say the least, but there is a sprinkling of red dust around the threshold and in the end she lifts Nonna over the offending step and the dog seems suddenly fine. Nevertheless, as she closes the front door behind her, Carys surreptitiously leaves it on the latch so that, should she have to, she can beat a hasty retreat.

'Come into my treatment room,' Ajay says.

Carys takes care not to sit in what she thinks of as the hypnotising chair and takes the sofa. It's a ridiculous choice – as if a piece of furniture could endanger her. But the sofa also gives her a clear route to the door. She notes the quartz crystal on its plinth, which she reckons she could use in self-defence if necessary.

Calmer now, Nonna settles at her feet.

Ajay takes the armchair at right angles to the sofa and leans forwards, his hands together, his elbows on his bony knees.

'Tell me about the photo,' Carys asks, adjusting her red stole around her shoulders.

'I needed to show you that I'm not deluded. That Alice and I were in love.'

'So perhaps you had an affair, but then she didn't want any more to do with you and you couldn't cope with it.'

Ajay looks up, teeth bared. 'No!'

Carys flinches and Nonna, sensing her fear, is on her feet, snarling.

'I'm sorry! I'm sorry, Carys, Nonna. It's just... I've not been dealing with things very well,' he says. 'Since we last met. Poor Lucy.'

'*You've* not been dealing well? It's your fault. You misled her, you misled me.'

He puts his head in his hands. 'I know.' He looks up at her. 'I'm so sorry.'

'So why did you do it?'

'I didn't mean all this to happen. I truly wanted to help her.'

'And to get at Bill.'

'I wanted to get the truth out.'

'You tracked me down, didn't you?'

'I've always felt I owed it to Alice to make sure Lucy and Sara were OK. And that last time, when Lucy cut herself so badly she nearly died, I knew it was time to step in.'

'How did you know about that?'

'You're still patients at the centre. I used to work there. I have contacts.'

'Sandra on reception, I suppose?'

'Ha. Yes. She called yesterday and told me that Tom had been round asking questions. I think he thinks I'm responsible for Alice's death.'

'But she's not dead.'

'Carys, she is.'

'No. No, I have proof, look.'

She gets the letter out of her bag and hands it to Ajay.

He looks at it, frowning and shaking his head.

'She didn't write that.'

'You just don't want to believe it because it means she wasn't the sainted goddess of your obsession.'

He gets up and walks over to the window, where he stands with his hands on his head. He breathes out and turns to her. 'Don't say that.'

'It's true. I'm sorry. Alice is the bad one in all this. She abandoned her family!'

He waves the letter at her. 'Alice didn't write this. I know it. It looks a lot like her writing, but it doesn't feel like it came from her hand. It's not her voice. And she calls me "a most unpleasant colleague". She wouldn't use those words anyway, but she certainly wouldn't use them about me.'

'What makes you such an expert?'

He thumps his chest. 'Just look at that photograph of us. I *loved* her. I knew her better than I know myself.'

He scurries across the room and sits next to Carys on the sofa, making her shift away, right up against the arm. He tries to look into her eyes, but she won't let him, scared that he might capture her mind.

'Look,' he says. 'I always thought Alice didn't kill herself. Now that I know her body was never found, I'm certain of it.'

'Why involve Lucy, though?'

He grabs her hand and holds it so tightly that it hurts. 'I genuinely wanted to help her. And I thought that by guiding her back to early childhood – which is what I would usually do with a patient with her particular mental health issues – I could also get some insight into what actually happened.'

'That's completely unethical.'

He nods, still holding on to her. His hand feels dry around her fingers. She tries to pull away from him, but he's got her too tightly.

'I know,' he says. 'It's not good. But I had no idea what we would uncover.'

'All that crap about poor Eve Bullock's daughter.'

'No, no. That wasn't crap. It was Lucy remembering.'

'Seeing Bill murdering a woman and a child?'

'Yes! The child was Lucy. By witnessing the actual murder of her mother, which is what came to her in the last session, the Lucy who existed before that moment – the child Lucy – died.'

'That's just crazy. You're bending it to suit your story. Let me go, please. You're hurting me.'

He ignores her request. 'We find our way to the truth through metaphor and narrative-building. Lucy was nearly there when she had that accident.'

'It was no accident. She threw herself under the train. I was there, Ajay. I saw it.'

'Oh God. Oh God. Poor Lucy.'

Carys nods. She feels numb, her heart hard. 'Yes. Poor Lucy.'

'I went to the police when Alice disappeared,' Ajay says. 'I knew – Alice told me – that Bill was jealous and possessive. I thought perhaps he could have pushed her off that cliff and made it look like she had killed herself. I couldn't believe, even with all the evidence the police claimed to have, even with her history of depression, that she would have done that. She was going to tell Bill about us, after Sara finished her A levels. It was only another year. She – we – had everything to live for.'

'Bill's not like that,' Carys says.

But even as she shakes her head, performing disbelief, she thinks back to the Airbnb scattered with her things, to how Bill reacted when he snooped and discovered that she had been in contact with Edina, how he was when she told him about Ajay...

'And who would the police believe, when the grieving white husband has already told them that the grieving brown lover was in fact a "most unpleasant colleague" who was stalking her?'

'Wait. Are you suggesting that Bill forged this letter?' Carys is almost speechless.

Ajay redoubles his grip on her hands. 'Yes! Yes! That's exactly what I'm suggesting.'

Nonna starts barking.

'He's right.'

Ajay drops Carys's hands as they look up and see a dishevelled, bloodshot Bill standing in the doorway of the treatment room.

FORTY-SIX

'So you're fucking him as well now, are you?' Bill says as he levers himself drunkenly across the room with his cane. He scowls at Carys, who has jumped up and pulled the dog with her to the other side of the room. 'If it isn't history repeating itself all over again.'

'How did you find me?' Carys says. Behind her, Nonna snarls. Ajay has risen slowly, his hands up as if Bill has a gun, which, although she knows it's hardly a possibility, Carys truly hopes he hasn't.

'Did you know that if you sit on that bench just beneath the apartment building, if I point Binnie's telescope in the right direction, I can see what's on your phone? And I have his address because it was on his business card, which you had not so cleverly hidden in the pocket in one of your notebooks.'

'Which you snooped in,' she says.

'Can you *blame me*?'

'Take it easy, man,' Ajay says, backing around the room so he is between Carys and Bill.

Bill moves towards him, his lip lifted into an ugly snarl. 'Hey, *man*. What were you doing sending my second wife pictures of you in flagrante with my first wife? Did you think it would turn her on? I mean, Carys is so fixated with Alice, it wouldn't surprise me if she fucked her too!'

'Shut up, Bill,' Carys says.

'Shut up yourself,' Bill says to her over Ajay's shoulder. 'Whore.'

'You forged that letter from Alice,' Carys says. 'I can't believe you'd go to those lengths.'

'Her handwriting was so obvious. It was so easy to copy.'

'But why the hell did you do it?'

'How else was I going to stop you sticking your nose in? With old lover boy's woo-woo charms here' – he waves his fingers in Ajay's face – 'you'd have started believing him sooner or later.' He pushes Ajay out of the way and puts his face right up against Carys's. She can smell the Scotch on his breath. 'Tell me, though. What's he got that I haven't?'

Ajay pulls Bill away from her. 'I haven't touched Carys.'

Bill turns and starts circling in on him. 'You touched Alice, though, didn't you?'

'You killed her,' Ajay says.

'Not this again.' Bill turns back to Carys. 'You don't believe this bullshit he's been feeding Lucy, do you?'

Carys looks at Ajay, then at Bill. Her husband, the father of her little girl and the baby inside her, the man she has built her life around: Could he really be a murderer?

Inside, she is boiling. She wants to rip out her heart and offer it up to the devil to make all this go away.

All she shows the two men, however, is her silence.

But that says it all.

Bill roars at Ajay. Before Carys knows what is happening, he has lifted his cane and brought it down on his back.

Nonna barks at him, but Carys holds her collar.

'Thieving bastard,' Bill says. 'You've poisoned my whole family against me, taken everything I ever had.'

Ajay cowers, trying to protect his head with his arms, but Bill lifts the cane and brings it down again and again.

'Bill, stop!' Carys screams. But Bill doesn't hear her.

'Please, stop,' Ajay says. He's in a corner, and with Bill twice as wide and twice as strong as he is, he has no chance to fight back or to get away. 'Please.'

Bill keeps on and on, crunching the cane down, beating Ajay until he is on the floor, curled into a ball, his long fingers clawing at his hair to protect his skull.

Carys watches, frozen in horror, as her husband attacks his dead wife's lover. Because she's certain now that that is what Ajay is. Nonna snaps at her hand and gets past her. Snarling, she launches herself at Bill, sinking her teeth into his leg. Bill cries out and tries to shake her off.

For Nonna, for Alice, for Ajay, Carys is wrenched from her paralysis. She lunges towards the pointed crystal and yanks it from its plinth. Swinging it like a club, she runs at Bill as he raises the cane to bring it down again on Ajay. He screams as she smashes his hand with the sharp quartz tip, swiping the cane from his grasp. He turns, cradling his bleeding fingers, and looks at her astounded as she swings it behind her like a baseball bat, aiming to bring it up onto his chin.

But she doesn't have the height to do it. As she lashes out in his direction, he roars and catches the crystal with his smashed fingers, taking the trajectory up and away. She doesn't let go until the last minute, when he has lifted her off her feet. She flies through the air like a swatted insect, slamming down on her back, the wind knocked right out of her.

Bill has done this to her. *Bill.*

And he did far worse to Alice.

None of it makes any sense.

Before she can gather herself enough to try to escape, he lands heavily on her and straddles her, his knees on her arms, which feel like they might snap under his weight.

'Oh Carys,' he says, grabbing the ends of her red stole, which is wound around her neck. 'You were too good, weren't you? If you'd left everything alone, if only you hadn't been such a concerned stepmother, such a perfect wife, such a devoted sister...'

'What?' Carys squeaks. This past tense. He's going to kill her, like he did Alice. Like Lucy said.

She should have believed her.

Nonna is doing her best to get at him, but Bill turns and orders her to the sofa, a command she knows well and reluctantly obeys, leaping up onto the cushions. Instead of lying down as she usually does, she sits poised, ears back, licking her lips and snarling. But she is too well trained to disobey her master, even if he is throttling her mistress.

'I knew you were fucking around, though, knew it,' Bill says. 'With Artur, with that ex of yours, with that homeless tramp I saw you with. With *that*.'

He points to Ajay, who is lying horribly still not three metres from her.

'No! I swear. I've not—'

'Lying bitch.' He wrenches her stole and she starts to choke.

'Please, Bill,' she splutters. 'Our baby...'

'Best not to bring it into the world. It's all gone to hell, Carys.'

She needs to keep him talking. 'So he's right, then?'

'Who?'

'Ajay. It was you who killed Alice.'

Bill smiles, leans yet more weight onto her arms and bends down towards her, his jutting chin almost touching hers.

'What do you think?'

She swallows as best she can. 'I think it was you.'

He suddenly bursts into tears. 'Oh God, Carys, look at you. All so neat and perfect and good. So good any man would feel dirty next to you. It's your stupid kindness that's made all this happen. If you'd just not meddled, we could have gone on being happy.'

'Lucy was ill!'

'Lucy is ill now, isn't she? Arguably in a worse place than she was when you started all this. So what have you gained exactly?'

'Why did you kill Alice?'

He lifts his upper lip. 'I had no choice. She told me she was leaving. I couldn't allow that. Not with the girls. We were the perfect family. I couldn't let her spoil that by going off with that weasel. And now you've given me no choice but to do the same to you, haven't you?' His tears fall on her face and run into her mouth, salty and alcoholic. 'I loved you so much.'

He pulls again on the stole. The edges of her vision blur.

'I love you,' she says desperately. 'So does Binnie, the baby...'

'Don't say that!' he says through his tears.

'Why Lucy, though? Why did you take her to Epping Forest?'

He relaxes his grip just enough for her to gasp in a breath. 'How do you know about Epping?'

'Sara told me.'

'She was asleep, though! I gave her Alice's pills in some hot chocolate. Enough to knock her out for a day and a night. I had to take her with me. Sara hadn't come back. I couldn't leave her on her own. I'm a good father, you know that. A good father. I panicked. I had to hide it, you see, because otherwise what would have become of the girls? I knew the place in Epping, that tree Alice loved; you can drive right up to it, deep in the forest, so I put her and Lucy safe in the car and buried her there.'

'And Beachy Head?'

'I thought of the plan while I was digging. I went back, hooked up the bike and sidecar on the trailer then drove out there, made it look like Alice had killed herself. And it was perfect. Perfect. No one ever knew until you started sticking your nose in. You should have kept quiet, Carys.'

He pulls tighter and tighter. She tries to plead with him, tries to ask him more questions, but it's too late, the room has turned monochrome, and red spots fly before her eyes, and all she can hear is Bill crying and apologising to her, telling her that what he is doing is necessary as he squeezes the last breath from her.

But then behind him there's a scuffle and a female voice that Carys, from the very edge of her consciousness, vaguely recognises. It's telling Bill to step away, and he's struggling, his knees working over the bones in her arms until she hears one of them snap.

But she's beyond pain now.

And then the weight is lifted from her and a male voice says, 'Bill Anderton, I am arresting you on suspicion of the murder of your wife Alice Herman.'

'Fuck you, Bunny Boiler,' Bill says.

Somewhere inside her slipping consciousness, Carys wants to laugh herself sick.

As she realises she doesn't have to hang on any longer, the woman's voice is there again, right by her ear. A hand unwraps the scarf from her neck.

'Carys? Carys? Are you OK?'

Carys forces her eyes open, and just before she slips away, she sees Sara's face leaning over her, her lips forming the words:

'I'm so, so sorry.'

FORTY-SEVEN

For the first time for years, the sun is shining for Alice's birthday. The brightly coloured clothes Lucy asked everyone to wear are on full display, not a raincoat or cagoule in sight.

She has just finished singing 'Amazing Grace' and Sara proudly helps her sit down again. It's been a long haul over the past eleven months, but she is almost back to full mobility and her short-term memory is improving every day. Best of all, she is happy.

And today, the final ghost is being laid to rest.

With Fig at his heels, Ajay steps forward with the urn containing Alice's ashes. He scoops out a handful and scatters it into the hole he dug earlier beside her blackthorn. He closes his eyes and says a couple of words. He too has had a long journey back to full strength, crediting yoga and acupuncture for getting him on his feet again.

Well, he would, wouldn't he?

He turns to Sara and beckons her forward. She reaches into the beautiful stoneware pot Lucy made during her occupational therapy and takes a handful of ashes. Her mother feels gritty under her fingers, and that seems absolutely right. She kneels on the grass and lets them fall.

'I love you, Mum,' she says. 'I'm sorry we took so long to find you.'

Then she and Ajay help Lucy out of her wheelchair, and supported by them, she tips the rest of Alice into the hole.

Ajay lifts the climbing rose the three of them picked out after much discussion over colour and places it in the hole. It will be a deep, dusky pink that will grow up over the black-thorn, greeting summer visitors to the Alice Herman Health Centre with scent and blooms.

He takes the spade Sara bought for the occasion and shovels the first clods of earth around the roots of the rose.

The others line up after Sara and Lucy to take their turn.

Bill of course is not here. He is at the start of a life sentence for murder and attempted murder. Despite everything he has done, underneath her anger Sara feels sorry for him. He is such a desperate, lonely man, and it's all his own fault. He wanted to control the women around him, and he didn't realise how impossible that was.

He is answering for it now, though.

Sara and Lucy have visited him twice, and both times he has been a mess of tears and contrition.

He is pathetic.

Carys steps forward for the spade, baby Marcus strapped to her front and Binnie and Nonna at her side. One day she will take the children to see their father, but she needs time.

He did nearly kill her and Marcus, after all.

She helps Binnie put earth on Alice's rose, then steps back in the sunlight with her two children, smiling at her stepdaugh-ters and the knot of friends who insisted on coming to support her.

Her arm is still weak from the break, but neither that nor all the police and court stuff around Bill has stopped her driving Five Oaks through to completion. She is especially proud of the deal she has struck with a housing association, which means the entire development is now going to provide homes for people coming off the street or out of addiction – or, as is more usually the case, both.

Some of the neighbours aren't best pleased, but the ones who would have put up the worst stink are also in prison and in no position to object.

Indeed, Eve Bullock, who is standing one person away to Carys's right, has sold her parents' house, and she and Carys have set up a trust to provide grants and support to help the tenants through rehab and into work. Their first client is Devon Stephens, who got in touch to repay some of Carys's gift and was quickly welcomed into the fold. He says that in Eve and Carys he has found two proper mothers. As if to prove it, he stands here between them, with Scout at his feet. Edina and her wife, Juliet, are also here, right behind him. They are regular visitors to the Muswell Hill house, which Carys has decided to keep on. She managed to turn the insurance-funded restoration into a total remodelling. With that and the fire, most of the ghosts have been exorcised and it has become a place where family and friends almost constantly drop in for coffee or wine or dinner.

Carys didn't realise how much she missed other people. She sees now how Bill cordoned her off, kept her for himself, starved her of company.

But no longer.

She catches Sara's eye. They smile at each other.

Sara has told Tom that he has to put away all hope of picking up their relationship, and Carys is so proud of her for that. As she and Sara are now proving to each other, it is far better to be single than with the wrong partner.

They both know that given time, Tom could have become a version of Bill.

The best part of all is that Sara is staying in the UK, and will be living with Lucy in the flat. She has transferred to the Met, and is a DC on a Community Safety Unit, specialising in domestic violence cases.. She's based in Tottenham, like Tom, but she keeps him firmly at arm's length.

He wanted to come today, but Carys gently told him it was family only. Even as loosely applied as in this gathering, he does not qualify.

Carys looks up at the clear blue sky. She hopes the weather will hold, because tomorrow she is driving up to Hull for her monthly visit to her parents. They know everything now. She expected them to be furious at her deception and deviousness. Strangely, though, their reaction was pride at what they called her resilience and resourcefulness.

Ajay gently takes the spade from her and neatens up the planting while Sara pours the gin made with last year's sloes. Binnie and Devon help her hand round the glasses.

Then everyone – including the two recovering addicts, who have blackcurrant juice – raises their glasses to the woman they have finally laid to rest.

'To Alice.'

A warm breeze ripples through the blackthorn, and like summer snow, its blossom falls around the newly planted rose.

A LETTER FROM JULIA

Dear Reader,

I want to say a huge thank you for choosing to read *The Daughters*. If you enjoyed it, and want to keep up to date with all my latest releases, just sign up at the following link. Your email address will never be shared and you can unsubscribe at any time.

www.bookouture.com/julia-crouch

I have always been fascinated by the way memory works. Psychologists claim that it's not physically possible to form memories before two years of age, yet I swear I can remember as a baby lying under the cherry tree in my parents' back garden, looking up at the blossom. My birthday is at the end of April, so I must have been at most two months old! Of course, the fact that my mother has told me this story many times to show me how 'good' I was as a baby *may* have something to do with it...

When it comes to memory, we love to make stories from scraps of information, and to place ourselves at the centre of them. This can be useful – indeed, it's how we make sense of the world, arguably even how we define ourselves – but if we are placed in the wrong hands, this tendency to construct narrative can lay us open to manipulation.

In this story, Ajay the hypnotherapist works with Lucy to uncover her memories. Hypnotherapy can be extremely effective for some people. Indeed, it is still used by police forces to help witness recall. Back in my drinking days, I once had hypnotherapy to try to help me control my alcohol intake through a full-on party December (remember those?). I thought I would be unhypnotisable, but instead I had an intense experience where I felt like I had rushed to the bottom of a deep cavern, and the words of the hypnotherapist sounded distant and meaningful. The session worked, and I didn't have more than one glass of wine at any event during that whole party season.

Having been made so suggestible, however, I realised how easy it could be for a hypnotherapist to abuse that power. Exploring past events in these situations has to be done so carefully – as Dr Julia Shaw explains in her brilliant book *The Memory Illusion*, it's scarily easy to implant false memories.

In *The Daughters*, I look at how the idealised memories of Alice, a brilliant, much-loved woman, are held by her family after she dies, and how these affect Carys, who steps possibly rather too quickly into her shoes. This would be a tall order for any woman, but Carys is also just a few years older than Sara, her elder stepdaughter. So despite her best intentions and genuine love for Bill, Alice's grieving widower, her relationship with her new family is complicated from the very first moment.

Then, years later, when questions arise about the nature of Alice's death, and Carys's stepdaughters start delving into the past and – with Ajay's help – putting their memories together, that relationship becomes even more difficult.

I hope you've enjoyed sorting out the actual truth from what the characters believe or maintain to be true. I'd love to know how your suspicions moved around!

I've really enjoyed connecting with readers through my other books, *Cuckoo*, *Every Vow You Break*, *Tarnished*, *The Long Fall*, *Her Husband's Lover* and *The New Mother*, so please, if you have any comments or questions, do get in touch on my Facebook page, through Twitter, Instagram or my website.

Finally, I would be very grateful if you could write a review of *The Daughters*. I'd love to hear what you think, and it makes such a difference helping new readers to discover one of my books for the first time.

Thanks,

Julia Crouch

www.juliacrouch.co.uk

facebook.com/JuliaCrouchAuthor

twitter.com/thatjuliacrouch

instagram.com/juliageek

ACKNOWLEDGMENTS

I'd like to thank Graham Bartlett (policeadvisor.co.uk), former senior detective, crime writer and police advisor, who has been so helpful with this, my first-ever book to feature the police in any meaningful way. Without him, I could have got so much wrong. With him, anything I *have* got wrong is my own fault.

I would also like to thank my first/sensitivity readers, Jeff Gayle and Maria McNicholl, and my soon-to-be daughter-in-law Eva Nella for putting up with me asking lots of questions about being an architect (always good to have one in the family). Thanks also to Laura Marshall of www.triptychpd.com for helping me with what happens when a body turns up on a building site – not, I hasten to add, something that often happens in her professional experience, but she knew who to ask, and to Janice McLeod for the Australian detail – most of which ended up on the cutting-room floor, but hey-ho. Thanks as always to Nel, Owen and Joey for teaching me about being a parent, and Tim for letting me know what a happy marriage is. And thanks too to the community of writer friends who have kept me going through the lockdowns, especially Colin Scott, without whom I would have sometimes felt horribly alone.

Thanks as ever to my brilliant, laser-sharp and twice-as-fast editor, Ruth Tross, and the whole Bookouture team, who make me feel like I am part of a family. Also, thanks to my wonderful agent, Cathryn Summerhayes at Curtis Brown.

Two publications have helped me enormously with this book: the *Great Trees of London Map* by Paul Wood, published by Blue Crow Media, which has guided me on walks real and imagined (via Google Maps) in London; and Dr Julia Shaw's *The Memory Illusion*, (Random House Books), which is both entertaining and full of astounding information. The colleague experiment Edina refers to is based on Dr Shaw's work.

All errors and omissions are entirely my fault.